A STONE'S THROW

Alida Winternheimer

Wild Woman Typing

Book cover by Camille Monk.

Author photograph by Jonah Castañeda Barry.

Second Edition

Visit the author's website at www.alidawinternheimer.com.

Wild Woman Typing

Minneapolis, Minnesota

Contents

For mothers and daughters.

October

Chapter One

Summer had gone. Simona's favorite time of year arrived in an extravagant show of rust and amber, scarlet and sienna. Matching shades colored her fingertips, used to blend and work the oil pastels that lay beside her in their worn out box. She sat on a lakeside bench, wrapped in a wool sweater and scarf, and gazed upward, her entire face lifted to better drink in the sky. Deciduous trees held their finery, clinging to delicate stems, at the peak of their glory. The barren season would follow soon enough. Simona let her gaze linger in the treetops. Eventually, she looked from leaves to trunk to the yellowing grasses on the banks of the lake, and at last into the sapphire waters. She only ever felt like painting landscapes in the fall, that time of year that inspired her to mix her own pigments. She believed every major life event should happen in autumn. Yet here she was, due to have a baby in June, the start of summer with all its green.

Time to move on, Hannah would be waiting. Simona put her drawing supplies in her bag and gave up the bench. She strolled, passed on both sides by a constant flow of people with clouded breath: runners, skaters, cyclists, everyone swished by her. There were also couples and parents with strollers, pumping their arms and legs as though the lake and trail only existed for their cardio benefit, the scenery disregarded as extraneous to their workouts. Simona's mind wandered as she walked the familiar course. She remembered biology class. Human reproduction. Two cells came together inside her body without her permission and without her knowledge. They became it. It found purchase in Simona's craggy interior. One divided and multiplied. And now, what was it? Blastula? Or was it already more than that? Embryo. She rolled the word around in her mind. It was round and smooth, oily, cleaved by the middle consonants, like a coffee bean. Was it already as big as a coffee bean? If she said it enough, it ceased to be real, became nonsense, a twenty-five cent toy from a gum ball machine—easily lost and forgotten. *Embryo-embryo-embryo-embryo-embryo-embryo-embryo-embryo-embryo-embryo-embryo....*

Simona came to a standstill. The person rushing along behind her was forced to suddenly divert, bumped her shoulder as he sidestepped, mumbled, "Watch it." She didn't notice. She was in her own space, turning overgrown boulders of thoughts. The biggest one left a deep impression in the valley of her mind. *It is becoming a person.* Traffic continued to flow around Simona, like water around a stone. "A person," she said to herself.

Slowly, Simona rejoined the current of people traveling the path, and soon left it for the sidewalk, took Lake Street a few blocks east, and arrived at the café where Hannah was waiting at a sidewalk table.

"You okay?" Hannah asked.

Simona pulled a wire backed chair away from the table, but didn't sit down.

"Want to tell me what's on your mind?"

"After I get our drinks. Latté?" She went inside the café without waiting for an answer.

Hannah stirred in honey, clinking the spoon around the glass, and stared at Simona with her brows lowered in concern.

After blowing into her mug a few times, Simona sighed and looked up. "I'm pregnant," she said.

"Oh!" Hannah's eyes and mouth formed circles. She drew in a breath and recovered. "Wow. How are you?"

"Terrified. I keep hearing my father's voice, 'only bad girls have babies.

No daughter of mine! You will be smart, keep the boys away.' I feel like a fool. Like this shouldn't happen to me. I should have prevented it."

"Yeah." The word was barely more than a mumble slid between Hannah's lips on their way to her coffee.

"What?"

Hannah's eyes flashed up, caught on Simona's, and she lowered her glass without drinking. "Sweetie, have you thought about the timing here?"

"Since it's unplanned...no."

"Yes, but you could change things. If the timing isn't right. I mean, *I* could never have a baby now. I'm too focused on my career. And your career is going so well right now. I'd hate to see you lose focus."

Simona looked at her friend: fair skin rosy in the autumn air, blonde hair pulled back in a ponytail, her weekend look. Hannah always dabbed perfume, something floral, but not sweet, on the back of her neck. Usually Simona liked the scent, but today it seemed to make her nauseous. Simona thought she might be getting sick, then remembered she had heard something about hormones affecting the senses. "Hannah," she said, "this isn't the reaction I expected from you. You know, support?"

"Of course. I'm sorry. I just meant...I didn't want to do the wrong thing. Gush like an idiot if you're not keeping it, or." Hannah stopped herself. "What should I do? Congratulate or commiserate?"

"I don't know yet."

"Is it a good thing?"

"I don't know yet."

Hannah leaned out of her chair to hug Simona. "Whichever it is, I'm totally supportive." She squeezed Simona's shoulders again before settling back into her own chair. Hannah tossed her hair back over her shoulder and sat up straight, slapping both palms on the table. "Okay, what am I?"

"You're scaring me."

"I'm a project manager, a planner. Let's approach this logically."

Simona rolled her eyes.

"Come on," Hannah urged, pulling a notepad from her shoulder bag. She wrote, "Life Changes" at the top of the sheet and underlined it twice. "Finances. Less. Time. No longer your own," she spoke as she wrote down her thoughts. "Dating..."

"Put hell there," Simona said, pointing to the paper.

"Dating, hell. Painting?"

"Same."

Hannah shook her head. "No. There's pressure to sell work now. You can't live on bread and tea if the patrons find a new sweetheart. You'll need diapers, baby food. They outgrow clothes every few months."

Simona stared past Hannah while she scratched her notes, leaving her friend to consider all the complications that hadn't even occurred to her yet.

"One last question. How do you feel about becoming a mother?"

"Like a total impostor."

"Im-pos-tor," Hannah wrote across the bottom of the page in large block letters. She turned the notebook so it faced Simona. "This doesn't even begin to cover it."

Simona laid her hand over the page. "I thought of something on my way here."

Hannah waited while Simona's hand remained, covering the list of arguments against her becoming a mother.

"This thing inside me is a person. Whenever that actual state comes into being, all the information is there. It's becoming."

"Yes, but..."

"Half of that information, that blueprint for a person, came from me. This *it* hanging out inside here..." she paused to lift her sweater and look down at her navel. "It's my family."

Hannah didn't speak. A car horn honked. People around them continued talking. Thick café dishes clanked against each other. A cell phone rang. Simona and Hannah sat in silence, sharing a moment of private understanding.

Hannah burst from her chair and embraced Simona with cheek pressed to cheek. "Congratulations! Can I be your birthing partner?"

Simona laughed. Her eyes again clear and bright.

"Unless," Hannah said, "the father wants to coach you through labor."

"He won't."

One of those stunted urban trees along the sidewalk gave up a leaf. It fluttered to the ground. Simona pulled her sweater sleeves over her hands and wrapped her palms around her mug.

"Cold?" Hannah asked. "We can sit inside."

"No, I like this weather."

They sat quietly, watching the traffic.

"Ummm..." Hannah eventually hummed. "Who is the father?"

"Immaculate conception."

"Have you notified the church?"

Simona raised her mug and felt the steam against her face. "I wonder if chai is good for the pores," she said, wondering how long it would take Hannah to piece it together.

Hannah gasped. "Oh my God, it's that English guy, isn't it? Peter-the-three-week-fling."

Simona pretended not to have heard and watched a motorcyclist zoom past, edging around cars in one lane and then the other.

"Are you going to tell him?"

"No. Even if I wanted to, he never gave me his number in London. We had an agreement."

"But you could find him. What about child support?"

"I won't need it."

"He'll never know his child exists." It was a statement. Simple. Final. Wistful.

Simona let Hannah sit, twisting a paper napkin into fine knots, considering the morality of not telling Peter about his child. It was the nature of their friendship. Simona did. Hannah considered implications and complications. Simona moved under her own power before it even occurred to her others might help. Hannah gathered support as a prerequisite. They balanced each other. Simona couldn't imagine a better friend and ally than Hannah Andersen. As for Peter, she still missed him.

They had met in Loring Park.

Actually, they had seen each other the night before at an opening. Simona had a show in the Jasper Gallery and the opening had gone incredibly well. Peter had been there, though she had no idea. He recognized her the next day in the farmers' market along Nicollet Mall and followed her in an almost stalkerish way into the park. Simona was prepared to kick him, or at least to scream her head off, but he opened his mouth first and spoke with an English accent. Then he gave her a cantaloupe from the market. At dinner that night, she informed him that he had narrowly charmed his way out of a bruised shin.

"Come on," Hannah said, "I have something to show you."

They finished their drinks, and Hannah drove them across Minneapolis to the north end of downtown along the Mississippi River. She parked in front of a large building with a limestone front. The stones had been quarried from nearby Nicollet Island. Greek columns supported the half-dome pediment. Inside the frame of the pediment farmers toiled in relief, scythes and cradles cutting a bountiful field. The figures moved toward the center where a stock of banded sheafs stood ready. The building had housed the grain market at the turn of the century. Here, farmers, millers, freighters, bankers, and government officials came together to set the practices and prices for the northwest grain trade. Two rows of large windows faced the street. Natural light would have been crucial to the work of inspecting grain samples that came in on freight cars. The building had sat empty and in need of repairs for decades. The city finally partnered with a number of granting agencies to fund a remodel and designate the building as a hub for social services for women and children. A number of agencies would have offices inside, from crisis centers to career counseling. It was an ambitious project, and Hannah was on the Board of Directors. She was instrumental in convincing the Board that they should use a relatively small percentage of the funds to commission a mural on a large wall of the lobby, and then she had convinced Simona to apply for the job.

The women climbed out of the car.

"Why are we here, Hannah?"

"Come inside." Hannah led Simona up the stone steps under the pediment. The doors were of solid wood with cast bronze handles in the shape of sheafs of cut wheat, beautiful and locked. "Over here." Hannah called Simona down to the far end of the portico where a standard door with a card reader had been installed. She unlocked the door and ushered Simona inside.

The lobby was cold and dusty. A scuffed wood floor of narrow planks had once gleamed under the heavy traffic of commerce. The chandeliers overhead would not be sufficient to light such a vast space, hence the windows, enough to ensure there'd be light even on a cloudy day. To the far left was a blank wall, two stories tall, unbroken by windows or doors, to the right a long, dark counter shaped like an L. Originally, the pit where the bidding on future grain markets took place, it later became a teller's counter when the building was owned by a bank. The frames and etched glass panes of the teller windows remained. Behind the pit, raised several feet off the main floor stood an office with windows that looked into the lobby. There a manager could survey his workforce. At the back of the lobby, directly across from the entrance, were two old elevators with brass dials above the gated doors. The building exuded the regal, masculine air of early twentieth-century construction. It had been built for the commerce of men. Simona thought there was an ironic beauty to it being repurposed to help women and children in need.

"We're thinking of putting a snack counter and coffee bar in the pit," Hannah said. "Wouldn't that be cool? With lots of tables here, then rugs and chairs in conversational groups over there under your mural."

Simona shook her head. "Say that again."

"People can grab a cup of coffee and sit down with a book or friend over there." Hannah gestured toward the blank wall, "We want it to be an inviting space."

"Go back a little further."

Hannah's smile broadened. "Yeah," she said. "Your mural. You got it."

Simona put a hand out and found Hannah's arm, gripped it. "I don't believe it. Oh, Hannah...." She covered her mouth with her hand, shook her head, and looked around the lobby again. "It's really mine?"

Hannah nodded.

Simona went to the wall and put her hands on it, glided them across the surface. Apart from a couple of large cracks, it was unmarred—the largest canvas Simona had ever worked with. She leaned into the wall, pressed her cheek against the cool surface and inhaled the dusty damp scent of plaster. She turned to face Hannah, her features spread in a smile of joy, and pressed her back against the wall. "Tell me everything."

"Everyone loved your work," Hannah said. "Really, the mural you did for the hospice was your coup de grace. And Elise Jasper's recommendation was outstanding."

"Really?"

"Of course, I voted against you."

"Naturally."

"I had to abstain. Conflict of interest and all that. Simona...."

"Yes?"

"You can peel yourself off the wall now."

Simona came to stand shoulder to shoulder with Hannah, facing the vast expanse of dingy white wall. The nothingness of it thrilled her. "When can I start?"

"Next week. What will you paint?"

"That wall. Duh."

"Ha, ha." Hannah linked her arm through Simona's. "Is this job going to be too much for you right now?"

"What do you mean?"

"The Center's grand opening is mid-June. And when is your due date?"

Simona laughed. "I forgot! I'm having a baby June eighth. I actually forgot about that."

"I'm sure it in no way reflects on your ability to be a mother. But are you sure you want this job right now?"

"You don't pass on a job like this unless you're dead."

Hannah looked at Simona with doubt, scanned the wall from bottom to top, her head tilted back to take in the upper corners. She wore the same concerned expression she had when Simona told her Peter would never hear about his child. Simona followed her gaze to the top of the wall. She saw pale blue.

"Come on, let's celebrate," Hannah said.

At the doorway, Simona paused to look back at the wall. It loomed at the far end of the lobby, waiting for her touch. A familiar thrill came over her that signaled the beginning of a work of art, that moment before brush touched paint that was pure, unlimited potential.

Chapter Two

It was raining. It always rained in her dreams. Gemma stared out her window at three young girls skipping rope in the street. Rivulets ran down the windowpane, blurring her view.

The girl skipping rope had long blonde plaits, just like Gemma had at that age, that bounced when she jumped. She wore a white pinafore dress with a tie at the back and a ruffle around the neckline. She stood in the middle of a large puddle and her bare feet made a splash each time she landed.

The girls chanted a rhyme. It was hard to hear through the window and the rain. Gemma desperately wanted to know what they were chanting.

She stood outside on her front steps. The rain flattened her hair and made her blouse stick to her. She went down the steps to the pavement, closer to the girls. The jumper had her back to Gemma.

"Pretty little Gemma went and got wed—"

The rope arced through the air.

"Then she did the nasty in her bed—"

The girl splashed down and Gemma felt large drops of water splatter against her cheek.

"Went to the doctor and the doctor said—"

The girl's plaits lifted off her back, following the arc of the rope.

"Feed that baby lots of bread—"

Splash. Gemma's heart raced.

"Tiny little baby with an empty head—"

The rope slapped the pavement.

"Born to Gemma already dead."

Gemma sank to the ground as the girl turned to face her. She shook her head, her mouth open, forming a silent "No." The girl had no face, as though someone had cut it away, leaving her head hollow. Blood pooled inside the empty cavity and when she jumped it sloshed about, spilling out over her chin and spattering everywhere. Gemma looked down at her lap. Her trousers were soaked. Everything was red.

She startled awake, damp with sweat, heart pounding wildly. She looked around in the darkness before sitting up and snapping on the bedside lamp. As she blinked back the light, Gemma realized it was only a dream—only that damned dream again—and calmed herself enough to get out of bed. Peter slept soundly through her discomfort. It was just like him to not wake up, and just like her to suffer it alone.

Downstairs, she plugged in the electric kettle and set a tea bag on the counter. Out the window she saw the bulky shadow of her gardening shed and the odd shapes of her now overgrown plantings. The tile floor chilled the soles of her feet. Normally inaudible, the clock ticked intrusively in the middle-of-the-night silence. Gemma carried her mug into the sitting room. Her hand trembled as she poured a jigger of brandy. Some spilled and she stared at the puddle stupidly. Would it matter if she left it to stain the old piece of wood?

Still, Gemma was Gemma and the thought of ruined furniture nagged at her until she looked around for a cloth to wipe up the mess. Nothing presented itself, so she used her nightdress, then carried the mug back to the kitchen with a golden-brown splotch staining the front of her gown.

When Peter came downstairs, several hours later, dressed for work in a bespoke suit, which signaled client meetings, he found Gemma sitting at the kitchen table in her stained nightdress, the empty mug before her. He lifted it to his nose and sniffed noisily.

Gemma didn't bother looking at her husband. She knew what he looked like well enough. If he ever went missing, she could describe him to a sketch artist in photographic detail, right down to the scar on his elbow. She told him that once, and he asked her why she wouldn't just hand over a photograph. Clearly, he didn't get her point. He didn't get her point more and more these days.

"I'm working late tonight."

"Of course you are, darling."

"What does that mean?"

"Only that you have a number of big projects since you got back from the States and work late a lot, it seems."

"Right. Well, I do have a number of big projects right now. Today I have three different meetings with prospective clients..." He let his voice trail off, sensing, Gemma knew, her disinterest in hearing more about his work life. That other life that did not include her and took him away for months at a stretch. "Go easy today," he said.

He left her there, his parting words, go easy today. Go easy today. She wondered on what she should go easy? On the drink? On the house? On herself? In which way did her husband mean for her to go easy?

When Peter first got home from the States, she thought absence had made his heart fonder and that things would be different. Their first night together was passionate in a way she had not seen for years, if ever. He was ravenous for her, and she responded, discovering that she had been starving for his attentions. But that had been it. He left for work the next morning and returned sapped of the desire that had driven them into each other's arms.

She could not understand it.

Gemma stood at the sink, her rubber-gloved hands sunk into the scaldingly hot water. She wore extra thick gloves—the green ones because she hated the yellow ones. Yellow—that intense bomb-shelter, police-line shade of yellow—was too garish, too institutional to be found in her kitchen. The heat rose and radiated through her. Perspiration was forming at her hairline. She had a double sink. Wash water on the left and the in-sink dish rack on the right. Clean plates were lined up, waiting to dry. Gemma had a dishwashing machine, but had gotten in the habit of doing the washing up by hand when Peter was gone because it took her a week to fill the washer by herself. Besides, it gave her something to do. Gemma put her gloved hands into the soapy water, let them slip under the bubbled surface, and then she forgot them, let them hang while she stared out at the back garden. Her garden was a shambles. She used to care about it so much. She had never had an idle hour with the garden to tend. Weeding was a meditation of sorts. The flowers in bloom, aromatherapy. And when friends stopped by, she proudly entertained them on the patio. But that was before. Gemma idly swished her hand and the tip of a knife caught the finger of her glove. She pulled back and peeled off the rubber sheath. There was a prick, just a drop of blood, but the glove was ruined. A wave of nausea surged, her insides pitched, and she hurled into the right-side sink all over the clean plates. There had not been even a second's warning.

She had thrown up yesterday, too, decided it was a stomach bug or something she ate, because she felt fine once Peter was home from the office. Now, it seemed like something else.

Gemma grimaced as she turned on the faucet and rinsed the vomit from her dishes. She tried to do it without looking. She would have to start the washing up over again. She went to the water closet and rinsed out her mouth. Under the sink, way at the back where she was unlikely to bump into it accidentally, Gemma had stashed a pregnancy test. It was leftover from the last time they were trying to conceive. She had found a special at the local chemist, two for the price of one or something. She had brought home six in a moment of determined optimism. They would make a baby, however many cycles it took to conceive. That had been folly. Or not. They had conceived and she only used five of the pregnancy tests along the way.

Gemma knelt in front of the vanity and reached past the pipes to the farthest corner, trying not to think of the spiders that liked to take up residence in such concealed places, and found the smooth, narrow box. She extracted it and sat back against the wall as another surge of nausea came over her. This time, being next to the toilet as she was, the surge passed uneventfully. *Figures*, she thought. She examined the box. It was already past the expiration date, but it would do for now.

Had she really skipped a period and not noticed? She tried to think back through the five weeks. Since they hadn't been trying, she hadn't been thinking about conceiving. She hadn't been fretting and planning and taking care to do everything right. She hadn't even noticed her period was errant. She set the test on the counter and washed her hands. The waiting was better if she did something to fill the time.

Gemma returned to the kitchen and turned on the kettle. Chamomile tea was the only thing for her stomach now. The faint odor of sick threatened to turn her stomach again. She turned the tap back on and let it run, flushing the pipes of any residue. That was better. The sun was shining on her garden, her shambles, her neglect. Too late for this year, but if she did some weeding, spread some compost, and maybe added some bulbs, things would come up fine in the spring. In the spring....

When the garden first bloomed, she would be entering her third trimester. Gemma's breath quickened at the happy thought. Her flowers and trees would be in bloom at the same time she was, a welcoming world for her child. She would nurse under the white blossoms of the apple tree. She would teach her child the names of the flowers, the colors, and the usefulness of bumble bees. They would read about Winnie the Pooh beside the pink azalea. But she was getting ahead of herself already.

Gemma returned to the bathroom and paused in the doorway to hold her breath. There was nothing to do but look, she told herself, and look she did. She had to hold the stick with both hands to keep it steady enough to read. When she turned it the right way round, she found a plus sign. Gemma fell back against the wall, bumping her head on a souvenir picture of Dover. She remained leaning for several minutes. She would have thought herself prepared for that plus sign, but really, even as she looked at her garden imagining her happy future, part of her had not believed it. Too much had gone wrong already for her to let herself get carried away. Winnie the Pooh was only a fantasy, after all, yet here she was, leaning against the wall beside the sink, her head against a picture of Dover, with another plus sign in her hands. It hardly seemed possible that her wish could be fulfilled so easily when so many things were wrong.

The night Peter returned from the States he had been different—so anxious to begin, then playful, and he was demanding, at moments rough. She wasn't able to refuse and before she knew it, she was caught up in his excitement. Remembering how passionate they had been still made her shiver. It was only fitting a child had been conceived that night. Still, something troubled her.

She and Peter hadn't made love in a couple of years, since the first miscarriage. There had been functional sex to conceive. There had been ritual sex that mimicked passion lost. And there had been the occasional attempt at true lovemaking, but it always failed, always left Gemma feeling nothing. Before Peter left for America, his lovemaking had been like an attack. When his anger dissipated, he became the rod and she the shaft: mere vehicles, sensation disconnected from emotion. It was punishment, his anger and his disinterest, but for what crime? They wanted the same thing. He had said so. No, he had professed it a thousand times on long walks, across the dinner table, with his head pressed to the flat of her belly. They both wanted a baby. And now, maybe, they could be happy.

The thing was, they had not made love since his first night back. Not even the perfunctory kind of sex that scratched the itch. She didn't understand how he could be so passionate that one night and then...it was like he had left her all over again.

She turned her head to face the vanity mirror. It seemed she hadn't looked at herself for months. Her hair had gotten away from her. She spotted a gray strand at her temple, which she would have to pluck. Thirty-two was too young to be showing her age. Gemma had been a model. It was a brief career; the camera loved more extroverted girls. Still, it meant she was beautiful. Through one of her limited jobs she discovered hand-modeling and was soon earning a decent wage at it.

She didn't mind all the gloves, moisturizing creams, and manicures. She continued for a few years after marrying Peter, for something to do while he worked, and tucked away the income in her personal savings. Peter requested she retire her hands after a vacation to Spain where Gemma wore long white gloves while sunning on the beach. In those early years of their marriage, Gemma was willing to make changes for her husband. She leaned across the counter toward the mirror, looking for a glow, but instead noticed the tiny laugh lines at the corners of her eyes. She had aged despite her best efforts. The last couple of years had worn her from the inside out until she felt like one of her mother's old crock cardigans. It didn't matter. The layers of grief and weariness she'd worn like a shield were soon to be cast off. This pregnancy, the baby she would get to keep, would rejuvenate her, erase the last couple of years and mend her and Peter.

Chapter Three

PETER SAT IN HIS office at International Marketing Strategies, staring with unseeing eyes at the cursor blinking away on his monitor. Just six weeks ago he had been in the States where it was hot and the sun was bright. Moisture hung in the air, making things cling together: his shirt to his back, his thighs to a vinyl chair, a woman's hair to her forehead. The only rain he saw in a month's time came at dusk when the air went still and the birds disappeared. He had stood on his balcony in the middle of downtown, where even sixteen stories up, Minneapolis's tall buildings shaped the horizon. Peter watched as jagged white streaks came closer and closer. Thunder rumbled in response, closing the gap between sound and vision as the storm moved over the city. Fat drops began pelting him. He stayed on the balcony drinking a Summit Pale Ale from the bottle until the rain came so fast it was difficult to see. The thunder clapped directly overhead, booming so violently that the building trembled. Soaked and exhilarated, he went inside, giddy with the sudden relief from the day's humidity and the spectacle he'd witnessed.

That afternoon, Peter had left a business meeting in a sober bespoke suit and found the midday sun miserably hot. The Farmers' Market had set up along Nicollet Mall, so he removed his jacket and lingered, despite the heat, to explore the offerings of American stalls.

While browsing the fruit and veg stands, Peter noticed a woman who looked familiar. She had long black hair that hung in a plait down her back and wore a tank top, cut-off jeans, and Converse pumps, the toes of which were covered with paint. When she turned to move on, Peter saw a small spatter of red paint up the back of her calf and realized he had seen her before. She had been at the Jasper Gallery, at an art opener one of his American contacts dragged him to. She had been striking in a pale pink dress, and now, seeing the paint on her leg, Peter impulsively decided to follow her.

He reminded himself of the only other time he'd followed a woman. He'd been nineteen and when he asked her for a date, she slapped him and railed at him for scaring her half out of her wits. This was different, he told himself. It had to be. Without so much as eye contact, he felt drawn to this woman. She moved with a confident stride: her head held straight, her plait bouncing. Maybe it was her certainty and confidence, or the fact that she lived with colors dripping on her shoes, that attracted him. He had never strayed from Gemma before and had no intention of straying now. He simply wanted to meet her, to tell her he admired her paintings. There was no harm in that.

The woman slowed her pace and cocked her head to one side before slowly turning to look over her shoulder. Peter kept moving, pretending not to see her. When she continued on her way, he dropped back slightly, told himself to stop behaving foolishly, but kept his course. She stopped at a stand. Peter did as well. He watched her select a pint of raspberries, and he bought a melon. He felt her looking at him, or maybe he only imagined it because he was red with guilt.

She left Nicollet Mall and Peter followed her down a street he'd never been on, past a Japanese restaurant with a blue tiled roof, then into a park. He'd broken a sweat keeping up with her and had to loosen his tie.

She sat on a bench facing a pond and took a baguette out of her bag. It occurred to Peter she might think he was threatening, or she might be married, or know judo. He sat at the other end of the bench despite common sense. The woman tore a hunk of bread off the loaf, her gaze fixed on a pair of mallards in the pond.

Peter cleared his throat. "Hot today," he said casually.

She swiveled on her seat to glare at him. "Why are you following me?"

"I...uh...um..." he stuttered. "I bought you this."

She had looked suspiciously at the plastic bag, then opened it as if it might contain a biting thing and peered inside. Her laughter had simultaneously surprised and aroused Peter.

His computer went into sleep mode. The photo of him and Gemma from their holiday in Spain drew Peter back to the present. He swiveled his chair to face the rain-streaked window.

His friend, Roger, had once told him about an affair he was having, and Peter had been no help to him at all. He didn't feel, morally speaking, that he could support his friend in the affair. But he couldn't bring himself to condemn Roger, or advise him that he must stop. It all seemed such a sticky complicated mess that Peter felt ill equipped to even form an opinion. Now he found himself equally ambivalent about his own guilt. He had left a troubled marriage, a troubled wife—were their troubles enough to excuse what he had done?

I am an adulterer.

Peter put his head in his hands and buried his fingers in his hair. No matter how often he thought it, it did not seem real. As though Peter Ledbetter had gone to sleep and another man went to the States and did all those things Peter Ledbetter would never do.

They had been honest together, hadn't even bothered to pretend. Three weeks. The finality of it, the brevity, fueled their passion. Simona...Peter pictured her long black hair falling, and...she made noise. Not like Gemma.

It was all that black hair, and in the painting she was brushing it. Peter didn't know why he had lied about his name at the gallery, probably because he was embarrassed. One wasn't supposed to buy a souvenir of one's affair. And it was shameful to have presented it to Gemma as a gift. She insisted on hanging it in their bedroom. It was, she said, a boudoir portrait. The subject sat at a dressing table, brushing her hair. She wore a blue robe and her face was reflected in the mirror before her. It was a melancholy but striking image, and Gemma liked it immensely.

"Hello, darling," Peter said as he entered the sitting room. He'd pushed back thoughts of Simona the entire way home and vowed to be good, to pay attention to his wife. He was troubled by the morning, finding her sitting at the table, a mug that smelled of brandy before her. Nonetheless, he stopped at the sideboard to pour himself a gin and tonic. "Can I pour you a drink?" He wanted her to decline because he thought she was drinking too much lately, but he would pour her a large G&T without comment if she asked for it.

"No thanks."

Peter raised an eyebrow and looked at her before capping the gin.

Gemma lit candles on the dinner table and went back into the kitchen. "Supper's almost ready," she called.

Peter sat down at the table, which was set for a formal meal, and noticed Gemma had placed a fresh arrangement in a crystal vase on the table. She set a plate in front of him: lamb chops, asparagus, and stuffed baked tomatoes. Their glasses, although stemmed, held only sparkling water.

"This looks lovely," he said, reaching for the bread. He looked at his wife finally and added, "And so do you."

"Thank you." She wore a simple, clingy knit dress in mauve. "How was your day?"

"Fine." Peter cut into his lamb chop. Gemma was certainly a better cook than Simona, who had once worked diligently at a vegetarian supper, but got her "tsp." and "tbls." mixed up so that the tablespoon of salt made the dish inedible. He smiled to himself. Certainly Simona's knowledge of local restaurants and ineptitude in the kitchen were related. She was tuned into city life and took him to a movie in a park, a play in a bowling alley, cycling around the lakes, and to one restaurant after another, each a unique experience.

"Pass the butter, please," Gemma said.

He obliged. They were quiet again. Peter wondered what the occasion was. Gemma never prepared a meal like this, dress and all, without a motive. Maybe she was going to ask him for a divorce. Were they that bad off? Or was it wishful thinking? He felt a tinge of guilt, but it faded when he heard Simona's laughter in his mind, so vibrant it made him feel like his life in England was happening in black-and-white. The weather was gray, his suit was black, his company car was brown, his dining room was beige—or "sand," according to Gemma. Everything here was dull and muddled. He didn't even know how he felt about his wife anymore, how much longer he could tolerate her depression.

"Darling, I have news."

"What?" Peter looked across the table at Gemma and noted that she was smiling.

"You're certainly preoccupied tonight," she said.

"Sorry. It's just...well, I have news too. Something happened at the office today."

"Something good, I hope."

"Yes, I think so." Peter smiled at his wife and thought how unfair it was to compare two such completely different women. Besides, this thing with Simona was just an adventure abroad—he was hardly himself in the States.

"You first," Gemma said. "Mine can wait."

"All right, darling. Mr. Perry liked my report on the States. He said the research and proposal were top-notch."

"Of course they were." She smiled and served herself a second helping of asparagus.

"He wants me in charge of opening the new branch. It's a fantastic opportunity."

Her smile withered. "Of course it is."

"I'd have to return to Minneapolis for about three months. I laid the groundwork this time, so mostly I'll be firming up relationships, hiring people, organizing things."

"You accepted it, then?" She scowled, her disapproval showing before receiving his answer.

"I saw no reason not to." Peter speared a piece of asparagus with his knife tip. "It's a huge responsibility. If I prove myself there, I'm that much closer to the vice-presidency. You know Netley is only two years from retirement. I'd be a fool to let them send another department head."

"When will you go?"

"After the holidays." Peter sipped from his drink, rather satisfied that his news had gone over without more resistance. "What's your news, then?"

"I'm pregnant."

Peter sat dumbstruck while a dozen conflicting thoughts raced through his mind, thoughts about Gemma and Simona, the new branch in Minneapolis, and a baby. He stood up from the table. "Why darling, that's wonderful. He went round it to lift Gemma into a tight embrace.

"Peter—you're—squishing me."

"Sorry!" He let go and stepped back to look at her. "How far along?"

"Seven weeks. I looked at the chart in the pregnancy guide, and my due date is June tenth."

"You've been to the doctor?"

"No. I only found out today. Besides, there's no hurry yet. I'll take my vitamins and get on the schedule—"

"Gemma, you know you should be monitored by the doctor," he said sternly.

"I know. I know. I'll call in the morning and make the appointment."

"Good."

Gemma laid her head on Peter's chest. The image of a black-haired woman sitting at a dressing table flashed through his mind and Peter swore he'd take the painting down. "Don't worry, darling. I won't take the job."

"But..."

"I want to be with you every minute of this."

November

Chapter Four

CLOTHING LAY OUT OVER the bed: flouncy tunic tops, trousers with stretchy panels, dresses with tie-backs, and everything barely worn. A box sat on the floor, one last piece neatly folded on the bottom. A posh frock, bought for a wedding during Gemma's third pregnancy when she was six months along, black silk with large pink flowers. Bright, cheery flowers that had reflected Gemma's happiness, her third-try's-a-charm confidence, the giddiness over safe passage through the second trimester. Somewhere tucked out of sight was a photo of Gemma at the wedding reception. She wore a hat with pink camellias decorating the brim and proudly displayed her belly. Everyone had declared to her how wonderful she looked, how well she carried, how she positively glowed. They had whispered that she looked happier than the bride and laughed and patted her round swell, as irresistible as Buddha's belly

No one knew. There had been no signs that only a week remained to her bliss. One week and then the painful sinking into despair. Congratulations turned to sympathy. The well-wishers who had swarmed her at the party sent cards or flowers, and then drifted away, suddenly close-mouthed and afraid to meet Gemma's eyes.

Peter received the firm handshake, the clap on the shoulder. For Gemma, condolences were sent long-distance by greeting card, or passed from friend to friend to Peter. It was the sick bed phenomenon, she decided. Nobody dared to come close, never mind that her pain and grief were intangible things that couldn't be seen under a microscope. They were contagions nonetheless. All that she needed was that touch, that eye contact they gave so easily to her husband. The words didn't matter. "I'm sorry," would have been enough, but they didn't know, and they left her isolated in a sick bed of heartache. For this she blamed them. So, the dress with the pink flowers remained in the box, a reminder of all those celebrants who had abandoned her to feast alone at grief's table, refusing to share even a morsel of her pain.

Gemma selected a pair of leggings and a dress with three-quarter sleeves and a tie at the waist in a lovely burgundy color, her favorite autumn shade. Her brown riding boots and a houndstooth coat completed her ensemble. It was a good day. She walked with her belly protruding, the slight swell accentuated by the maternity dress. She unconsciously pushed her hips forward, let her stomach, normally so taut, protrude. Pride drove the display, and confidence. Everything was all right this time. Gemma couldn't help smiling in the elevator as she unbuttoned her coat, grinning in the hallway as she walked, baby first, to the doctor's surgery. She entered the waiting room and found Peter sitting in a corner with his attention focused singly on a newspaper.

"You escaped the office." She leant over to kiss his cheek.

"Yes, and I didn't think I'd beat you here."

"Traffic was worse than I expected."

"Isn't it always?"

"Mrs. Ledbetter?" a nurse called from the surgery doorway.

Gemma and Peter followed her back to the examination room.

"You don't have to undress today," said the nurse as she took Gemma's blood pressure and temperature. "One-twenty-two over seventy-one. Ninety-nine degrees," she announced before exiting.

"'Breast Self-Exam,' 'Nutrition During Pregnancy,' 'Prenatal Exercises,'" Peter read the titles of brochures on display. "I guess there's not much call for men's literature back here. This season's rugby line-up, or how to build a boat."

"You've never wanted to build a boat in your life."

"True. But I'd rather learn about that than 'What You Need to Know about Your Uterus.'"

Gemma laughed. Not the polite chuckle she'd been forcing for the last year—a genuine laugh, light and amused. Peter smiled and touched her knee. It occurred to her they were happy. It occurred to her she wasn't the only one aging as the overhead light caught a showed the lines over Peter's brow. Perhaps he had shared in her experience more than she gave him credit for. She smiled at her husband. At last, things were improving.

A balding man with reading glasses tucked into his lab coat pocket came in. "Good day. Sorry to keep you waiting." Dr. Saunders shook Peter's hand before sitting at the foot of the examination table. "You can lie back and relax, Gemma."

She obliged and exposed her abdomen. "The other day, going upstairs, I got a stitch in my side," she said.

"A stitch?" Dr. Saunders palpated her abdomen. "Not a cramp?"

"A stitch, here." She poked herself in the side.

"You were probably dehydrated. Don't exert yourself too much and drink more water."

He took a tape measure from his pocket and ran it from Gemma's pelvic bone to her navel. "Twelve and a half centimeters. Your uterus is growing appropriately." He scanned her chart. "Your weight looks fine."

Peter squeezed Gemma's hand.

"Now for the fun part." Dr. Saunders smeared jelly on Gemma's abdomen and placed a microphone against her skin that was attached to a small speaker. He turned the machine on and adjusted the volume. They heard a low, rhythmic whooshing sound. "Your heartbeat," he said, moving the microphone. They heard a gurgle from her stomach. The doctor moved the microphone again, paused to listen, and again, pressing it harder against her abdomen.

Gemma looked at Peter. He smiled reassuringly. They both knew what they were supposed to hear: their baby's heartbeat, like a tiny horse galloping at full speed.

Dr. Saunders cleared his throat.

Oh God, not again. Gemma looked out the tinted window behind the doctor. It had clouded over and rain blurred the glass.

Peter moved to Gemma's side and took her hand.

"Don't panic, Gemma," Dr. Saunders said. "We'll just have to perform a sonogram to find your little one." He paused to look at her. "It's too early to assume anything," he said before he stepped into the hallway.

"Darling, you've gone all white," Peter said.

"It can't happen again. It just can't!"

Dr. Saunders returned with the nurse, wheeling in the sonogram machine. He kept his head turned toward the monitor as he searched with the apparatus, but Gemma could see the nurse's face and she watched it carefully. The nurse opened her mouth in surprise at whatever she saw in the gray swirl, then quickly snapped it shut and focused her attention on the machine so deliberately that Gemma knew she was avoiding her gaze.

The doctor proceeded quietly, freezing and printing images on the monitor to go in Gemma's file, muttering occasionally to the nurse. When he finished, the nurse carefully wiped Gemma's stomach, focusing her gaze on her own hands. She replaced Gemma's top and escaped through the door.

"He's dead," Gemma said.

"No, Gemma." Dr. Saunders leaned in closer to lock his eyes with hers. "There is no baby."

"What?" Peter exclaimed.

"I feel sick." Gemma sat up, a hand on her stomach.

The doctor held Gemma's chart lightly, as though it was as fragile as his patient, and shook his head. "It's called pseudocyesis, also known as a phantom pregnancy. In essence, you wanted to be pregnant so badly that your body has been behaving as though you actually are pregnant. But there is no baby."

"But I missed my period. I've had morning sickness. I took a test!"

"Each of those symptoms is possible in the absence of pregnancy. A fetal heartbeat is considered the only true way to confirm pregnancy by many doctors."

"Doctor, my wife is not prone to hysterics or fantasies," Peter said, recovering from his shock. "Surely there's a mistake somewhere."

Dr. Saunders looked at Peter for some time before speaking. "You are welcome to a second opinion, of course, but the sonogram showed clearly that there is no baby."

"Can I see the pictures?"

"Of course." Doctor Saunders handed Peter the printouts and explained what he was looking at.

The doctor's voice faded away as Gemma's head rang with questions, questions she already knew could never be answered. She held her breath, not knowing what to do next. *This isn't happening. It's impossible.* "This kind of thing is associated with mental illness," he said. "I want you to guarantee she'll see someone." He scratched something on a slip of paper and handed it to Peter. "What are you saying?" Peter said. *Not again. Not. Again.* "That it is possible Gemma is suffering from a mental crisis of some kind. She needs to see a specialist to be certain." "But, doctor..." *I've been through this before. I know the signs.* "It's a lot to absorb at once, Peter. Just take her home. Call me if you have any questions and make certain she sees that psychiatrist." He pointed to the paper in Peter's hand. "If nothing else, she can help Gemma through the grieving process." *Grieving! I don't want to go back there.* "Thank you, doctor." "Take good care of her, Peter," Dr. Saunders said from somewhere miles away.

"Darling?"

She and Peter were alone. His eyes were tinged pink and she knew he had held back his emotions in front of the doctor.

"I'm sorry," she whispered and broke into sobs.

"No. No, love." Peter pulled her head against his chest and cradled her. "It's not your fault."

Chapter Five

"I'M AFRAID I NEED a couple of days medical leave," Peter said into the hall phone.

"Are you sick?" asked a gruff voice on the other end of the line.

"No, sir, it's Gemma. She's not well and I need to look after her for a bit."

"It's not too serious, I hope."

"It is troubling, but she'll recover. Of course," Peter added, "I'll be able to work from the house."

"Of course. Give Gemma my best."

"I will, sir."

"Peter, you haven't changed your mind about that job in the States, have you?"

"No, sir."

He hung up the phone and returned to the sitting room. He stood at the sideboard, watching Gemma while pouring them both a tall scotch. She sat on the couch, hugging her knees to her chest. He knew he should say something to his wife, something comforting, but he couldn't think of anything. He simply didn't understand. What Peter wanted to say was, *How could you?*

Chapter Six

SIMONA ARRIVED AT THE Center, relieved to find the lobby empty. It had been cleaned so there wouldn't be dust drifting off the chandeliers while she worked, and a steel scaffold had been built with casters so that she could safely reach the top of the wall. The bottom row of windows had also been covered in paper at her request, so that she could work in privacy without curious passersby stopping to stare. The lobby was then declared off-limits so that workers wouldn't track in dirt. They would come and go through the back of the building, sparing her constant interruptions. Hal, the on-site building manager, was the only person she could expect to see in her lobby, since he used the old bank manager's office.

Her first batch of supplies had been delivered and she pulled everything out of the boxes, taking stock as she organized each item: polyethylene sheet, washing solution, gloves, putty knife, filler, sandpaper. There was a certain pleasure to be had in ordering the tools of her trade, preparing for a new work of art. After the cracks were filled and the wall was prepared, she would prime it with an acrylic gesso wash, then paint on a warm white ground coat. It would be a full week's work to prep the wall, but it was a critical step that Simona wouldn't allow anyone else to handle. At the bottom of the box was a ventilator mask, which she had not ordered. She turned it around in her hands, examining the capsule-shaped filters that sprouted off the mouthpiece like industrial mushrooms. It had two padded straps—one for the top of her head and another for the back of her neck—clearly this thing would get heavy. Simona held the mouthpiece in place and tried to breathe. Immediately she felt the warm humidity of her breath trapped against her skin and felt like she couldn't get enough air through the canisters. She gave a Darth Vader wheeze and tossed it back in the box. Hannah meant well, but Simona couldn't work with that thing hanging off her face. A simple paper mask would do. Simona congratulated herself on this compromise. "See?" she said to her belly, "I can make good choices for other people."

It was the first time she had spoken to the baby and the realization was strange. *I'm going to be somebody's mother.* The weight of that thought forced her to the ground. She made it safely to the floor, crossed her legs and put her head in her hands. "Okay. Okay. Get it together, girl." Simona did some deep breathing to calm herself, the kind she had once learned from a therapist before quitting him. She believed in action, not talk. She might have continued therapy if they could have talked while riding bikes around the lakes. At least the breathing thing helped whenever she felt overwhelmed. The way to not feel overwhelmed by this, she decided after several meditative minutes, was to focus on what was real and present. And *that* was the mural.

Simona stood, collected herself again, and went to stand before the wall. She ran her hand over it. The old, cool plaster had a smooth, slightly chalky feel. Light from the upper row of front windows gave it a matte appearance and showed the gentle waves of plaster smoothed into place by builders, craftsmen with trowels, who were all long since gone. Simona would add her ghostly imprint to this wall with her handiwork just as they had. She believed in that, the imprint the artisan leaves behind through her work. Simona stood still and let the lobby fill with silence.

Time to begin.

The last of the ground coat was finally on and the large brush she held dripped on the toe of her Converse high tops. Simona was lost in thought, staring at her wall, considering potential and possibilities, reveling in the limitlessness of creation. The Center for Women was going to provide so much for so many. Between the counseling, classes, and daycare facility, hundreds of women would be passing under Simona's mural each week, thousands each year. She traced the wall's edges with her gaze, sizing up her canvas, and a shiver of excitement ran through her.

Sheets of drawing paper lay scattered about Simona's studio, torn away from the sketchpad and abandoned recklessly. She tried sketching famous women and role models, composites of women she'd known, as well as imaginary figures. She tried sitting at her drawing table next to the window, on the couch, at the breakfast bar, and on the floor. Nothing she drew pleased her. Nothing, except one sketch of a woman she'd known as a teenager, but one woman would not fill that entire wall.

That night, tired and frustrated, Simona leaned on the kitchen counter, staring into the side of her stainless steel teakettle. In that convex mirror-like surface, her face bowed around the curve of the kettle and she saw herself as a sixteen-year-old girl again. She had been so alone. Simona's father had worked hard to provide for the future, and in the meantime they went without. Each night he withdrew into a bottle of cheap Chianti, which was, for Gilberto Casale, a necessity. A truly nice Chianti was a luxury that he only allowed himself on Christmas Day, when he toasted his dead wife with the first and last glass that he poured.

She remembered Christmas dinner that year, when she was sixteen. Her father had sat at the kitchen table, his half-eaten plate of spaghetti had long gone cold and he was on his third bottle of Chianti, his favorite from the local estate in Grosseto, where he had grown up.

"In Italy, we would never pay fifteen dollars for this." He held the bottle overhead for emphasis. Simona sat across from him, picking at a piece of crusty bread. "We take old milk jugs, olive oil cans, whatever we have, and we fill them with this same wine for nothing! Nothing, I tell you."

Simona had heard how wine was sold back home a hundred times already. She had once even passed along the tale to a teacher as a point of interest in seventh grade. The teacher, an over-eager recent hire, became concerned and passed her name to the school counselor, who then grilled her about her father's drinking habits.

"A great jug cost us only pennies. And look at this..." He searched the bottle's label. "1994. For the Americans, they hold the wine two years. Never in Italy. Chianti is meant for drinking."

A captive of Christmas dinner, Simona sat with her arms folded across her chest while red lights strung around the apartment twinkled and cast her father with an unnatural glow. Under the table, she wore candy-apple red combat boots, defensively shod in steel toes. She'd managed to wear them to Christmas mass by convincing her father they were festive. Beneath a plaid flannel shirt, she wore a black T-shirt with a skull printed on the chest. Solely for her father's benefit, Simona had applied extra mascara and eyeliner before mass. When she served him dinner, instead of thank you, he said, "You look like a ghoul."

Simona glanced around the studio and knew that everything she had came from her art. It had been the thing Gilberto most disapproved of. She would grow up to abandon the purple streak in her hair. She would stop dressing like a depressed corpse. But this art, he must have realized, she could not outgrow. It was integral to her being, and so he disapproved of it more than anything else.

"What good is a degree from this College of Art and Design?" he had yelled, shaking Simona's crumpled acceptance letter in his fist before tearing it up. "You will attend the U and get a degree in business, something so you can earn a decent living." The school had offered her a scholarship and invited her to meet with a financial aid counselor. They needed her answer by January, so she had saved the letter for weeks, waiting until Christmas when she thought her father would be in a generous spirit. Simona took the pieces of the letter out of the trash after Gilberto fell asleep on the couch, *It's a Wonderful Life* making its annual Night Owl Theater appearance on channel 9. She shoved the scraps into her pocket and climbed onto the fire escape. She might have left home right then, her mascara running down her cheeks, but when she turned around to flip off her father through the window, to declare, "Fuck you," she saw that she was not alone.

"I do not believe my children ever flipped me the bird. For one thing, their papa would've whupped them good. For another, I do not believe our differences were ever as big as all that."

Simona spun around, her boots clattering loudly against the metal grate of the escape. In the shadows, wrapped in a large comforter, sat her neighbor. After getting over the shock of finding this woman she barely knew beside her, Simona sat and talked until her teeth were chattering and her fingers numb. The cold drove her inside to her own bed and she left her escape for another day, a day in summer about nine months later, when she moved out of her father's life to pursue her dream.

In the morning, Simona went to the Center. She dug around her box of supplies until she found a set of charcoals. Twelve new square sticks lay in a neat row, separated by the folds of their paper tray. She plucked one up from the middle and turned it over in her fingers, enjoying its smooth and familiar feel.

She pulled the sketchpad from her satchel and turned back several pages. "Hello, Clarice," she said to her drawing. After that Christmas, she and Clarice met frequently on the fire escape. Clarice had helped Simona through those difficult months, and Simona could still hear her voice, "Well now, Miss Simona Maria Casale, come and sit with me. Tell me your woes."

"Well, Clarice Abigail Washington, you don't make a mural, but you're my start," Simona said, touching the paper gently.

She sat on the floor and studied the grid she had marked off on the wall and tried to visualize, hoping more subjects would come to her. At this rate, she figured she would need more than the seven months before the Center opened to finish her project and would be painting with a baby strapped to her chest. After sketching for several hours, Simona settled on a composition of a large group of women, row upon row, standing shoulder to shoulder, each one with a story on her face. Simona did not yet know who they were, but she had the outline for a start. She wanted every woman who entered the Center to recognize herself somewhere in the painted crowd, to lock eyes with one of the figures and know that she was represented. Simona taped her sketch on the wall and next to it, the drawing of Clarice. Clarice would stand one-off, to the right of the central figure. Simona transferred the sketch to the wall, roughing in the life-size figure.

When finished, Simona dug in her supply boxes. She peeled the tag off her new palette and arranged neat blobs of color on it, mixing Van Dyke Brown and Raw Umber for Clarice's skin. As she worked, Simona wondered whatever had happened to Clarice and if she ever thought about Simona.

She arrived early the next day, excited that her work was begun. Simona blended paints, turned Ultramarine and Alizarin Crimson into violet and set to painting Clarice's dress. The daytime hours came and went quickly with Hal coming and going. Simona worked for hours without a break, detailing the shades of Clarice's skin, the shape of her knuckles, the light reflected in her brown eyes.

Painting was nourishment. Simona slipped easily into a different place where all that existed were brush and canvas. She paid loving attention to the work she created, naturally infusing the work with mood, her mood. And this portrait was dear. Simona had forgotten about Clarice and all the help she'd given her in recent years, but now that Clarice was remembered, and with a mature perspective, Simona revered the woman and projected love with each brush stroke.

Eventually, her hunger turned to nausea and became a distraction. Still, she pushed on, ignoring her queasy stomach's insistence that she feed herself and her baby, until Clarice was complete. Simona stood back and looked at the portrait. The woman painted on the wall was realistic and natural, beyond that, she was exactly how Simona remembered the real Clarice: warm, with gentle hands and deeply caring eyes, broad shoulders and a strong frame. Clarice could embrace the world.

"You look pretty good," Simona said to her painting.

Clarice gave a little nod.

Simona pressed her eyes shut, then blinked them, "Whoa, I'm tired." She shook her head, then, giving no more thought to the portrait's impossible movement, she packed up her things and left.

The next day, as Simona entered the Center, Hal came out of the office in the back corner of the lobby. "Miss Casale, that's wonderful work," he said.

"Thank you. You can call me Simona."

"All right, Simona. I'm heading out for the day. I'll lock the front door so nobody can wander in off the street. You can exit through the back any time."

"That's good to know. Thanks, Hal." The front doors had yet to be updated with push levers, a noncritical item this early in the renovation process, and there was some concern about spoiling the aesthetics of the old doors that still had to be worked through.

Left alone to work, Simona crossed the sad old floor, worn and streaked with heavy gouges from the last time the building was vacated, and set down her bag of supplies. She was grateful for the tall row of windows that faced the street. Even with the bottom papered to block curious passersby, she had plenty of light as long as the sun was shining.

She looked at Clarice, pleased with the portrait, but it was only a beginning. Simona would build out from and around Clarice's figure, which would serve as the anchor. The next portrait could be any woman, but Simona needed that spark of something tangible before she began.

"Talk to me," she whispered.

A ripple ran through the picture of Clarice. Simona turned around to see if the lighting had changed behind her, a black cloud passing before the sun, perhaps. *That's weird,* she thought, then knelt and opened her bag.

Another ripple passed through the painted figure. Her fingers moved and Simona looked up. Clarice nodded her head. Simona fell backward, her mouth gaping. A hand came out from the wall. The fingers spread and stretched, then curled into a fist as the arms reached out, one after the other, and Clarice's head pushed out from the plaster.

Simona's mind went blank, struck dumb by the utterly impossible.

Clarice pushed a leg out and placed her foot firmly on the floor. She peeled her torso away from the wall and stepped into the lobby, free.

Simona's eyes rolled back and she collapsed.

"Oh my gracious!" exclaimed Clarice, rushing to her side. "Come on, baby." Clarice fanned Simona with her hands. "Wake up. It's all right now."

Simona moaned.

Clarice jumped to her feet. "Hang on, baby!" She shuffled across the lobby, arms pumping, and ducked into Hal's office. "Ah-ha!" she yelled. "Hang on, hang on!"

Emerging from the office with a blue metal box in her hands, Clarice ran back to Simona and opened the first aid kit. Tucked under gauze pads and a carefully packaged scalpel were two vials of smelling salts. Clarice grabbed one and snapped it, then waved it under Simona's nose. Simona's eyelids fluttered and she turned her head away from the stinging smell before opening her eyes.

Clarice smiled down at her. Simona pushed away, scooting across the floor, eyes wide.

"Oh no, baby, don't be afraid," Clarice said. "It's only me."

"You're.... How can you be here?" Simona scrambled to her feet.

"I've near scared you to death. Hang on, let me think." She placed her palms on her thighs and bowed her head, searching for words.

Simona backed away.

"I'm sorry," Clarice said finally, "but I can't explain it."

"How?"

"I'm not sure, baby, but the head and the heart have powers we don't yet understand. I guess you wanted me to come help you with something and here I am." Clarice smiled a broad smile that made her dark eyes crinkle and her cheeks lift into brown apples. "It's so good to see you."

"I must be nuts!"

"No-oo," Clarice soothed and reached toward Simona. "Just look at you all grown up! Little Simona Maria Casale," she said the name in a singsong voice. "Go on, ask me something. You got me here for a reason, and I don't know how long I can stay."

The woman standing before Simona was real. As she moved, shadows on her body, cast by her body, changed under the lights. Her dress shifted and swung about her calves, flowers showing then hiding themselves in the folds of the skirt. Her face was mobile. When Clarice spoke, the shape of her mouth changed, wrinkles shifted, teeth flashed. Her eyes. Simona focused on Clarice's eyes. They shone with life—spirit—a depth and resonance that was only possible in the living person. No portrait, no matter how lifelike, could capture that human essence that shone through the eyes.

The portrait she'd stepped from was faded, yet a perfect likeness, as though Clarice had been birthed from her own reflection. Her Afro was cut short and graying at the temples. Her dress was a simple sundress with a V-neck and short, fluted sleeves. Clarice had once told Simona....

"Honey, it don't hurt to show off a little asset. Me, I like to cover my upper arms and show some cleavage. That's my most flattering."

"You read my mind," Simona gaped at her.

"No. I just read it in your eyes. The way you were studying me, I could tell where you were. I like this dress, honey, it's real pretty."

Beginning to trust in Clarice's familiar warmth, Simona felt her shoulders sliding back into place as her muscles relaxed. She was being drawn uncontrollably, inexplicably to this apparition. Perhaps Clarice sensed Simona's fear receding, because she looked for a place to sit, settled on the floor, and patted the floor beside her.

Simona took a step away from the wall and moved slowly. As she drew closer to Clarice, she became aware of a sound, as though someone was humming softly in the background, but there was no recognizable tune. Standing perfectly still, not quite trusting, she listened and puzzled over it. Unable to determine what the sound was or where it came from, she sat at arm's length from Clarice and looked at the first-aid kit still open on the floor.

"Don't worry, honey. I'll put that back," Clarice said. "Now then, who else are you going to put on that wall with me?"

"I'm not sure. I haven't thought of anyone specific yet."

"You will soon enough." Simona flinched when Clarice reached out to pat her knee, and Clarice withdrew her hand. "Maybe you'll think of who to paint while we talk." She paused, but Simona did not speak. "Tell me about that baby girl you're carrying."

"How do you know it's a girl?"

"I'm a woman, ain't I? You hang around as long as I have and you can sense these things."

Simona couldn't be certain, but she wanted to believe that she was carrying a daughter. It occurred to her that Clarice was a mother who could teach her something about this new life looming before her. She began with a simple question, nothing intrusive. "How many kids do you have?"

"Three," Clarice said.

"Three? Not two?"

"Well, not all of them were still in this world by the time we met."

"Oh, I'm sorry." Simona was surprised she didn't already know that, but supposed it wasn't the sort of thing a grown woman discussed with a teenage girl. She waited for Clarice to explain, suddenly eager to hear all that she could about mothering, about the trials and the joys.

"Michael, my first baby, died when he was only a week old. I came to about three a.m. one morning because my bosom was hurting something fierce and the milk had soaked all through my nightgown. I was gripped by a fear stronger than anything I'd ever felt before, so great that it paralyzed me. I woke my husband and told him to bring me my baby. While he was going for our son, I squeezed my eyes tight and prayed. Let him be alive, I said over and over. But I already knew. I already knew." Clarice shook her head. "James stood frozen to the spot, staring down into the cradle. Finally he just picked up the baby and carried him over to me. I sat there in bed and cried and cried and rocked him in my arms all morning long. He was so tiny, so new to the world, and yet his leaving broke my heart into a million pieces.

"I didn't let it go until Sara was one year old...I guess some of the fear left me then. Sara grew up and married a good man, but he moved her away from here so I don't hardly see her any more. At least she's good about sending pictures of my grandbabies.

"Tomas works construction in the summer then does odd jobs over the winter. He does his best with what he's been given.

Clarice fell silent and Simona didn't know what to do with this palpable grief of a woman who had lost a child, a husband, and was left alone by adult children busy with their own lives. Grief was not unknown to her—her mother's absence from her own life sometimes rushed her, overwhelming her with the pain of an injury that had occurred when she was too young to even register it. Yet, confronted with Clarice's grief, Simona felt helpless. She looked up at the ceiling, at the gilt chandeliers, and the humming she had forgotten came back to her.

"I didn't mean to spoil our reunion," Clarice said. She took a deep breath and exhaled slowly, releasing some ancient pain associated with mothering, then focused on Simona. "Do you have a name for that child yet?"

"No. I could name her after my mother. But..." Simona shrugged.

"What was your mama's name?"

"Carina."

"That's a lovely name. Tell me something about her."

"Right before he died, my father told me that I look just like her. He said it was hard to look at me because all he saw was her ghost. He used to talk to her when he was mad at me. He'd say things in Italian like, 'Carina!' Simona raised her hands and looked toward the ceiling, imitating her father's accent, 'What will I do with this child? Make her see.'"

"He loved your mother so much. You know he lived in a world of pain."

"So did I, and it made for a very lonely childhood."

"Some folks just have a hard time showing their love."

"Yeah..."

The front door rattled with the turning of a key. Simona gasped and looked toward the entrance as Hal entered with a gust of cool autumn wind. She was about to explain, to introduce Clarice as an old friend, but Clarice was gone. Or rather, she was just a portrait on the wall.

"Hello," Hal called to her. "I'm not done here today, after all."

Simona lifted her hand to wave as she remembered the first-aid kit. It had vanished along with Clarice. In a moment of confused silence, wanting to explain herself but knowing there was no reason to, Simona realized the humming had stopped.

Hal closed his office door and Simona turned to face the wall and Clarice's image in her own recognizable brush stroke, a portrait and nothing more. She went close, stared at the painting and looked into Clarice's eyes, but they were only paint, unable to return her gaze. Simona reached out a hand and touched Clarice's. It felt cool and flat as a wall. Feeling silly, she glanced over her shoulder to make sure no one was watching.

Clarice's visit—or Simona's vivid hallucination—reminded her of her youth. Clarice had introduced Simona to another neighbor, another kind and generous woman, Rosa Martinez. Simona took up her charcoal and began to sketch Rosa.

Simona cleaned up early, making sure she was ready to leave before

Hal. After wrapping herself in her coat, she grabbed her bag and noticed a scrap of something that had been hidden underneath it. She picked it up intending to toss it in the garbage, but stopped and looked, her heart beating fast as she read the paper wrapped around a small plastic vial. *Smelling Salts: For the prevention and treatment of fainting.*

Chapter Seven

GEMMA LAY CURLED ON the bed in her dressing gown with a teddy bear clutched to her chest. Peter had gone to fetch some files from the office, leaving her alone with only the sound of her own shallow breathing.

Light from the window fell across the painting he had brought her from the States. She stared at *The Self Less Mother*. The artist's mother and the Mother of God merged together, one representing the other, an attempt to fill a void. The artist sat despondent in a gloomy room, her mother out of her reach, on the other side of a portal. The artist's mother was dead, gone to Heaven, and faith in Mary had been no replacement. Gemma saw it in the neglected rosary and unlit candle. There the artist sat, the motherless child. And here she was, the childless mother.

Her art history degree had helped to develop her eye. She was quick to analyze, interpret, and understand. She could have been successful as a critic, but the degree had been a disappointment. She meant to be a painter. Flawless in technique, but none of her professors could teach her that creative magic that made the difference between being skilled and being brilliant. Gemma realized her limitations early, changed her major, and concentrated on finding a husband.

The painting was beautiful and she enjoyed the melancholy mood. What Gemma could not understand was why Peter had bought it. Perhaps because "mother" was in the title he thought it would comfort her, but could he really be that thick? He meant well, she knew, but he didn't see deeply, always satisfied with the first impression. He was right about one thing, at least, it did match the bedroom colors.

There was something about that painting. Something in those layers of paint, under the gold leaf, something she had to see, something she would see if only she looked hard enough. Gemma went to it, stared at minute sections, her eyes traveling inch by inch across the canvas. She memorized brush strokes, knew the weight of the artist's hand, felt the careful attention paid to detail—she noticed a white hair hidden in the artist's curls, just one hair painted with the finest brush. By the time she finished studying it, Gemma could have painted an exact copy.

Was the pain of losing a mother more or less than that of losing babies? Gemma tried to compare her pain to that other woman's, thought about what kind of painting she would make of her loss, putting herself in competition with the artist.

She suddenly remembered Peter standing in front of the mirror, tying his tie, his eyes turned away from the glass so that he could see the painting. She suddenly didn't want the painting in her house. Gemma placed her hands on the heavy frame and as she lifted it away from the wall, the unmistakable smell of a cat box came from somewhere. She returned the frame to its hook.

The tangy odor penetrated the membranes of her nostrils and made them itch. She so loathed the smell that she couldn't even stand to clean with ammonia. Her mother had always kept at least two cats, and it had been Gemma's chore to clean the litter. Percival, a snobbish white Persian, and Princess, an aloof Siamese, had tormented her teen years. Gemma looked around the room, desperate to find the source, but the odor followed her, growing more potent, until her temples throbbed. She sat on the bed again and picked up the teddy bear. Her brows pinched together as she scowled, puzzling over the odor. Her fingers dug into the plush sides of the toy, squeezing it to half its size. Then another blast of the stink sent her reeling and she fell back across the bed.

When she sat up, she found herself in a large room with an old marred floor of wood planks. Gemma looked at her hands and was shocked to see the nails were clipped short and naked. She tried to speak, but had no voice. A heavy-set woman stood in front of her, speaking with an American accent, and she smiled as though acknowledging Gemma's presence.

"Michael, my first baby, died when he was only a week old," the woman said.

This is some kind of dream. She fixated on the death of this woman's baby, on the horror of holding that still little body. That large, homey woman's voice enveloped Gemma and she stopped listening to the words. She felt the vibration of human notes as this woman, Clarice—the name came into her mind—spoke of her children. Somewhere beneath the voice was a sort of humming noise that Gemma noticed when Clarice wasn't speaking.

"You should rely on your inner strength," Clarice said. They were parting words as the empty room surrounding them dissolved into a kaleidoscopic array of color.

Gemma's bedroom emerged from the mutating shades and, as she came back to her senses, her eyes focused on the painting. The cat-box smell remained, burning in her nostrils. Her entire head throbbed. Gemma moaned. She still held the little bear and her hands were stiff from gripping it so fiercely for so long. She tried to knead the poor thing back to its original shape while she sorted out the strangeness of the experience.

Gemma remembered something Dr. Saunders had told Peter: *This kind of thing is associated with mental illness.*

Chapter Eight

SIMONA PEDDLED THROUGH THE city, bundled against the wind in a short coat and scarf. As long as there wasn't snow, and sometimes even then, she rode her bike. The streets were already congested with the morning commute. Along the way, she remembered, or continued remembering, her youth. The memories had begun with Clarice and continued through the night and into this new day. Simona left home early in order to arrive at the Center before Hal. She pumped her legs against the cold, her mind again turning over what had happened the day before. Instead of talking herself out of believing it had happened, she found herself remembering.

During their conversation, Clarice had mentioned Rosa, another woman who had been kind to that lonely, troubled girl, the one without a mother in apartment 326. That spring, the two women had invited Simona into Rosa's kitchen. Rosa's table was covered in a yellow cloth and she poured them iced tea from a ceramic pitcher she'd brought from Mexico. It was hand-painted with simple brush strokes in cobalt blue and sunny yellow. Her glasses were blue Anchor Hocking. Later, Simona had seen the same glasses at the grocery store for about sixty cents each and asked to buy some. Papa, however, saw nothing wrong with their glasses. "Glass doesn't wear out," he had said. At Rosa's table, Simona's grunge trappings went seemingly unnoticed while the women gossiped about people she'd never met. They complained about men and money troubles. Sometimes they asked Simona if she knew so-and-so, or how school was, or if Gilberto was as bad as most men about picking up after himself. Mostly, Simona sat and listened.

Rosa often made flour tortillas during their visits. She mixed the dough, then sat at the table while it rested. Without looking at a clock, she knew when it was ready and sprang up from the table. She put dinner plates in front of Clarice and Simona so they could form the dough into balls. Then Rosa laughed and chattered away while spreading the dough with her rolling pin. Once it was rolled out, the tortilla was laid on the *comal* to cook while she rolled the next one. Simona remembered the deftness of Rosa's hands with admiration. When they were finished, the women snacked on Rosa's tortillas, rolling them around her fresh tomatillo salsa.

Rosa was generous and cheerful, yet she was guarded, too. Simona realized, looking back, that she didn't really know anything about Rosa. It had seemed strange to her that Clarice never spoke of her children in front of Rosa. Then, one day on her way to the bathroom, Simona noticed a photo. A girl with long black braids stood smiling in front of a red adobe house. She had a balloon tied to her wrist and wore a white party dress with a lace collar. The girl, dressed like a child of six, had the figure and height of Simona herself. She knew then, whatever Rosa's story, her heartache had been framed and hung on the wall.

Simona set her bike inside the door and made sure it was locked. The wall was a giant on the other side of this chamber, rising up vast and empty, void but for the two women Simona had painted. Clarice stood life-size at the bottom of a white field. She looked ready to walk across the lobby and give Simona a hug.

"You're being silly," Simona told herself as she slipped off her coat. She slowly approached Clarice's portrait, reached out and touched the hand, half-expecting her contact to spark some magic and bring the painting to life. It felt cool and dry, just as paint and plaster should feel. She giggled nervously at her own foolishness. It had been a fantasy, she assured herself. The smelling salts wrapper had already been there on the floor and she had simply incorporated it into her dream.

She laid out her painting supplies and prepared her palette. She worked alone in the quiet without so much as a flicker from Clarice. Before she knew it, Hal arrived, said hello, and retreated to his office so that she could work in peace.

Simona painted Rosa with a broad smile on her face and her mouth slightly open, as though she were at the beginning of a hearty laugh. Since Simona couldn't paint Rosa standing at her stove, flipping tortillas onto the *comal,* she put her in a sun-yellow blouse and added a touch of cobalt blue jewelry to her costume, the other color so prominent in Rosa's kitchen. As she worked, Simona savored her memories. She could almost smell the tortillas heating on the *comal*, almost taste the salty butter blending with Rosa's salsa *cruda*. As she worked, her desire grew into a craving for Rosa's black bean burrito.

Throughout the day, workers came and went from the back of the building, bringing saws, drills, pipes, wires, and who-knew-what into the building. She could hear them, clunking around in heavy boots, but the sounds became a background of no importance and Simona hardly noticed the quiet that came with their departure until Hal stood outside his office pulling on calfskin gloves and saying good night. She wanted to ask him to stay, to wait so she wouldn't be alone. Pride kept her from saying anything other than a simple, "Good night."

She stood with her back to the mural, staring into the empty space, looking after nothing, waiting for something. Despite her morning experiment, she was no longer convinced she was alone, or that she had imagined her visitor. Her heart rate accelerated until the beats came one on top of the other. "You are not going nuts," she said aloud. Simona closed her eyes, waiting for a sign, counting the moments until she could give up and laugh at her own foolishness. A different scent came into the air. Simona's back stiffened as she drew in a breath and held it. It was the prickly sweetness of Halston cologne that filled her nostrils. Every day that Simona had known her, Rosa had dabbed herself with that drugstore perfume.

"*Mija.*"

Simona recognized the voice from long ago, and knew that both Clarice and Rosa stood behind her. She turned and stared at them, unable to speak.

"I know this doesn't make much sense, but you need something from us," Clarice said. She'd always been direct and plain spoken with an unmistakable tender note to her voice. Simona looked at Clarice, then past her at the wall. Her portraits of the women were faint imprints, remnants of the women who stood before her.

"Let's sit down," Rosa suggested. "We'll visit—like we're back in my kitchen making tortillas. Okay?"

Beneath the fear and uncertainty, she wanted them. Simona nodded and sat on the floor, because she didn't know what else to do. These women before her, whatever they were, she welcomed them. She picked up her sketchbook and stared at a blank page, waiting for someone to begin. In the quiet, she heard the strange humming noise.

"You know, I was thinking about home, and my childhood," Rosa said. "My home in Sonora was a beautiful place. We lived in the country very near a river. When I was a little girl, I thought if I followed that river it would bring me right to the sun. I would climb up on that old sun when it was even with the earth and I would ride it through the sky, past my home, every day. I would sit there on a throne of gold like a princess. I thought I would not come down until my prince came and beckoned to me."

"She likes to tell stories," Clarice said, sticking her thumb out in Rosa's direction.

"I told that to my little girl almost every night."

"Your daughter?" Simona asked, looking up. She thought of the girl in the photo, the one with Rosa's eyes. They were reddish-brown, the same as Rosa's skin, the same as desert clay.

"She is in Mexico with *mi madre*. When Mama dies we will sell what is left of our little farm and bring my daughter here. In only four months she will have her *quinceañera*. For us, a girl's fifteenth birthday is very special, it is like Confirmation and Sweet Sixteen combined. I am saving money for her party, but I do not even know if I'll have enough to go home for it." Rosa tucked her hair behind her ear. "I never expected to be apart so long. My mother, I sometimes think, has been visited by Death many times. But she is so stubborn she sends him away." She laughed and nudged Clarice with her elbow.

"My mama could hardly wait for Death to come," Clarice said. "She said she had buried a brother, three babies, a husband, and a grandbaby—and it was about time somebody buried her. And three months later, I did just that. She got her affairs in order, called me up one night and told me I'd been a good daughter to her—that is the closest that woman ever came to saying she loved me. Then she told me to come by the next morning. When I got there the place was dark—every curtain drawn and every light out, but she had the gospel station playing on the radio. I found her in her bedroom, laid out in her best dress with makeup on and a pearl necklace—ready for her grave. I'm sure if she could've, she would've died standing up so as not to muss up her hair-do." Clarice laughed. "My guess, she laid down like that, closed her eyes and died of her own stubborn will."

As Clarice and Rosa talked, Simona sketched quick pictures of them and their mothers. She didn't look up from her pad, just listened and drew. She sketched a young Rosa riding the sun through the sky. She drew Rosa's mother holding a fistful of dirt. She drew Clarice's mother standing before a mirror, preparing to leave this earth. Never having met the women she drew, she imagined older versions of Clarice and Rosa, thinner, more severe women.

Eventually Simona grew tired and hungry. As she finished one last sketch, she became aware of the silence. The humming was gone. She looked up and saw that Clarice and Rosa had returned to the wall as silently as they had come. Simona stood and stretched, stared at the portraits and was satisfied with her day's work.

After cleaning up, Simona got out her phone to call a cab. The building was a dead zone, so she went into Hal's office to use the land line. She stood outside the office and looked through the dimly lit space at her work. "Goodnight," she called to Clarice and Rosa. They did not respond. She left her bike at the Center and let a cabbie drive her home.

Simona sat at an antique dressing table in her bedroom, looking at an old black-and-white photograph. The date stamped in the border was Oct 1966. Carina and Gilberto Casale were on their honeymoon in Rome. It was the only photo Simona had of her mother, who was wearing a hat, her face deeply shadowed. Simona's mother stood in front of a fountain, pigeons surrounded her, a man on a scooter zipped through the background. Her father had told her she looked just like her mother.

"Mama," she said, and stopped, uncertain where to begin. "I'm pregnant, but you already know that." Simona felt like she was reaching out to a friend after years of absence. "You must know what's happening to me," she said. "I don't know what's going on. When I'm there, talking to Clarice and Rosa, it feels so natural. Then I leave and I think I must be crazy." Simona stared at her reflection, hoping the mirror would fill with heavenly rays and her mother speak to her from the other side, or to step from the photo as Clarice and Rosa had stepped from their portraits. Nothing happened and she returned the memento to a jewelry box that had belonged to her mother. She climbed into bed and fell asleep.

She walked through a garden of vibrant flowers in full bloom. In the center grew a tree with a great gnarled trunk that twisted upwards, ladder-like. The branches spread wide, forming a canopy over the garden, and the roots reached just as wide, coming out of the ground, laying across it like so many dead giants. It reached from the heavens to the earth.

A great serpent lie coiled in sleep at the tree's base. Its body was as thick as the gnarled roots that spread around it. Simona noticed the iridescence of its scales, the many shifting colors running its back, and the milky white of its belly. She came close and reached out to touch the snake, to see if she could feel the energy flowing through its rings of muscle. Before she laid her fingers upon it, it moved and the many yards of thick coils shifted and separated, revealing her mother's head, arms, and torso.

Simona stared, and her mother stared back. She saw herself in her mother's face, and understood the regeneration taking place inside her own body, the creative act of bearing a child.

"Simona," the Serpent-Mother spoke. "Why did you think I was not watching you? Do you think a mother ever leaves her child?"

The Serpent-Mother rose from her coils, disappearing into the canopy of the tree. When she returned, the Serpent-Mother held out her open palm. A golden orb hovered above her hand, glowing so brightly that Simona had to cover her eyes. "A gift," she said.

Simona accepted it. The heat from the orb seared her palm and she cried out. The Serpent-Mother looked on calmly as Simona absorbed the light. Simona felt a great heat spread throughout her body. It moved and pulsed in waves, touching on every cell, then it centered in her womb, enveloping her child with a fierce maternal love.

Chapter Nine

PETER SCOOTED AWAY, CLOSER to the edge of the bed, barely asleep. And still, Gemma rolled over, curled herself into a ball, and pushed her knee into his back. She moaned. Peter was unwilling to wake Gemma, to comfort her again in the middle of the night. This restless, fitful sleep of hers had to be better than nothing. And he pitied her. What else could he feel for a woman who invented a baby? Whose body behaved as though pregnant when it wasn't? In the morning, he would not be able to bring himself to complain about the bruise on his back or how little sleep he himself was getting. Since he could not help her, he tolerated her.

Chapter Ten

Her dreams, since Gemma had learned that her baby did not exist, had been dark, shapeless horrors that escaped her in the morning. They left their mark all the same. Each night she took a fresh nightie from the bureau, knowing it would be damp with sweat in the morning. She woke tired with an unsettled feeling, a sense that her entire life was wrong. Every decision on her path, to veer right or steer left, to move uphill or ease down, was wrong. Ultimately, she had come to this horrible place by her own design and the road ahead was filled with broken glass and flanked by high walls. It was too late for Gemma.

The smell of cheap perfume tickled her nose and she rubbed it with the back of her hand as she rolled over. A picture came before her mind's eye. Two women. A dream? The women came into focus. Clarice and another woman. They were talking. Gemma listened, finally lying still in bed. She was certain they knew she was present and they welcomed her.

While Clarice talked of her mother's death, Gemma looked down at what should have been her hands. One hand held a sketchpad balanced on a lap that wasn't hers—a host whose hands and lap, whose eyes and ears she borrowed—and the other hand sketched with a soft artist's pencil. The swift flowing lines formed pictures of Clarice and the other woman, who was called Rosa. The fingers of the hands were blackened from blending and shading, and there was paint under the nails and spatters of color on the backs of the hands. These hands were never pampered as hers were, with their ragged cuticles and the sun-deepened lines about the knuckles. The hands-that-were-not-hers belonged to an artist.

Clarice's mother had willed herself to die, a woman who decided she had seen enough of life. Rosa's mother refused death, a woman who was needed. Gemma felt like neither. She could not list accomplishments, could not claim anyone would have trouble surviving without her in this world.

She listened and watched the artist's sketches take shape. It felt like a long time she was there, in that place of both light and dark. When she awoke, she remembered it all clearly and knew it was more than a dream. She turned on her bedside lamp and took a notepad and pencil from beside the phone, then sat up and made her hands work. She moved quickly, copying the sketches the Artist had made, trying to keep the originals sharp in her mind's eye. The pencil she used was dull with hard lead, but Gemma was unwilling to go in search of a more suitable one, afraid the images would be lost if she stopped drawing. Her pictures filled several pages as she captured the strange women of her visions.

When she finished, Gemma looked at her hands, one holding a notepad and the other a pencil. The fingers were slender, the nails long and manicured, the skin smooth and delicate, so different from the Artist's. She suddenly felt ridiculous for spending years pampering those hands, investing so much pride in such silly useless things. Those hands that had never made anything, never signed any important document, never held a baby. Gemma sat back against her pillows and held the notepad up, her unblemished hands trembling. Her copies were good for quick scratchings. She stared at Clarice and Rosa's faces. *Why do you come to me? Why now?* She tore the sheets of paper from the pad and slipped them between the pages of a book. *No. They're only dreams. They don't mean anything,* she thought, trying to comfort herself.

Gemma parked in front of a handsome house with red brick along the ground floor and white stucco with black timbers above. The semi-detached residence sat just yards from the Heath. A small plaque on the garden wall read: E. Hamilton, M.D., Please use side entrance. Gemma followed the crazy paving around the house. As she drew closer, her progress slowed, delaying the unavoidable.

She banged the knocker sharply three times and turned to look at the street. She didn't think she knew anyone who lived in this neighborhood. She hoped, anyway, as she searched for a crack in the curtains next door.

Dr. Emily Hamilton opened the door and held it for Gemma. Gemma noticed the woman's hands. Her nails were unvarnished and trimmed short, so short Gemma thought it mannish. Remembering that her own burgundy-colored nail varnish was chipping and didn't complement her aqua blouse, she curled her fingers into her palms before stepping inside.

"Welcome," Dr. Hamilton said as she stepped aside and put on a pair of black wire-framed glasses. The frames matched her straight black hair, cropped short. Apart from a smearing of red lipstick, she didn't wear makeup. Dr. Hamilton led Gemma through to her office. "Please, take your coat off," she said.

The office was lined with bookshelves. On one shelf, encased in glass, sat a mounted brown trout. The plaque on the wood base read "The River Dove." Gemma looked at the spots on its back and the butter-colored sides that melted into a white belly. Its mouth was open and its tail bent as though it was fast coming upon the fly, yellow, tied with copper wire, that shared its case. The trout would forever be poised thus, ready to gulp down the fly. The fish couldn't have known that the fly was no fly, but a bit of fluff concealing a hook, and not only was that meal its last, but it wasn't even a meal. Next to the case sat a framed photo of Dr. Hamilton in waders, waist deep in a river with a fishing rod. The rod was bent and the line stretched taut. A copy of *The Compleat Angler* by Izaak Walton stood on the shelf, its spine well broken.

"Do you fish often?"

"When I can." Dr. Hamilton smiled pleasantly and moved toward an armchair in front of the fireplace. "Please, sit down."

Gemma sat opposite the doctor on the pale green settee, her back straight and her feet flat on the floor. Dr. Hamilton balanced a note pad on her lap and uncapped an elegant fountain pen with silver filigree overlay along the cap and barrel.

"Mrs. Ledbetter, tell me why you're here."

"Don't you know?" Gemma asked.

"I'd like to hear your version of things."

"I..." Gemma cleared her throat and laced her fingers together. "I need to be analyzed, to see if I'm ill."

"A lot of people think you need to be ill to seek therapy, but there are plenty of people who come simply to sort things through. Let's say you're one of those people. Now, tell me what you'd like help sorting through."

Gemma nodded, then began to talk slowly, forming a rough outline of hopes and expectations that gradually filled in with details of aching losses and a failing marriage. She told the Doctor that nothing made sense anymore. She had a great ambition once, when she was very young, to be a painter. She was good. Everyone said so, practically perfect—well, her dad said that. She amazed him. Her mother clucked her tongue every time she touched a paintbrush. Gemma couldn't stand her mother's pragmatic ways. So simple. So dull.

Dr. Hamilton's silver pen caught the light and flashed momentarily. Gemma realized she was talking about her childhood and her parents. She suddenly felt foolishly cliché. Wasn't she there about a pregnancy that ended only days before? Was she about to blame it all on her mother? Still, the Doctor did not correct her and it felt good to talk. Gemma continued with her story.

At university, her professors complained and nagged her. Technically speaking, she was very skilled, but there was no creative spark, they said. No genius. No true originality. They advised her to find her gift. She tried. She tried and tried and tried again. In the end she became an art history major. Art history degrees were not known as moneymakers, and Gemma could not stand to prove her mother right, so she pursued the one remaining option: marriage.

She spoke as though to the air, only vaguely aware of Dr. Hamilton capturing her words, making note with that silver pen. Still she talked on, letting truths tumble from her mouth like clay blocks. They were newly formed and rough, shaped in the dark so that Gemma barely recognized them in light of day.

Peter's money meant comfort. She would be one of those affluent few, the non-wage earning woman who did charity work and attended functions. It would be fun. It would not be her mother's life. Ultimately, however, it did not matter what color she painted her sitting room, or how current her wardrobe. She was a pool untouched, reflecting bright blue skies, but beneath the surface, the bottom was dark and somewhere, buried under everything she'd lost, was herself.

One day, flipping through a magazine, she had an idea. Such a nothing act. Flip. On the page was a woman with bobbed blonde hair. In her arms was a baby, bundled in a soft white blanket. The scene was gleaming. The woman was smiling. Gemma didn't remember—what were they selling? Something to clean with: *Clean enough for her, clean enough for you.* Gemma didn't want the product. She wanted the baby. She wanted to feel the love and joy and serenity projected on that woman's face.

She would have a child. She took out a calendar and planned: three months to get pregnant, nine to be pregnant, and in one year, her happiness would arrive in a package of about seven pounds with ten fingers and ten toes. A girl with dark blonde hair. Of course, anything so long as it was healthy, but Gemma pictured a daughter who resembled herself more than Peter.

It began so innocently with a glossy magazine advertisement. One moment Gemma was studying the latest trend in handbags and planning her next trip to Harrods. Flip. She began that very night. The diaphragm was tossed out and Gemma greeted Peter with a special dinner, candles, wine, and beneath her dress, the chemise that would slip so easily to the floor. She made a game of it.

Her failure increased her drive. She made demands on Peter. He did his duty each time he impregnated her, and so the losses she took on herself, blaming her body. With each one she became less.

Gemma sniffled, and Dr. Hamilton held out a box of tissues. She felt a complete fool recounting it all. How much she had taken for granted! If she had known that one magazine ad, a model smiling at a baby, would lead her to Dr. Hamilton's pale green settee, questioning her sanity, Gemma would have dropped the entire magazine into the dustbin and walked out of the house.

"Now?" Dr. Hamilton asked.

Now. Gemma considered now. The past two years, the babies and the not-baby, had crippled her. When she tried to stand up, her knees buckled. All the pain had wedged a boulder between her and Peter at the same time that it forged a chain and bonded them together. The links of the chain were called guilt, incrimination, pity, fear, blame, loss, but they were no less strong than those other bonds people claim, the desirable ones.

And what did Gemma want? A life that was neither cold nor sharp. And maybe the occasional moment of happiness.

A smooth, empty, gray sky stretched over Hampstead, a backdrop to the store windows that twinkled with Christmas lights and doors hung with wreaths sporting bright bows. The cheeriness of the decorations irritated Gemma. She looked up at the red brick houses so familiar to her. The street-side windows hung in neat rows, and each house differed from its neighbor only in the color of the front door. The way buildings stood shoulder to shoulder all up and down the street reminded her of sentinels, blocking the rest of the world from view. If it weren't so cold, she would have walked on the Heath. The Heath helped her feel less penned-in. She supposed, like any kept animal, she was comforted by her cage at the same time she longed for her freedom.

A woman about her age with two children, a boy and a girl, passed by. The children wore matching scarf, hat, and mitten sets. Their shoes were shined, and each had pretty curls poking out from under their knit caps. The woman was pregnant, radiating that mother's glow that came with the security and confidence of having healthy babies. Gemma couldn't help but stare as the trio passed. The children were as well behaved as they were groomed. Her heart swelled with envy, pushing against her chest like a water balloon about to burst. She bit her lip as she watched them turn into a shop. The little girl paused at the door and looked back at Gemma, a troubled expression on her face. Gemma tried to smile and waved her fingers, but the girl did not return her gesture as she disappeared through the doorway.

Gemma inhaled, filling her lungs. It seemed she wore her frailty like a badge pinned to her coat for all to see, even a little child, and it was wearisome.

On the way home, she pulled into an empty parking space in front of the Black Bear. She seldom went to pubs and had never drunk alone in one before, but it seemed better than going home. A bookshop was next door and Gemma went in, grabbed the first appealing paperback she saw on the way to the counter and bought it, just to have something to occupy her in the Black Bear.

She ordered an Irish coffee at the bar before finding a booth near a window. People talked quietly over their pints and bags of crisps in the dark pub. A couple of men sat sullenly at the bar, staring at a television.

Leaving her coat on, Gemma opened the book to the first page and prepared to forget herself. She read, "Jessica Vernon ran away from her life when she was thirty-five years old." *The problem with running away,* she thought, *is that you need somewhere to run to.*

As the coffee warmed her, filling her chest and stomach, she let the cover of her paperback flip closed and wrapped her hands around the footed stoneware mug. Gemma was always cold in winter. When she and Peter were first married, she liked to lay her head on his shoulder and press her icy hands to his bare chest until they warmed. She knew it wasn't pleasant for Peter, but he never complained. Then, one day, she stopped, and he didn't ask why, like they were children who'd suddenly outgrown a silly game. She realized that she'd been pulling away from Peter for some time. It occurred to her now, looking out at the red brick walls of Hampstead, that he was doing his part as well to widen the chasm between them. She couldn't exactly say he was pushing her away, it was more that he wasn't trying to bring her back to him.

Gemma opened her book and read again, "Jessica Vernon ran away from her life when she was thirty-five years old."

The sessions with Dr. Hamilton, nine so far, were helping. Gemma had regained enough confidence to get out of the house without imagining herself under the whole world's scrutiny. At the last meeting, the doctor had asked Gemma a string of specific questions about her sleep patterns and nightmares, about her level of distress when encountering pregnant women, about avoiding places where children were likely to be, and about her withdrawal from family and friends. They also discussed her depression since the stillbirth of her third child—the fetus, Gemma called it—her drinking to get to sleep, and her feelings of guilt. Dr. Hamilton had said she would review her notes and have some ideas for Gemma next time.

Any minute now, Gemma would know if she was crazy.

Dr. Hamilton sat across from her in the usual armchair, her silver pen scratching away, while Gemma reported the events of the last few days. Did she think Gemma wouldn't remember her promise? That it wasn't agony to sit there waiting for a verdict?

"Now, Gemma, last week I mentioned that I'd have a diagnosis of sorts for you."

Her heart seized at mention of the word. She wished Peter were with her. He'd be able to listen rationally to bad news, ask the appropriate questions, and he could hold her hand.

"Generally," the Doctor continued, "women who experience pseudocyesis are histrionic, someone seeking attention, someone unstable, impulsive, and usually suicidal. They possibly have a borderline personality. Or they are suffering from post-traumatic stress disorder," Dr. Hamilton explained.

Gemma sat stiffly, uncertain whether she could stand to hear the rest of it.

"You have been suffering from post-traumatic stress." The doctor waited for Gemma to resume breathing.

"So...I'm not...mentally ill?"

"Not the way you mean it, no. Your phantom pregnancy was brought on by a series of extremely traumatic events: three failed pregnancies. The cause was circumstantial, not organic."

The fear that had been haunting Gemma finally dissipated. Muscles that had been tensed for ages relaxed. It had been so long living with that idea of insanity, taunting her from the recesses of her mind during the most mundane activities: slicing bread, selecting clothing from the closet, walking out her front door, and whenever she saw a pregnant woman on the street.

"We still have work to do," continued Dr. Hamilton, not giving Gemma a chance to dwell on this good news. "You must have had friends at university. Were any of them also art history majors?"

"What do old school friends have to do with this, Doctor?"

"Bare with me, Gemma."

"Well, there was Miranda."

"Miranda." The doctor jotted the name on her notepad. "What is she doing now?"

"I don't know," Gemma lied. Miranda Richardson was one of London's most successful gallery owners. If Gemma had become a painter, she'd have done anything to maintain that friendship.

"See if you can't find her again. Find out what Miranda has made of her art history degree." Dr. Hamilton's instructions were always received as commandments, spoken in the voice of quiet suggestion, but something about them, about her, left no doubt that one should do as she bid as soon as possible. She scribbled something on her notepad, then looked at Gemma. "I want you to do something else. I want you to write a letter."

"To you?"

"No, to the babies, maybe to Peter. It's up to you, really. The thing is, nobody has to read it, so feel free to say anything you like."

"What's the point of this, doctor?"

"Don't worry about that just now. Write the letter, and we'll talk about it next time."

Gemma stared at the unconverted fireplace and the sooty black remains of a long-ago fire, so long ago she thought of its remains as archaeological. She had the urge to pick up a lump of the burnt log and crumble it into dust. She made a loose fist in her lap and wondered what it would feel like to dirty her hands, and then maybe wipe them on her trousers.

"Gemma?"

"Sorry." Gemma looked at Dr. Hamilton, who had removed her glasses. The doctor's eyes were hazel.

"Remember, there are no rules for this letter. You can be yourself."

Peter was safely tucked out of the way, trapped in his office at IMS for a few more hours at least, maybe longer if traffic was horrible. Gemma laid her monogrammed stationery on the kitchen table. How glad she'd been to drop her maiden name. She made coffee, strong coffee, and set it above her pen. She was about to sit when she changed her mind. At the sideboard, she poured a shot of whiskey. *You don't drink like this anymore,* she thought. *Shut up,* she thought, and set the shot glass next to her mug.

Darling Baby,

How can I explain to you what happened? How can I accept Dr. Hamilton's pronouncement that I am not crazy, and yet, right now, admit that I miss you—figment of my imagination. How can I explain that my greatest failing as a woman resulted in this terrible fabrication, this sick attempt to get what I want?

I think about you each day. I can't help it. It's easier to pretend you were real and I lost another treasure. When I let the truth in, it frightens me. How do a mind and body conspire so wickedly against a person? How could I have done this to myself? A thousand questions. Not one answer.

Gemma sipped her coffee, but it wasn't enough. She decided it was easier to pour the whiskey into her coffee and stir than to hold the pen. She drank again.

She wrote on through three mugs of Irish coffee and eight sheets of paper.

Gemma finished when sobs shook her body, made her vision blur, and her hand tremble. She hated the letter and all of its misery, but writing it was a relief. Gemma slowly headed up the stairs. She had just enough strength left to run a bath.

Coming downstairs in her dressing gown, hair wet and combed smooth, she was surprised how much better she felt. Peter had come in while she was in the bath and she expected to find him reclining in the sitting room, but the room was dark. Gemma continued down the hallway to the kitchen.

She faltered. Her hands felt for the belt of her dressing gown and cinched it tighter. Peter stood at the table, the last page of her letter in his hand.

"Oh hello, darling," he said. "It was lying out. I thought..."

"Never mind." Gemma hurried to the table to straighten and order the pages of her letter. "It's silly."

"No, not silly. We've never really talked it through." Peter placed his hands on Gemma's to settle them. "We should talk. Please."

She looked into Peter's green eyes. They had a depth she had never penetrated. If she could be honest with him, maybe she could go deep enough to salvage their relationship. His gaze calmed her. Her husband had finally asked to talk about their babies. Gemma took two wineglasses out of the cupboard and Peter, following her cue, opened a bottle.

They sat across from each other. Gemma fingered the stem of her wine glass, nervously running her fingers up and down then around the foot as she prepared herself to be honest. She expected, when they had both exhausted the subject, that it was Peter who would save her from this horrible lonely grief.

"I knew all this had taken a terrible toll on you," Peter began, "but I didn't know you felt so alone. I thought your sister and your mother helped you."

"You know my mother better than that. As for my sister, she's never lost a child. Just being a woman doesn't make someone understand," Gemma said.

"But surely they're sympathetic."

"It's not the same. To them I didn't lose children, I lost pregnancies, things. It's completely intangible to them. Mum thinks I should be able to just get over it, like it was the dog that died. I haven't even told her about this last one."

"I didn't know."

"No, but you should have," she said gently.

Peter looked puzzled.

"Peter, you're my husband." She emphasized *husband* as though the word carried intrinsic meaning that would make her case for her. "We made four babies together—"

"Three."

Gemma's face dropped. She took a sip of wine and avoided the thought that Peter had made an accusation with only one little word. "Yes, I suppose I made that last one all by myself. The point is that you are the one person who has been at my side through all of this. You should understand better than anyone."

"You're right." Peter sighed.

They sat in silence. He stared past Gemma. She knew the window behind her, the way the garden looked as dusk approached. She naturally pictured it tidy, at its best. She reminded herself how poorly she'd kept it of late. Peter was staring at the garden and thinking she was a mess. She'd given up. He was right, wasn't he? Gemma had let go of everything and then expected Peter to do all the work, to keep them together. She decided she would apologize for expecting too much of him, for being difficult, for filling holes with imaginary babies.

But Peter spoke first. "Gemma, is it true? What you said about me." He flipped through the pages of the letter, scanning each one. "Sometimes I think," he read, "that if I'd married someone else, none of this would have happened. I'd never have suffered. Perhaps the problem is with Peter, and not me."

"Peter, please."

"If it's his fault we can't have children," he continued, "then I only have to forgive him, and I think I can just manage that." Peter set down the paper and lifted his wineglass.

"You were never meant to see that," she said. "No one was. They're only thoughts. I only wrote the letter because my therapist said to."

"I see. Then it is true."

Gemma looked at Peter's eyes again. They were impenetrable. "I don't blame you, Peter."

"But you would like to."

"Only so I wouldn't have to blame myself."

"You know the doctor said it was a combination of factors, that neither one of us could be blamed." His voice was calm, but beneath the rational tone, Gemma recognized the hardness of anger and hurt so poorly concealed.

"It seems that it has to be somebody's fault..." she tried to explain.

"So it has to be my fault. If you'd married Nick instead of me this never would have happened to you."

"That's not what I said," Gemma insisted.

"It is, right here in this letter."

"If you read the whole letter, then you know I blame myself. I just said that because..." Peter stared at Gemma, waiting, but there was no way for her to continue honestly. She had said it because she felt it, and on some level, against all logic, she believed it. The air in the room was heavy, making it impossible to walk away from her husband and the half-truths that stood between them. The complexity of what each really thought, of all the things they had hidden from each other, connected them at the same time it drove them apart. At last, she refused to be defeated by a silence. "I thought we were going to talk and come to some understanding. Not just throw out accusations. Let's start again, please." Gemma held her hand out across the table.

Peter kept his folded in his lap. "Gemma, I'm tired. I don't know if I can go through this again."

"*You're* tired? Of being pregnant? Of having awful bloody messes born from your body?" Her voice rose shrilly. "Or delivering a brainless child that had been dead inside of you?"

"Of course..."

"Of course not! You're tired of *me*."

Peter leaned on the table, pressed his elbows against it and hid his face in his palms. "Has it occurred to you that this has been hard on me as well?"

"Of course, but it's different." Gemma tipped the wine bottle to her glass, the two clinking together, a crisp accent to the cutting tone of her voice. "You get to leave."

"I get to leave what?"

"Everything. The house, for one. You go to work and have this other life I don't have. This..." She gestured with her arms sweeping overhead to take in the entire kitchen. "This is my entire life, here in this house.

This is where they were all conceived. This is where I was pregnant. This is where I went into early labor three times. This is where I have nightmares." She paused to glare, to set her meaning. "All of it is right here. You even..." Her voice cracked as tears came and she struggled to finish the sentence, "...get to leave *me*."

"Gemma, I haven't left you."

"No, you just ran off to America for a month. A lovely vacation, I suppose. Meanwhile, I'm stuck back here. Do you know that I made a list..." her voice faltered again.

"A list?"

"...of ways I could kill myself and when I should do it so that I would be found before I rotted."

"You weren't serious," Peter said. "It was only a dark moment."

"I considered hanging myself, but it seemed too risky. What if I didn't do it right? What if instead of snapping my neck, I strangled myself? Pills seemed the natural choice. That's how all housewives do it, isn't it? But slitting my wrists held a certain appeal, more dramatic I think, all that blood. I would have done it in the nursery."

"I think you have too much time on your hands." Peter's right hand held his left, his right finger rubbing over the smooth surface of his wedding band.

"You could have found me dead!"

"Honestly, Gemma, resorting to emotional blackmail."

"Call it what you like, but you know I'm right. You're never around. You never see how much I need you."

"I've tried to help you, Gemma. I've done what I could, but I can't be responsible for your depression."

"I didn't ask you to be responsible for me, Peter." Her voice thickened with emotion.

"Just tell me what you want." His neck muscles strained under the skin, tendons pulled like tent ropes.

"What I want? What I've always wanted, Peter. It's nothing new. I want a baby, don't I? I want for you and I to have a baby together, to make a family. That's all I want."

"Really?"

"*Really*?"

"Gemma, you're a liar."

"Uh!" she spluttered, unable to form an actual word. Her hands shot up, then down, slapping the table, rattling the wine glasses. "What are you talking about?" she shrieked.

"You do not simply want a baby. It's become this prize that you can't quite get hold of. Instead of looking at our lives, at what we really need, you barrel on."

"I barrel on?"

"You barely lose one and it's 'Come on, Peter, knock me up. Quick cause Gemma needs a baby.'"

"How dare you!"

"Did you ever ask me if I wanted to go through it all again? Did you ever ask if I still want a baby?"

"You've changed your mind? You don't want a baby anymore?"

"I don't know. But I would like to be considered on occasion. I'm surprised you haven't asked me to bed you yet."

Gemma stood and reached across the table, her open hand swinging for Peter's cheek. He caught her wrist and held it. They glared at each other, hated each other for that frozen moment. In the silence, the world shrunk and they each saw nothing but the other in their singular focus, and they were steaming.

Gemma twisted her wrist free and sat. "That was a horrible thing to say," she said as she refilled her wineglass.

Peter held his glass out and Gemma filled it too, though she'd rather have struck him over the head with the bottle.

"I feel like a failure," Peter said.

Gemma laughed, a hysterical burst. "Then we've something in common: a couple of failures."

"Do you still want a baby? Truly?"

"Yes, Peter. My desire hasn't changed, but we don't have to try again right away. Tomorrow will do." She smiled, making light.

Peter did not smile. His eyes did not even soften. "Gemma, I've been thinking, perhaps we could use another break."

Her mouth fell slightly open before she regained control and composed her features into an emotionless mask.

"It seemed to help when I went to the States last time. It gave you room to sort things through."

"You're taking that job," she said.

"Maybe."

"Of course you are." Gemma stood and leaned toward him, her hands spread on the table. "This is your cowardly way of telling me. I've no doubt your flight has been booked for days." She straightened up and brushed past Peter, trying to look indignant, while inside she crumbled at the prospect of being abandoned again.

"I think it's for the best," he said without turning.

"Don't worry," she called from the hallway, "Mum can look after me!"

January

Chapter Eleven

SIMONA LOST HERSELF WHEN she painted. The world disappeared and she moved without a conscious thought. Words sometimes popped out, words like: there, yes, nice. Words that emphasized a stroke of the brush or approved a color choice. When her head cleared, she knew she was done, either because she was exhausted or the work was finished. A deep breath. A moment for her eyes to readjust, to take in a distance further than her canvas, to see something other than color. Only then did she step back and look at the whole, to see what it was she had created.

She picked up vermilion with her brush, loading it heavily. The brush hairs touched canvas. The stroke was fat with energy. It left a rich swath of color. Simona worked quickly on the plump figures, each a different vibrant hue. They nestled up together, rubbed thighs and buttocks, sensual, abstract, it was—

The intercom buzzer startled Simona and she quivered. She set the brush on her easel and wiped her hands on a rag as she walked to the intercom.

"Yes?"

"Simona? It's Peter."

The sound of his voice brought goose-flesh all up and down her arms. She stood frozen, her finger poised over the button.

"Simona?"

She buzzed him up and waited, listening for his approach. The elevator arrived, its metal gate clanged open, then nothing. Moments passed. Simona reached for the door just as Peter rapped against it and she jumped back. He knocked twice more. She looked through her peephole. Peter stood there, his head slightly bowed by the lens of the spyglass. He was rocking back and forth nervously or impatiently. There was nothing to do but open the door. Simona grabbed the handle and slid the steel door aside on its track, a vestige of the building's life as a garment factory and warehouse.

Peter stood before her, the slush on his fine shoes drying into the leather, leaving a crooked salty line around the toe. He had a cantaloupe clasped to his chest in both hands, a bright orange bow tied around it. A lock of hair fell over his eyes. She had the impression of a schoolboy who'd at last found the courage to approach a girl.

Simona laughed, and as she laughed her fear slid away. She took the melon from Peter. "Most men would have gone with flowers," she said, cradling it in her arms.

"Hello, darling." He gave her a quick kiss. "You've got paint on your cheek." He licked his thumb and gently rubbed it away. Simona held her breath until he had finished and held up his thumb, displaying a burnt orange smudge.

Peter pulled the door shut. He removed his overcoat and hung it on her coat rack, which was overburdened by coats, wraps, bags, scarves, even mittens that stood floppily propped on the rack's pegs.

"Shall I cut the melon?" she asked, and carried it into the kitchen area of the studio.

"Not yet."

Simona held the melon to her nose and inhaled deeply. She could tell it was heavy with green rind, being out of season. Still, the scent roused memories. She looked over the curve of the melon at Peter. Could they just...without any formalities or pretense? It would be a game, a continuation of their summer affair, a folding of time to obliterate the last four months. She knew it was what they both wanted.

Simona circled the breakfast bar and returned to Peter. The silence was growing tense with delicious anticipation. She met his eyes, then lifted her hands to her shirt. She unbuttoned a button, just one, while watching Peter watch her. He lifted his own hands and pulled his sweater off. He dropped it to the floor. Simona hastened the unbuttoning, and her shirt landed next to her feet.

Peter removed his pants.

Simona slid off her black mini skirt.

They stood in their underwear, next to his and hers piles of clothing.

Simona felt his eyes on her breasts and followed his gaze straight into the depth of her cleavage. She knew her body was changed. Before she had time to feel self-conscious, Peter placed a hand on her waist. The feeling that shot through her erased any thought of confession. She let him pull her forward and press their bodies together.

The curtains over the window were pulled back. Dusk in the winter came early, and in moments the sky had changed to an orange glow that tinted their skin, made a landscape of Peter's form. As they kissed, Simona and Peter turned in a slow, rocking step, the movement complementing the waves of emotion that ran through them. The only light in the studio came from the city outside and the pale glow of Simona's fish tank across the room. Over Peter's shoulder she saw the fish. A half-dozen cobalt discus with their bright blue veined markings swam lazily about the tank, while Red George, the pigeon blood discus, hid amongst the floating plants. They hovered in the warm water, round eyes bearing silent witness.

She immersed herself in the moment, held on to the heat between her and Peter. For now, it was enough to pretend nothing had changed.

Simona's fingers danced on Peter's chest as she gently pushed, moving him toward the kitchen area. When he stood in front of the breakfast bar she stepped closer to him. Her eyes softly focused on the curve of his shoulder, his biceps. All thoughts vanished but one, and that one was not even a thought. It was a primal half-formed urge that resonated in their minds. Nothing was withheld. They allowed themselves every luxury of sensation.

They had been quick to perfect their technique during Peter's first visit. They knew what they liked and weren't afraid. After all, there was *the understanding*. It had been a brief affair, a respite from their real lives, and when the adventure was over, they would slip comfortably back, never to see each other again. If either admitted it was different this time—different because he had come back and because she had wanted him to—it would be ruined. It would become as complicated as real life. So for now, they sweat and worked their bodies. They pretended it was hot outside. They fucked like it was August.

Dark coffee, something rich with a nutty, slightly burnt taste to it, always appealed to Simona after sex. Often enough, she had been sorely disappointed to rise from a lover's bed and find no coffee, or worse, something in a can. She got up from the floor and left Peter lying across her rug, staring up at the fish tank. She softly crossed the cold tile of the entryway and stepped into the ring of her discarded skirt. She pulled it over her hips, then bent to lift her shirt. Her darkened nipples showed through the white chemise, rouged circles, reminders of the passion spent.

The kitchen light lit her flushed cheeks and disheveled hair. The stray and unruly hairs caught the light and fringed her face with a glow. Simona poured beans into the grinder, stared at Peter across the room while the machine buzzed. She sighed, the sound lost in the whirring of the grinder.

"Coffee?"

Peter retrieved his pants and once they were on, came behind the breakfast bar, wrapped his arms around Simona and squeezed gently. "There's a little paint on your earlobe," he said. "I hadn't noticed it in the dark."

After kissing her earlobe, he went to her easel and inspected the canvas.

"This is very sensual. The figures are so voluptuous."

"Yes." Simona took mugs from the cupboard.

"Is it finished?"

"I don't know. I'd have to look at it again." She stayed near the coffee maker, waiting for the aroma of the first coffee to pour into the carafe.

"You know what they look like, these figures?" He turned to Simona and his eyes accented his question, but they did something else as well—they took her in. Simona was holding her breath, waiting for Peter to answer his own question. At last his gaze returned to the painting. "They look like those fertility dolls with the round hips and bosoms and big pregnant stomachs." He moved his hands, making a full arc in front of himself.

Simona was glad Peter wasn't looking at her when he said that. He would have caught her looking shocked and guilty both. She went to stand next to Peter, to stare at her own work. "They do, sort of. I hadn't thought of that while I was painting."

"I like the colors." He moved behind her, rested his chin on her shoulder and wrapped his arms about her waist. "Why did you paint it?"

"Don't know." She pulled away from his hold and returned to the kitchen, putting the breakfast bar between them, and poured their coffee. The aroma alone went far toward satisfying her yen. "I could live in a coffee house. Smell that?"

"Sex and black coffee."

Simona smiled. She handed Peter a mug, then led the way to the couch.

The couch faced the fish tank. Lying between the two was a large Persian rug and a coffee table. The tank stood in front of floor to ceiling bookshelves that housed an expansive collection of books and music. Simona had built the shelves herself, and after months of hunting, found an antique rolling ladder from an old, condemned country library.

The studio was not decorated, so much as it provided the housing for a number of things Simona either needed or loved. The couch was needed, bought at the Salvation Army without a thought as to color or size or shape. The bookshelves and their contents were loved, carefully constructed, neatly stocked with an eclectic collection of reading material and a collection of sketchbooks stacked on one shelf that were never opened, but served as a historical record of her life as much as any diary would. She also had odds and ends, a rock picked up on a camping trip in Colorado some years ago, and somewhere, on an upper shelf and out of sight, sat a small music box. It was carved from a single piece of wood and the lid slid back, revealing the little silver drum and pins that played "Waltz of the Blue Danube." Clarice had given it to her when she left her childhood apartment in the "Nordeast." It had been forgotten, then found mixed in with things she couldn't remember gathering, trinkets of times worth forgetting. She rescued it before sending the rest of her junk to a dumpster. She placed it on a high shelf, where it would be forgotten again, but at least it had been spared the garbage heap.

Simona tucked her feet under herself on the couch. She wrapped her hands around the mug and absorbed its warmth through her palms. Her anticipation, fueled by the aroma, was as pleasurable as foreplay.

"Tell me..." Peter said and then said no more. "I've changed my mind," he said. "I don't care what you've been up to since we last did that." They both smiled. "I'd rather pretend I never left. Can we do that? Carry on the same as before?"

Simona nodded and took the first careful sip of her coffee.

Chapter Twelve

GEMMA LIFTED A BAG of rice from the grocery shelf and considered its weight in her hands. Her stillborn child had weighed about a pound. Ignoring the tightening in her chest, she dropped it into her trolley, then rounded the corner into the next aisle and stopped to browse the frozen foods.

"Gemma?" a man's voice said with a note of astonishment.

She spun around and in an instant recognized the speaker. "Nikolai Mylanos!" she cried, throwing her arms about his neck. "My God," she said, stepping back, "it's been," she counted, "*eight* years, hasn't it? And after all this time you simply turn up in the Waitrose frozen foods aisle." She eyed Nikolai's black hair and olive skin, darker than she remembered. "I thought you were in Greece."

"I came back to visit my sister and mother and take care of some business."

"They're still in London?"

He nodded. "Diane lives close to here. In fact, my niece has a sore throat, so I came to get her ice cream." He held up a carton of strawberry ice cream. "It irritates Diane to no end the way I spoil the children." His smile reminded Gemma of old feelings. "I was just off to find the chocolate sauce."

"Your hand must be freezing. Put it in my trolley."

Nikolai slipped the carton in next to Gemma's fava beans. "I can't believe I haven't seen you in all this time."

"Yes, and all that time in Greece has given you a slight accent."

A woman pointing her empty trolley at them cleared her throat loudly. Nikolai nodded to her as he and Gemma stepped aside, but Gemma couldn't pull her gaze away from Nikolai's face. She studied him as they walked along, side-by-side, slowly maneuvering between shoppers and their trolleys. He had added laugh lines about his eyes and mouth, the kind that vanished when he was attentive, but sprung into place with the slightest smile and deepened to the sun-laid crevasses of mirth when he laughed. His hair was still thick and shiny with that touch of boyish curl. Gemma remembered catching her fingers in those curls, which had been long coils when they were students, a symbol of his freedom and youth before he was shipped off to Greece to work in his father's family business.

"What's next on your list?" Nikolai asked.

"Runner beans."

Nikolai held a bag open while Gemma filled it with beans. She dumped in handful after handful while they recalled the night she and Nikolai had met. It had been the first month of her first year at university, and she was constantly afraid that her working class background would show, that people would care. She had been reserved and off-putting with everyone, until she wound up at a party.

"I'll never forget that party. Well, not the parts I could remember anyway." She laughed.

"You were quite fun once you had a few drinks in you," Nikolai said.

"I know I've never been so pissed." She placed the bag of runner beans in the scale; it registered an absurd two and a half pounds, but Gemma barely noticed. "How did we ever end up on the roof of the science building?"

"Franklin had a key, for his job cleaning out the labs."

"Oh yes. We're lucky none of us fell off."

They moved on, ticking items off Gemma's list. Nikolai took a bottle of chocolate sauce off the shelf and set it atop Gemma's growing mound of food.

"You're buying quite a lot, aren't you?" he said.

Gemma cleared her throat. "I don't care for grocery shopping, so I get as much as I can as infrequently as I can."

She realized, now that Nikolai had unintentionally pointed it out, that since he first said her name, she'd felt completely normal. In the last thirty minutes or so, Gemma had smiled and laughed and shared memories, space, breath even, with another human being without so much as damp palms. She smiled at Nikolai while he went on, ignorant of her recent troubles, about that night, the chill air, the stars on the black velvet sky, the way the drunken partiers had paired off and retreated to distant corners of the roof. But it wasn't that far-off night that made Gemma smile. It was Nikolai.

She rose on her tiptoes to reach for a jar of sauce on the top shelf. Nikolai reached it easily. Their hands wrapped around the glass at the same time, fingers overlapping. They paused, smiled, and together placed the jar in the trolley. Gemma saw the moment in her head as though watching a movie, and knew how it looked. How silly and romantic, trite even: *their hands accidentally touched around a jar of sauce.* For once, she didn't care.

Gemma opened her car and smiled as Nikolai loaded her shopping in the boot.

"Your ice cream." She held it out for him.

"I completely forgot. How much do I owe you?"

"I wouldn't hear of it."

"Then why don't you give me your number? I'd love to take you to dinner."

"Fantastic." She handed him her card.

"Gemma Ledbetter," he read. "I'd almost forgot. Of course, Peter must come along as well."

"Nikolai?"

"Yes?"

"That first night we met, what did you think of me?"

"I thought you were beautiful."

He held the card up, a confirmation of his intent, and then slipped it into his coat pocket and turned. Gemma watched him walk up the row of cars to his sister's green wagon.

Nikolai leaned back comfortably in his chair, a glass of red wine held in front of him. He swirled the wine about the glass, squinted to inspect its color, then tipped it to his nose and inhaled. "My uncle has wine tastings at his vineyard four times a year. They are fantastic parties. You and Peter should vacation in Greece soon, come when a tasting is scheduled." He pulled his chair forward to let a server pass, bringing him even closer to Gemma.

"Peter is in the States on business," Gemma said. Nikolai looked mildly surprised. She had let him assume Peter would be stuck in the office when they arranged a weekday luncheon.

"How are you getting on without him?"

"Perfectly fine." She took a sip of her wine. "Do you have a wife waiting for you in Greece?"

"No, only a housekeeper. I never found a woman I could love as much as I loved you."

Gemma blinked, unsure how to respond to Nikolai's casual confession. She shook out her napkin and set it on her lap.

"You're surprised?" He seemed amused.

"Yes. I thought you would have settled down by now."

"That's just the thing, I've never been able to settle."

Again Gemma froze at Nikolai's words. She looked at his face, at his dusky eyes, and believed he was sincere. She wondered if she hadn't begun dating Peter immediately would they be together now? She could have moved to Greece after graduation. It had been her—hurt, angry, stubborn, foolish—who had ended the relationship.

"I'm sorry," he said. "I've become too forward living in Greece all these years. I forget the English are more reserved."

"No, it's only..."

"It's all right, Gem."

Gemma twitched as a little shiver tickled her spine. She had never allowed Peter to shorten her name, claiming she didn't like the sound of it. In truth, she'd always loved Nikolai's pet name and had reserved it solely for his use.

"I'm just being honest," Nikolai continued with a gentle smile, as though conceding defeat. "I know you love Peter."

"Of course I do." Gemma spread her party smile across her face, the well-practiced one that concealed her thoughts.

After a rather long lunch, Gemma invited Nikolai inside for a coffee. They continued to reminisce and then discussed Nikolai's life in Greece, the import-export business he inherited from his father, and how frequently he traveled while working remotely, thanks to technology and a number of competent managers on site. Given the nature of his business, almost any trip could combine business and pleasure. Nikolai had seen most of the world over these eight years, while Gemma had mostly seen her kitchen. She was impressed by his success and his freedom. She thought if only she had gone with him, she could have seen the world by now, too. Perhaps there was still hope for her.

Nikolai reached out to touch her cheek. He cupped her face in his hand tenderly and she moved closer to him on the sofa. She tucked her leg underneath herself, raising her skirt to accommodate the position. Facing Nikolai, she felt like she was eighteen again and about to be kissed. They leaned toward each other and Gemma let her eyes close. Their lips touched, tentatively at first, then with purpose. She smelled him, his scent coming from inside his shirt collar, so different from Peter and just as indescribable, but his scent had a potency Peter's had long since lost. Gemma wanted to press her nose against his neck and inhale the Mediterranean.

Nikolai put his hand to the back of her head and moved his mouth from her lips to her neck right below her ear. He moistened the spot with his tongue and she whimpered with pleasure. Her secret erogenous zone, so discreet yet so crazy-making, and he remembered. His lips massaged her neck with firm kisses. She moved her hand to his lap and felt a stirring erection.

"Cooey!" The call rang shrilly through the house. Gemma leapt off the sofa, eyes wild. She spun about to face the sitting room door, adjusting her skirt and blouse as she turned. There was no time to put her shoes on.

Beth Warner bustled into the sitting room, a bundle of overcoat and homemade rust-and-olive striped scarf that wrapped about her neck three times and still managed to trail to her knees. She stopped short when she saw a man sitting on the sofa, her face opening wide with shock.

"Mother," Gemma said dryly, crossing her arms over her chest. "I see you've brought the scarf out for another year."

"Yes, luv. I just can't seem to part with the dear old thing." Beth unwound her scarf and piled it on a chair, keeping her gaze locked on the man sitting behind her daughter.

"I thought a bus dragged it off last winter."

"Yes, it did. Caught the tail of my scarf in its door as I was stepping off. Nearly pulled me over and dragged me along as well. But I managed to get untangled and didn't get run over somehow by God's own grace." Beth had her coat off and sat down, her pile of garments behind her on the chair. "A lovely gentleman who got off at the next stop retrieved it for me. He noticed the label I'd sewn on it, had it cleaned and mailed it back to me with a nice note, asked me to meet him for tea, he did." Beth looked at her daughter, her face serious. "Your old mum can still turn a few heads, you know."

"Yes, Mum."

Beth's hair set on her head like a helmet of steel wool. Her face was puffed and red, her hands chapped and her nails bit away to nothing. The old red cardigan she wore was missing the second button down and it puckered open over her large bosom. The blouse underneath had been nice when Gemma gave it to her mother six years ago.

"Walk in on something, did I?" she said.

"Mrs. Warner, how lovely to see you again." Nikolai uncrossed his legs, stood and extended his hand across the coffee table. Beth stared at it as though sin were contagious.

"Mum, you remember Nikolai," Gemma said.

"Of course." Beth took his hand at last and permitted only a hesitant parting of her lips that fell short of a smile.

"Gemma was kind enough to meet me for lunch, for old time's sake," said Nikolai.

"We were just having a coffee. Mother?"

"Oh yes, dear." Beth couldn't take her eyes off Nikolai, as though staring at her daughter's first love would reveal the extent of their guilt. Her interrogation began innocently enough. "How is Greece these days, Nick?"

Gemma slipped into the kitchen to pour her mother's coffee, moving quietly so as to listen to her guests. She admired how expertly Nikolai handled her mother, charming while gently teasing her.

"I just asked Gemma to run away to Greece with me," he said.

As Gemma came in, Beth swiveled in her seat, her features suddenly exaggerated into a look of shock. Gemma handed her a coffee cup. "He's kidding you, Mum."

"Honestly," Nikolai said, "I told Gemma she and Peter should visit me. I have a lovely villa in the hills with a heated pool and a view of the ocean." Gemma gave Nikolai a warning look and mouthed "Shut up!" He winked at her. "You should come along, too, Mrs. Warner."

"Oh, it sounds lovely," Beth said with real enthusiasm.

When Nikolai had finished his coffee, he politely excused himself, told Gemma to give his best to Peter, and then kissed her casually on the cheek. After walking Nikolai to the door, she returned to the sofa and glared at her mother, boring holes into her suspicious mind that even now would be adding two and two to make seven.

"You don't have to look at me like that, Gemma. I might think you hate your old mum." Beth sat up straight and held her cup over one knee to hide the tiny hole in her brown corduroys. She had a mother's keen eye and sense of propriety to back her and, hole or not, she faced Gemma square on.

"I don't hate you, Mum. I'm upset at you."

"Were you going to tell me Nick was in town?"

"Is it your business?" Gemma felt her face grow hot, cursing her fair skin's betrayal.

"Seems to me if you've nothing to hide, you'd mention it to me, and to Peter."

"I see. So I can't have lunch with an old friend..."

"Nick is more than an old friend," Beth insisted.

"And because of that, you automatically assume I'm bonking him."

"There's no need for vulgarity, Gemma. You shouldn't have a man in your home when your husband is away."

"Says who? Your 1962 ladies' handbook to keeping a man happy? Why can't you accept that nothing happened. Or at least give me the benefit of the doubt?"

"I don't see why you're so defensive. The way you looked when I came in! Clearly glowing."

"Honestly, Mum!"

Beth thrust a fingernail into her mouth. "Sorry, luv. I might have over spoken."

Gemma pressed her lips into a thin line, refusing her mother's apology. "Let's sit in the kitchen. I'd like another coffee." Gemma didn't want the coffee so much as move her mother out of the sitting room where Gemma could still smell Nikolai's scent as though it had lined her nostrils to tease her after his departure.

Beth sat at the table with her coffee, plunking into the chair without an ounce of grace.

"Mum," Gemma said, filling the kettle with fresh water, "how'd you get in? I thought the door was locked."

"Peter left me a key. He thought I ought to have one in case of emergencies."

"He did? What sort of emergencies?"

"Oh I don't know, Gemma. *Emergencies.* I suppose you could tumble down them stairs and break something, couldn't you?"

"But you wouldn't know I'd fallen down the stairs."

Beth's hands fluttered across the tabletop like wounded moths. "I suppose I wouldn't, now you mention it. Still, that's what he said, *for emergencies.* And I didn't ask if he was expecting you to have a specific emergency, now did I?"

Gemma put new coffee grounds into the French press pot and filled the carafe with steaming water, keeping her eye on it while she spoke. "And is this an emergency?"

"No, this is a visit. I thought I'd surprise you, but if you mind I'll be off right away."

"Of course I don't mind, Mum. It's just that Peter didn't mention he'd given you a key."

"I should have a key anyway." Beth stuck her chin out. "I'm your mother. If something happened to you, who would care more than me?"

Gemma depressed the plunger, forcing the grounds to the bottom of the pot. "You're right, of course. Keep the key. Only don't surprise me, right?"

"Honestly, Gemma, you're making me sorry I came!"

"Sorry. I don't mean it." She poured herself the coffee she didn't really want and sat across from her mother.

"Ta, luv. How are you getting on without Peter?"

"Is he gone? I hardly notice. He spends so much time working when he is here that it's barely a change."

"That's a shame. Your father was always around when we needed him. Still, he didn't provide for us like your Peter does for you." Beth looked around the kitchen and tilted her head toward the dishwasher. "There's a luxury I've never had."

"Would you like us to get you a dishwasher, Mum?"

"Oh no, dear! Goodness, I wasn't hinting at that. Besides, I'd have nowhere to put it in my little kitchen. I only meant you've done quite well for yourself."

"Money isn't everything," Gemma snapped.

"I know you've had a few false starts, but you and Peter will have a baby soon enough."

"No, Mum," Gemma sighed. "I don't think so."

"Why not? I thought your doctor said you could."

"We can..." Gemma narrowed her eyes to slits as her mother began picking and scraping at what little nails she had. "Things haven't been that good between me and Peter lately."

"What's happened?" Beth's eyes flashed with incrimination, a look that said, *what have you done now?*

"Nothing. We simply don't connect anymore."

"Is that all? Gemmania..."

Gemma cringed at the sound of her given name, all her life she'd envied her sister, Molly, her plain, sensible name.

"Most couples don't connect. That's no reason to get mopey. Peter's a decent enough bloke. He works hard, earns plenty of money, gives you plenty to spend. Honestly, Gemmania."

"Mum, call me Gemma."

"Gemma. In my day, a girl would count herself damn lucky to have such a husband as yours."

Gemma stopped herself from getting into an argument she didn't have the energy for and stared into her mug. Beth shoved a finger into her mouth. When the nail proved too short to satisfy her urge, she began gnawing at the knuckle of her left index finger. "Quit that," Gemma snapped, then clucked her tongue in disapproval. "It's disgusting. Just look at that callus on your finger." Her tone was overly harsh and said much she would never actually put into words.

"We can't all be hand models," Beth muttered. "Some of us has to work for a living."

"What?"

"I said your father raised you too soft. You're positively spoiled and you fall to pieces over a couple of miscarriages—"

"Four. I had another one in November." She looked coolly at her mother, with no intention of elaborating on the truth, her mouth set in an acid expression.

"Oh! Sorry, luv, I didn't know." Beth raised her hand to her mouth, but stopped herself and settled for fussing with a button on her cardigan. "Thing is, Gemma, you've got so much. Why let one bad thing ruin so many good things?"

"*One* bad thing? Is that how you think of it? Four dead babies can go a long way toward ruining a marriage, Mum." Gemma stopped herself from saying any more. Beth would never understand anyway.

Beth gnawed at her stubby nails, nibbling feverishly, while the tension between them waned. "Is that why Nick was here?"

"Oh, Mum!" Gemma cried, exasperated. "Nikolai. *Nikolai*," she added for emphasis, "is an old friend. We had lunch and coffee. That is all."

"Fine. But if that is all that happened, I don't see why you were flushed when I came in. Honestly, Gemma, the way you greeted me!"

"I was upset because you came inside my home unannounced and I knew as soon as you saw him, you'd be assuming the worst."

"Well," Beth looked taken aback, put a nail to her teeth and took it away, held it firmly in her other hand. "In my day, a woman didn't have men in her house and she didn't do anything that would cause others to suspect."

"Mum, it's not your day anymore. Women are free to have friends. People can be in a room together without having sex!"

"Oh, Gemma."

In the quiet that followed, Gemma was aware of how many lies she'd told that afternoon. Of how close to the truth her mother really was and how she wanted to believe nothing untoward had happened, that the kiss was only a kiss and would not have led to more if Beth hadn't come in. The disturbing thought of what could have happened next and what would have happened if Beth had walked in on them later caused

Gemma to blush. She rose to dump her coffee down the sink. She stared out the window at her garden and the birdbath Peter had bought her when they were first married. She had neglected it this past year, like so many other things, and left water in it. It froze and the basin cracked.

"I've brought you something." Beth's voice was quiet and hopeful.

Gemma returned to the table, frustrated that every argument ended the same way, with Beth burying the issue under a peace offering. Still, she couldn't bring herself to refuse her mother and waited quietly while Beth retrieved her tote bag from the entry. She extracted a book, which she lay on the table facing Gemma.

"It was on clearance, and I thought of you."

"Flower arranging?" Gemma pulled the book closer and flipped through it.

"You're a right dab hand at those flowers, Gemma. I know you haven't done as much in the garden lately."

"Thanks, Mum. There are some very pretty arrangements in here."

"But wait, there's more," Beth said, forcing herself to sound chipper. "Know what today is?" Gemma shook her head. "Well, nothing really. But next week..." She sang out "next week," her voice tinkling like broken glass.

Gemma dropped her gaze. *Here's Mum with some present and I'm acting like an absolute prat.*

"I know you get busy with all your friends around your birthday, so I thought I'd better come along today." Beth reached into her cardigan's large patch pocket and produced a brightly wrapped jeweler's box. She set it on the table and slid it toward Gemma, then put her little finger in her mouth and bit at the stub of a nail.

The foil paper was meticulously folded and taped. Inside the box lay a four-strand choker of black crystal beads and matching earrings. "It's lovely, Mum."

"It ain't diamonds or anything fancy, mind you."

Gemma went out to the entry and stood in front of the mirror. She put on the necklace and admired the way the beads caught the light. Beth came and stood to the side so that her own tarnished reflection would not show in her daughter's gilt-framed mirror.

"You have a good eye, Mum. This really suits me."

Her mother shrugged modestly, and Gemma gave her a quick squeeze, as awkward as it was tender.

Chapter Thirteen

SIMONA WORKED ON THE mural during the daytime hours that Peter worked and she didn't see Clarice or Rosa once. That was as it should be. Normal. She also didn't see Hannah or anybody else. When she wasn't working, she was with Peter. Their time together was a blur of activity: restaurants, theaters, bars. On their second night together, Peter had brought over a bottle of Syrah. She told him she'd given up alcohol. It was part of a healthy vegetarian diet. An experiment to see if she felt more energetic and needed less sleep as a non-drinker. She had even believed herself. So they went to bars to play darts and shoot pool and hear local bands, and Simona dutifully stuck to water and juice.

At the end of the week, Simona was uncomfortable in her skirt, the waistband seeming snugger at the end of the night than it had when she put it on. She was also exhausted and overly sensitive to the noise and bustle of the restaurant she had chosen for a late dinner. They retreated for the night to Peter's corporate rental along the river, because it had been closer than Simona's loft. She'd been so tired, despite her not drinking, as Peter pointed out, that she slept through the phone ringing, through Peter leaving the bed, but it had jarred her enough to bring her sifting through layers of sleep, ever closer to consciousness.

"Yes, darling," Peter said.

He was in the living room, speaking quietly into the phone. She rolled over to listen. There had been a time last summer when she'd played with Peter while he was on the phone to his wife. One of those funny games that actually masks some minor cruelty. A barb disguised as a joke. Resentment passed off as nonchalance. This time Simona stayed in bed, where it was warm, and waited patiently for Peter to finish.

"Are you still seeing Dr. Hamilton, then?"

Simona did and did not want to know anything about his wife. Knowledge of that woman would only make her feel terrible about something she could no longer help. It had all seemed harmless over the summer, a chance encounter that led to an affair. A brief, sexually turbid but emotionally lucid affair with only one unstated rule of engagement: do not talk about the past or the future. Simona and Peter never swapped life stories. They never suggested a future together. They never acknowledged Peter's wife. She was present only as a simple gold band, a shiny high-karat ring that adorned Peter's finger.

He'd jammed the finger playing rugby or some such ball sport, probably fractured one of the metacarpals and never had it looked at. Now he couldn't take off the ring. It would have to be cut off. The story came out one night over martinis because Peter had asked her which body part she would least like to injure. Simona said her hands. She said she didn't think she'd be a success painting with a brush between her teeth. One remark led to the other. Perhaps he'd taken the opportunity to apologize, in a way, for keeping it on, to explain why the thing shone from his hand like a beacon, why every gesture seemed to brandish it between them. The truth was, Simona didn't care. It was only metal formed into a circle.

That holy union it symbolized, that woman it reminded Peter of, didn't exist for Simona. She preferred life uncomplicated and if she had tried to analyze what they did, all the ripples their stone's throw might send into the world, she would falter. She might change her mind, miss out on life, or worse, feel guilty. Over those few weeks, while Peter was in Minneapolis, he was hers. When he left Minneapolis, she opened her hand and let him go, waved him out of her life and back to that other life that was not hers.

Then he came back and everything was different. Simona didn't have a choice about being serious now. And neither did he, whether he realized it or not.

Peter hung up and went to the kitchen to put on water. Simona stayed in bed, in case he needed a moment to regroup. She needed a moment herself. She pulled a pillow over her face and groaned into it.

"Hello?" Peter called from the kitchen.

"Morning," she called back.

The pregnancy was tucked behind a curtain in her mind, the one she'd drawn when Peter asked if they could pretend. It had been easy to seal herself off from the pregnancy, at least for a while. It was like taking a vacation. For the time being, she didn't have to worry about whether she could handle a baby, or afford a baby, or if she would be loved by her baby. She got to pass baby things in stores with only a secret glance, instead of finding herself at a full stop, staring like an idiot, rubbing a bit of pink or blue between the pads of her fingers. How best to end the game? A parting of the curtains, a peek behind them, and Peter would be blown over by the inconceivable and life-changing mistake. Simona shook her head to clear away her last thought. She didn't like the word mistake. Whatever her numerous doubts and overwhelming uncertainties, she never wanted her child to feel like a mistake.

"Here, love." Peter slipped sideways through the half-opened doorway, a mug of tea in each hand.

Simona sat up to take it. She decided to start with the wife. At least Peter already knew she existed. "That was your wife?"

"Mmmm," he affirmed. "It seems life continues in London without me."

She would have joked, they didn't have the decency to put everything on hold, only she'd just decided to end the game, so instead, she asked, "What does she do?"

"Gemma paints, keeps a garden..." Peter shrugged. "I don't really know."

"She's a painter?"

"Sort of. Gemma's terribly precise, but there's no spark. I think she could make a fortune doing forgeries."

"She's that good?" Simona couldn't hide the surprise in her voice. From the snippets of information she'd gathered on Peter's wife, she had never imagined the woman to be an artist.

"Yes, when she copies someone else's genius. The originals she brings home from classes are, well, they lack something. Her paintings at school didn't pass muster, so she got a degree in art history."

It had been Simona's greatest fear entering art school that she'd end up an art history major. Over the years she had decided that was the cliché of art school, a version of "those who can't do, teach; those who can't teach, teach gym." Yet here was someone for whom it was a reality. They sipped their tea and glanced around the bland room, decorated for corporate rentals, completely inoffensive. "When you left," she said, "I thought I'd never see you again."

"Likewise. I didn't mean to come back to you, but..."

"Here you are."

"Quite."

"Do you and Gemma have any—"

"Dogs?" Peter cut her off. "No. Gemma wouldn't like the mess they make. And no, we don't have any of what you meant, either." He nudged her knee. "Come on, don't go all serious on me. Let's get breakfast somewhere, shall we?"

She nodded.

"Only I'm terribly hungry so let's go to one of those places with a two-hour queue and nowhere to sit while you're waiting."

Peter cut a small bite from his toast and dipped it into his egg yolk. Simona shoved a hunk of omelet into her mouth and washed it down with orange juice. At the table closest to them, a couple sat largely silent, eating, looking at other people, occasionally reaching out with some ill-fated topic of conversation. Simona wondered if that was what Peter and Gemma were like. She wondered if all married couples wound up in that same rut.

"Are you quite all right this morning?" Peter asked.

Simona looked up from her plate as a bit of egg slipped off her fork.

"You've been rather quiet," he said.

She set down the utensil and smoothed a paper napkin over her lap. She'd worn a corduroy jumper and was thankful there wasn't a waistband digging into her middle. "I'd like to talk about something," she said, "but not here. Not in public."

"What is it?"

"Not here, Peter."

He looked around, raised his coffee mug to the crowd. "They're all busy with themselves. Nobody is going to listen to our conversation."

Simona followed his gaze around the diner. "All right," she said. "What happens in three months? Do you just go home again?"

"Yes. Maybe." Peter shook his head, tossing away the carefree look he'd worn all morning. "What are you really asking, Simona?"

"I want to know if there could be more to our relationship than..." she dropped her voice, but kept her eyes on Peter, "great sex."

"Aaah." He stabbed his fork into a pancake lying helpless on his plate. "So that's it. The fun is over and it's time for the commitment speech. The will-you-leave-her-for-me million dollar question, is it?"

"Well..." She was surprised by the change in his tone, the bitterness of it. "Yes, I suppose that is what I'm asking. Would you ever consider leaving her for me?" There. She had said it. If he said no, he would never leave Gemma, then she would have her out and could move on with her life as though he'd never reappeared.

"I...I didn't think that was something you wanted. I thought our thing was so good because neither of us wanted a permanent commitment."

"That doesn't answer my question, Peter."

"No, it doesn't." He lifted and set down his fork. He looked at Simona intently.

"It's a yes or no question."

"Is it? Because what we have is brilliantly simple, unless you ask that question. Then it becomes a huge international mess, doesn't it?"

"Well," she smirked, "it's not exactly a nuclear peace treaty."

"Fine. A *small* international mess. You're asking if I am willing to change my career and my country, as well as my wife and my home."

Simona was taken aback by his blunt assessment, by how little emotion seemed involved, as though everything they were could come down to which country he preferred. "I see," she said quietly, looking at her plate and feeling overwhelmed by an emotional rush she blamed on the hormones. Most of all, she did not want to cry in a restaurant. She swallowed and looked Peter in the eye, prepared to challenge him. "I didn't ask you to move here. I didn't ask you to change careers. If we decided to be together, my moving to England would be just as viable as you moving here. I only asked you if you would leave her."

Peter deflated, looked at his lap and sighed. "I don't know. It's not simple."

"It's a simple question. Peter, would you rather spend the rest of your life with me or with her?"

He was silent.

The server came by with a coffee pot in her hands and refilled Peter's cup. He looked at his plate. Simona looked at him, determined to have an answer. The server left the table quickly.

"It's not..." he had to clear his throat. "It's not simple, is the thing," he said.

"It never is, but I need to know. If you don't want to be with me, then I think we'd best move on."

"I see." Peter's face darkened. "You've suddenly become the marrying kind and you can't afford a few months to play around? You need to commit or quick get back on the hunt?"

"You don't have to be nasty about it, Peter. Things change."

"Things change? Is that so? What has changed? Are you in love with me now? And you need to get a commitment before your heart gets broken? Have your girlfriends been giving you love advice and telling you to run from the married man?"

People at nearby tables were beginning to listen in, their own conversations going quiet, heads turning to better hear. Simona glanced around, her entire body flushing with heat. It seemed, since the pregnancy began, that any sort of emotion triggered a reaction far greater than she expected. She wiped her hands on her napkin to remove the damp of nervous sweat. "Please keep your voice down."

"I just don't understand," he insisted.

"I...I have a lot of work now. With the mural. I can't risk that project by spending all this time with you. I need to know it's worth it." It wasn't a complete lie. She hadn't spent enough time painting since Peter reappeared in her life.

"Bollocks."

Simona sighed and put her hands to her head, smoothing back her curls. Aware of her heart pounding, she didn't know how to respond to his anger. She tried a question, "What is wrong with asking you to make a choice?"

"Because that was not our arrangement. I have a life. Commitments. A future."

"So do I!" The tears started down her cheeks. "But you aren't willing to address my concerns, only yours. We have to do what is best for you and...and Gemma."

"What are your concerns?" he demanded. "You haven't told me anything other than you want me to choose between my wife and you."

"Things have changed." She wiped her nose with her napkin and glanced at the tables around her again. They had become a spectacle. Shame burned her cheeks and her hands began to tremble with uncharacteristic nerves. Everything seemed out of control. For a moment, she wished she weren't pregnant and a fleeting thought crossed her mind: if she had chosen differently when she had the chance, her life would be normal now. This wouldn't be happening.

Simona reached for her bag beside her chair.

"What has changed?"

Simona stood up from the table.

Peter reached across it and grabbed her wrist, his grip firm. "What has changed, Simona?"

"I'm pregnant!"

His hand went slack.

Simona twisted her wrist free and fled the diner. She felt the stares of everyone on her back. Once outside, she ran. A bus pulled up at the corner and she joined the line of people boarding. She swiped her pass and dropped into the first open seat. Simona turned her head to the window and wiped tears from her cheeks. She looked back at the café and caught sight of Peter emerging to look up and down the street. The bus rejoined the flow of traffic. She collected herself, looked at the passing shops and all the people on Lyndale Avenue with their own lives, their own problems. The bus was heading south and she lived north.

She rode the bus out of the city into a first-ring suburb, past strip malls showing their wear, overshadowed by new condo buildings hoped to reinvigorate the neighborhood, that only, as far as Simona could see, made the squat older buildings look that much more shabby. She got off the bus at a shopping center with a pet store and went in to buy a can of fish flakes. She crossed the street with her purchase in her coat pocket and waited for a northbound bus.

Simona climbed the stairs to the Center for Women, exhausted from that morning's event. She sat in the canvas camp chair she'd brought in, still bundled into her down parka and mittens, and stared in the direction of her work without seeing, her mind tumbling continuously over Peter. She replayed their breakfast scene and then she recreated it. So many different ways it could have gone. She could have stayed in the diner. He could have caught up to her outside.

Since Peter's reappearance, Simona had achieved little on the mural. Clarice and Rosa had been lavished with attention as a matter of avoiding new portraits, preventing the need to admit that she had nothing new to paint. She spent three hours one day putting a wedding band on Rosa's finger. And she'd begun another woman, one who had never existed, behind Clarice. And she'd made sketches. Mostly, Simona had sat in her camp chair with a mug of tea and drawn. Her romantic fling distracted her more than she had thought. Only now, reviewing her progress, did she realize how much. She decided Peter had gotten in the way of her work, diverted her creative energies, and this was an opportunity. Simona could return to her life, unhindered by the complications of loving a married man.

She took a deep breath and slowly leafed through her notebook, pausing at each page. The drawings of Clarice and Rosa's mothers held her eye the longest, so she tore the pages out and taped them to the wall. She began with Marguerite, sketching her opposite Rosa on the far right.

When the charcoal sketch was complete, Simona roughed out Clarice's mother, Alma, next to Marguerite. The two women stood side by side, but a narrow gap was maintained between them: separated by country and culture, they were nonetheless united by their generation's sensibilities and their reliance on their children. Whatever their differences, they would understand each other.

Simona squeezed dollops of paint onto her palette. She mixed them and put brush to paint, then brush to wall. It felt good to work again. Her hands brought the color of life to Marguerite, who stood stiff in a high-necked dress with her hair, a mix of black and gray, in a tidy bun. One hand was held at her waist, cupping a fistful of dirt. A single slender stream of earth poured through her fingers.

When Marguerite was finished, she added a girl of fifteen in a childish party dress standing slightly behind her grandmother. Rosa's daughter was created partly from imagining what Rosa looked like as a girl and partly from memory as Simona pictured the photo that had hung in Rosa's hallway. Flora Blanca wore patent leather shoes with a red dust coating the scuffed toes. Her braids were tied in wide satin ribbons, one in a bow, the other trailing undone. Her face was marked by simplicity and innocence.

Simona's immersion in her work suppressed thoughts of Peter and the pregnancy, even hunger and time, so that Simona didn't notice the hours passing until Hal stood across the lobby, pulling on his coat, and called goodbye. She waved with a paintbrush sprouting from her hand. There was no one she had to meet, nowhere she had to be. That freedom had been missing since Peter reappeared.

Simona stood in the empty building, satisfied but exhausted, squeezed her eyes shut and rubbed the aching muscles at the back of her neck. The charcoal she'd used to sketch the ladies still marked her fingertips, rubbed into the layers of her skin. Brown and black blotched her hands and forearms. Simona enjoyed ending a day with paint spattered on her shoes or smeared on her jeans. It was proof that the work had claimed her.

A wave of nausea came over Simona, reminding her it had been hours since she last ate. She sat down and closed her eyes, waiting for it to ease up. The scent of Halston cologne enveloped her, as though someone had just sprayed the air. Simona opened her eyes, and smiled weakly at Clarice and Rosa.

"*Mija*, you don't look too good."

"Hi, Rosa," Simona said. "I just need to eat. I have a sandwich in the office fridge."

"I'll get it," Clarice said, and went to the office.

Rosa turned to study Simona's work. Simona watched as she paused and her hand floated up to her chest. Rosa slowly made her way up to the wall and stared at the portraits of her mother and her daughter. It seemed like a long time she stood there in the silence, Simona holding her breath, afraid that it was somehow hurtful to paint Flora Blanca.

Clarice came out of the office, Simona's lunch bag swinging in her hand. As she neared Simona, she looked up and stopped short. "Oh good Lord!" she exclaimed. "You're putting Mama on the wall."

"Is that a problem?" Simona asked.

"No. I guess not. I dealt with Mama all my life, I might as well have her here, too." Clarice handed the bag to Simona. "Here you go, honey."

"Thanks."

Rosa turned at last, tears running down her cheeks. "She is beautiful, *mija*."

Clarice handed Simona the lunch bag and stood beside Rosa to study her mother's picture. "Mm-mm-mm." She shook her head. "You've got a way with people. I can see it even in this sketch, even without the color and all." She turned to look at Simona and pointed a finger in her direction. "You got busy today. What happened?"

"*Si*," Rosa added, wiping her cheeks. "This is the first you've made time for us in a while, and the most you've put on the wall in just as long."

"I just..."

"No, no, no. None of this, 'I just...' When a person starts an explanation with 'I just,' it's usually because they're about to blow smoke you-know-where. I just felt like it. I just in the mood. They ain't real answers. I want the *real* answer." She paused to draw breath.

"*Si*."

"Now, Miss Simona, what is different today?"

"I..." Simona smiled as Clarice's finger shot into the air, delivered with a warning look. "...*told*..." Clarice dropped her hand. "...Peter that I'm pregnant."

"Oh *mija*!" Rosa rushed to kneel beside Simona and wrap her in a hug.

"Now, Rosa, does the girl look upset?"

"If he had picked her, she would not be here painting so hard all day long. She would be out celebrating with the father of her child."

"She's right," Simona said. "It was horrible."

"I am sorry to hear that, baby," Clarice said. "You take a break from all that painting. Have yourself a snack and sit with us."

The women settled together on the floor. All those years ago, half of Simona's lifetime, she had sat with these same women around Rosa's kitchen table, only a girl does not fit easily into the world of two women, married, mothers, experienced in so many things. Clarice and Rosa had recognized the hole in Simona's world as a sort of starvation, and they gathered her into their kitchens to feed her on tortillas and the talk of women. Now Simona had become one of them, and while they were still elder and she younger, she was grown. Their world opened to her. There were no taboo topics, no coded words, no secret looks. She wondered if every woman experienced the same awe at the moment she realized she was accepted as an equal among a circle of women, especially those women who had been present to shape her girlhood.

"Do you love him?"

"I don't know yet. I think I do, but he has to choose me, too."

"*Mija*, the important issue is the baby. Would he be good for the baby?"

"Would he be good for *you*," Clarice said.

"I..." Simona looked at where her sketchbook lay on the floor, out of reach. She wanted it. If she could hold a pencil, it would help. If she could draw while they talked, she could better make sense of her jumbled feelings. Simona leaned over, stretching her arm across the floor to hook the spiral bound pad with her finger and dragged it to her. The pencil was still tucked inside the pages. Clarice and Rosa waited while Simona situated the pad on her lap.

The soft graphite tip touched the paper and she stroked it across the page. One line.

"I think," she started, "that I missed my mother so much that I want my baby to have both parents, to not miss out on one of us." Lines crossed and connected, swept and curved over the page. "What if this kid ends up hating me because she never had the chance to meet her father?"

"Let's not forget, he ain't gone yet."

"He could call you tomorrow," Rosa said.

Simona pressed her pencil against the paper, thickening the line. "He might be back. That's the worst part. He might be back, but he might not."

"Baby, do yourself a favor. Don't wait on him. You'll make yourself crazy trying to figure out if he's coming back or not."

"She is right," Rosa agreed.

Simona continued to draw while Clarice and Rosa discussed her life. She listened, weighing the advice, and drew. Pencil strokes shaped into faces. Gentle curves outlined brows. Rounded lines turned chins. Darker, thicker strokes swept together as dark curls of hair. Eyes were made big and round. The pad of her thumb shaded apple cheeks. "How do you know the difference," Simona asked, "between what you really want and what you've been trained to think you want?" Her hand was still moving quickly along the page.

"I know one thing," Clarice said. She pointed at the sketch in Simona's lap. The women stared at it. Central on the page was a picture of an infant's face, sweet and new. On either side, with less detailed attention, were sketches of Simona and Peter—the adoring parents nestling their young between them. It was an idyllic portrait, except that Peter's portrait had elements missing, as though half of his face had faded off the page. "You and that baby of yours have your whole lives together, mother and daughter, with or without Peter involved. I think you ought to just focus on what's for sure, and that's you having this baby."

"She's right, *mija*. If you can't be sure of his love and support, then you will be better off alone. A man who does not want you, or your child, is no good for you."

Rosa was right. Simona often thought that her father had only wanted his wife and that the wrong person had died at her birth.

"When your man doesn't support you," Rosa continued, "it is very difficult to be a mother. I could not leave my husband, so my daughter is being raised in Mexico by *mi mami*. It is better for her to be raised where one person loves her, than where one does not." She paused and the sadness of her words lingered. "Sometimes what is best for your baby breaks your heart. When my little flower was born, I had a hard time and she didn't get enough oxygen. She was very blue, but the midwife was able to save her. She looked so pale I named her Flora Blanca, my white flower."

Rosa was quiet for a moment, staring at the stone floor. "My husband is ashamed of Flora Blanca. I can no longer bear him children. He thought it would be too dangerous to migrate with her. Sometimes the jobs we found were not nice. And when you are in the fields all day, or sometimes a canning factory, you can't keep an eye on a child like her." Rosa pressed a hand to her heart as her face fell into a despairing look.

"We're settled now, but I don't know how she would survive in the city. In Mexico she has a little burro that walks with her everywhere. He is her special friend, and *mi mami's* farm is a safe place. I leave her in Mexico even though it breaks my heart to be away from her."

"That's awful," Simona said.

"No, mothers make sacrifices for their children," Clarice said. "You'll see."

"*Si*, being a mother is never easy."

Clarice looked over at her mother's unfinished portrait on the wall. "When Mama was almost fourteen, her daddy sent her to work as housekeeper for a rich widower. Her wages went straight to her daddy, so she had nothing coming for her work, except for a cold little room and a plain black dress that she wore every day. But that widower thought Mama was pretty enough to marry. She was too young to know anything better might be out there; besides, her daddy had agreed to it before she even knew the widower had feelings for her.

"He brought her a dress all wrapped up in plain brown paper with a pretty ribbon and proposed to her while she was opening it. She decided it was better to marry him than keep cleaning his fireplace. She thought once they were married, he'd hire a new cleaning girl." Clarice smiled at her mother's girlish naïveté. "What does a fourteen year old know?"

Simona followed Clarice's gaze up to the sketch. She'd imagined Alma severe, hard even. Her opinion softened as the image of that woman who had willed her own death was tempered by the thought of a girl, with no control over her own destiny, being given a pretty dress and a marriage proposal.

"Daddy had gone and bought the most fashionable, most expensive dress he could find, and she married him in it. It was a pale dusty-rose silk chiffon." She sighed. "I still have their wedding picture. Mama had used pieces of the ribbon from the package in her hair. She don't look especially happy. Daddy was sitting in an old armchair and I guess she was shadowing him, cause you can't hardly see his face. She was married to a man three times her age and had his baby at age fifteen. That woman had ten babies, three of whom she buried before they'd had a chance to turn two." Clarice shook her head as though to acknowledge the hardness of her mother's life.

"She used to make us clean the house. She cooked the meals and we girls did the cleaning. Mama was a tyrant about it too." Clarice raised her voice to a slightly shrill pitch and imitated her mother. "'When I clean that floor, you can see yourself in the shine,' she used to say. Then Daddy would come in and say, 'No you can't, Alma. I married you cause you're pretty, not cause you're a good housekeeper.' Mama used to get so mad at him!" Clarice chuckled and walked up to her mother's portrait. "Oh, Mama, you did pretty good with the life given you." She kissed her fingertips and touched her mother's face.

Chapter Fourteen

PETER TOOK A SIP of scotch and picked up the phone. He listened to the dial tone, an incessant droning buzz like an audible headache. He thumped the receiver against his head a few times before hanging up. He didn't know who to call. It was midnight here, six o'clock in the morning there, and a call would wake either woman at this hour. *Pregnant.* It certainly explained a few things. The subtle change to Simona's figure, soon to be obvious to the world since she was almost four months along. And the tiredness. And the moods. Nothing so extreme as to be glaring, but if he'd been paying attention he would have understood. He wandered through the living room and onto the balcony, leaving the sliding glass door open wide. He stood perfectly still, his fists and jaw clenched against the cold, arms drawn tight against his sides. Minnesota was having a hard winter and it was twenty degrees below zero, Below, the river park lay heaped with snow, picnic tables and dust bins just indistinguishable mounds of white under an indigo-colored sky. The ground was crisscrossed with ski and snowshoe tracks, anonymous marks that reminded Peter he was alone in this country. Each inhalation froze his nostrils and left ice crystals hanging in his lungs. He exhaled slowly and his breath drifted away from him in a white stream. Every second he lingered in the icy cold was penance for his crime, but like any bastard, self-preservation soon won out and he turned back. The glass door jolted on its track as Peter slammed it shut. He snatched a rug from the sofa and wrapped himself in it. *Bloody fool,* he thought, *acting like a lovesick kid as though there was something poetic about frostbite.* At least he'd made himself miserable.

He and Gemma used to have fun, but it was so long ago and so far out of reach.

When they met at university, Gemma was vibrant, liked by everyone, and she loved Nick Mylanos—perhaps more than she'd ever loved Peter. That small fact had never really bothered him because Nick walked away and he won.

It had been spring, the end-of-term Peter's junior year, and exams had given the campus a subdued air. It was as though the campus held its breath, waiting for that mighty outburst when the students went collectively mad. They fled the hallowed halls and raced to the river. Books, shoes, and assorted articles of clothing left a wide trail, a testimony to mayhem, down Old College Hill.

After a mass swim the students headed to the nearest pub, Pat's Tap, each and every body dripping wet. Old Pat only barely tolerated the ordeal because it brought in a sizable annual flux of cash. Granted, most of it was soggy, but after the first few years in the 1920s when the tradition was begun, Pat learned to be prepared, and each subsequent generation of Pats despised the last day of exams as much as they loved the students and their cold, wet cash.

Peter stood in the crowded pub shoulder-to-shoulder with his school chums, all of them leaving puddles at their feet. They were laughing at something Charlie had said—it didn't matter what because anything was hilarious on the last day of school. There wasn't a person in the place who wasn't intent on getting pissed in celebration of his or her own achievements.

Someone started belting out the school rugby song and the crowd joined in enthusiastically. "We'll bring the old school to glory, make the masters proud!" Peter was in the middle of the second verse when someone at the bar caught his eye. Gemma Warner. She stood next to her boyfriend. A thin curl of her wet hair stuck to her face, curving seductively along her jaw line. She was wearing a white blouse that clung to her and Peter could make out the lace pattern of her bra along the curve of her breast. They'd had a couple of classes together. She was witty and ambitious in class. Outside, she constantly hung on Nick's arm—that was about to change with Nick moving to Greece. Peter had never seen Gemma look more beautiful or more sad, and at that moment he vowed he would have her.

Chapter Fifteen

BRR-BRR...BRR-BRR. GEMMA REACHED OUT from under the duvet and swatted at her bedside table, knocking her paperback to the floor before finding the phone. "Hello," she said in a froggy morning voice.

"Gemma."

"Peter? What time is it?" She had never been one for conversing before her morning coffee and a look at the paper. "Why are you calling at this hour?"

"I was thinking about you is all."

"Oh."

They were quiet. Gemma cleared her throat trying to get rid of the croak in her voice.

"How are you, love?"

"Fine." Gemma rubbed her eyes. "Peter, can you call me back later? When I'm awake enough to actually talk?"

"Right. I should have waited until you were up. I was just remembering the day we met at Pat's Tap and I wanted to hear your voice."

Gemma rolled her eyes. "That's sweet, but I'm not awake yet. Call me later today."

"Maybe. I don't know if I'll be able to call later. Work..."

Gemma knew she should sit herself up and talk to her husband. She felt Peter reaching out for a connection, but she couldn't reconcile that knowledge with her petty annoyance at being woken up. As the receiver settled into place, she heard the ping of another strand of their marriage snapping. The thread that had once held them together was frayed and tired, and Gemma was losing interest in its maintenance.

She made her way to the shower and stood under a steady, hot stream. As it relaxed and revived her, Gemma's thoughts turned to the day Peter had mentioned, the day they had met. She and Nikolai stood at the bar in Pat's Tap, dripping wet. It was their last day together. Gemma was going home for the summer break and Nikolai would stay on a few days for the commencement, visiting with his mother and sister, then head off to Greece to work for his father.

The pub was roaring with noise and Gemma wasn't the only person with Nikolai's attention. They were surrounded by friends, all toasting their futures with pints of stout, cursing old man Foley in the Physics department, or Crawford in Archaeology, or whoever had given them trouble that year. It wasn't long before someone started singing the school rugby song and everyone was going along. Except Gemma. She looked at Nikolai, his pint held high, belting out the school song with a look of nostalgia. She was losing him to an island with warm beaches and olive trees, his father's business, and dark-haired girls. She, and their three years together, were a part of his glory days at university. It was at that moment Gemma knew Nikolai wouldn't come back for her and she decided not to wait for him.

In the next moment, Peter had elbowed his way up to the bar and stood next to her. "Hello," he said. Gemma had turned her back on Nikolai and smiled at Peter.

Gemma laughed at the strangeness of life. Here Peter was overseas, practically gone from her life, and Nikolai turns up in a reversal of history. But had she already turned her back on Peter? She wasn't sure yet. She did know that now, just like then, she was interested in a new possibility opening before her. Gemma wrapped a towel around her hair and went to her closet. She was meeting Nikolai for breakfast and felt like wearing a skirt, something that would show her calves.

Gemma snuggled onto the sofa, wrapped in a rug, a romantic film in the DVD player, a bowl of nibbles, and a Milk Tray ready.

The smell of cat box filled her nostrils and her muscles tensed. She looked around the room with wide eyes, suddenly aching for company. The stench intensified and she knew she was helpless to stop it. She stayed on the sofa with her fingers digging into the overstuffed cushions, bracing herself against the coming journey. She spasmed, knocking the chocolates onto the floor. Gemma was only vaguely aware of her body going rigid, then softening against the couch.

She was again looking through a stranger's eyes, watching hands that weren't her own moving in front of her. The Artist was painting a portrait on the wall, *Clarice's mother*. The ammonia scent faded and was replaced by that sickly-sweet cologne. Clarice and Rosa came into focus as her head cleared.

"I named her Flora Blanca, my white flower." Rosa was quiet for a moment, staring at the floor.

Gemma looked past her to the mural and saw that new figures had been added.

"My husband is ashamed of Blanca, and I can no longer bear him children." Gemma felt a kinship with Rosa and at the same time envy that her daughter had survived. She had thought about it a thousand times—would she rather have a failed pregnancy or a disabled child? Each time she'd drawn the same conclusion. Any child, no matter how needy, would be better than suffering that loss.

While Clarice told of her mother's hard life and her strength, Gemma watched the Artist draw, her hands moving with an intuitive rhythm that seemed to accompany the women's stories, keeping time for them all. It occurred to Gemma that she might be weak. That other women suffered her loss and carried on. *Necessity*. The word came, whispered in Clarice's soothing voice, delivered exclusively to Gemma.

Necessity, she thought. Those women did what they had to and carried on because they had no choice. Gemma had the luxury of being sick and depressed, and of seeing a therapist. If she were not so comfortable, how would she manage, she wondered.

After the women said good night to each other, Clarice looked into the eyes of the Artist, but her stare seemed to penetrate and pass right through to Gemma. "You know, baby, there is a time for everything," she said. "You got to believe that your life will work itself out the way it's supposed to. If you two is meant to be together, you will be. If your relationship has run its course, then trust that you can survive without him."

Gemma spiraled back with Clarice's words still echoing in her mind. Panting softly, she slumped onto the sofa. Gemma felt like she'd just sprinted a twenty-yard dash and her chest hurt from the exertion. Her television came into focus again, a blue screen with the words "DVD Player" scrolling across it. She had been out quite some time. Her spine cracked as she stretched. When the fear and exhilaration that came with each vision had settled, she went to the sideboard and poured herself a drink, repeating Clarice's words. "You can survive without him."

Wearily, she climbed the stairs to her bedroom.

Gemma and Peter walked side by side through a meadow under a blazing sun. They approached an orchard of bent and sagging trees as the sky turned red. Wormy apples lay in decay over the ground. Gemma was afraid to walk in the orchard, afraid to feel the squish of putrid fruit beneath her bare feet. She looked at Peter for help, and he disintegrated into a pile of ash. A gust of wind swept him away, toward whence they came. The moon rose toward the sun and the air cooled. Gemma stood alone, waiting for the impending eclipse.

She woke from the dream, her sheets binding her legs and her nightshirt wrapped around her middle. Now that she was used to Peter being gone, she moved quite a lot in her sleep, sprawling over the whole bed and twisting in the covers. Instead of enjoying the newfound space, Gemma was disconcerted by the state of her bedding each morning. She saw her movements as a sign of stress and contrary to her progress with Dr. Hamilton. Or perhaps it was simply her dreams that made her so restless.

It was still early, only five o'clock. She might not have been well rested, but at least she'd have plenty of time to get ready for her lunch date with Miranda Richardson. It had been Dr. Hamilton's idea for her to get in touch with an old school chum. Getting in touch was easy, but scheduling had been difficult. The date finally arrived and Gemma was already feeling awkward. She got out of bed and straightened her nightshirt, then put on Peter's old terry cloth dressing gown, the one thing left of the man that gave her comfort. After spending an hour in a wardrobe crisis, Gemma settled for a taupe pantsuit. The jacket was long and belted, worn over a dark camisole. She added a silk scarf for some color. Every time she passed a shop window, she stared at her reflection. The more she inspected herself, the more certain she was that she had chosen entirely wrong.

First to arrive at the restaurant, Gemma sipped a still water with lemon and inspected the English prints hung on the gray chintz wallpaper. She'd always liked English landscapes and romantic portraits. Miranda, she remembered from their school days, had only been interested in contemporary art.

"Daar-ling!"

Gemma was afraid to look.

"Gemma Ledbetter, I'd know you anywhere."

Miranda swooped down to the table. Gemma stood, prepared to offer the obligatory double-peck on the cheek, but Miranda landed in the chair opposite her with a breathy little huff as though she'd just jogged to the restaurant.

"Sit, darling." Miranda extracted a phone from her coat pocket and laid it next to her silverware. The case matched Miranda's turquoise leather skirt. "Wow-ee Gemma, you haven't changed at all. Still very trim," she said approvingly. "No children, then?"

"Ladies." The server saved Gemma from having to answer. "What can I get you to drink?"

"I think wine. Something dry. Something white," Miranda said.

Gemma nodded to the server. "That would be fine."

"You know," Miranda said, once the server had left, "I was in Texas last week, visiting an American friend there. Everything is bee-er," she dragged out the word, imitating a Texas drawl. "But I did fall in love with the margarita and with Mexican cuisine. Did you know there are three types of Mexican food? Interior, authentic, and Tex-Mex. My friends tell me if they speak English in the kitchen, it's not worth eating."

Miranda gave a well-practiced chuckle that turned Gemma's stomach, yet she felt the need to respond with feigned amusement.

Miranda ordered the venison in ginger and Madeira. Gemma opted for the chicken breast in pimento and chili sauce. Halfway through the meal, she finally had the opportunity to ask Miranda about her work, or more specifically, how she had come to own a successful gallery with any number of artists clamoring to hang their work on her walls.

"Well, darling, mostly you have to be in the right place at the right time, and you need a good eye for talent, of course. Why do you ask?" She looked at Gemma, her chin tilted.

"It's just that we have the same degree, don't we?" Gemma said. "Only we've chosen such different paths, and I...I'm considering doing something new. Something professional."

"It's about time! I can't imagine spending the last decade of my life doing some man's laundry. I mean, it's really doing nothing with your life, isn't it?"

"I wouldn't say I've done nothing." Gemma was starting to hate Miranda and her turquoise leather skirt.

"No, no, not *nothing*. I only meant, well, being a housewife isn't exactly a profession, is it?"

"You make it sound like I've been kept prisoner by my husband." Gemma felt her cheeks growing warm. "I chose to not work."

"Yes, and now you've called me because you're ready for something new. Why is that?" Miranda stared with one well-shaped eyebrow arching into her forehead, the answer blatantly simple, if only dull-witted Gemma would catch up. "Because being a housewife is not fulfilling for any woman with half a brain in her head. Who wants to putter around a house all day, then throw parties for her husband's friends on the weekend, when she could be out there, making her own friends? And her own money?"

"But..."

Miranda's cell phone rang and she plucked it off the table. "Yes?...Fraaa-nco," she purred. "How is Madrid?"

Gemma cut the remainder of her chicken breast into small bite-size pieces, carefully sawing through each piece until her knife touched china, halving it—an experiment in division—until the piece before her was too small to cut. "No, nothing, just lunch with an old school chum," Miranda's eyes flicked up as she flashed a smile at Gemma. Gemma stabbed the tiny chicken piece on an outside tine of her fork and looked at it. *This is my ego. My life's accomplishments. My reward for being an executive's wife. This is Miranda's heart. Her talent. Her brain. Her ridiculously minuscule tits.* Gemma put the fork in her mouth and closed her teeth over the tines, then delicately slipped the chicken off the utensil. She swallowed without even tasting it. "Love to Basil. Kiss, kiss." Miranda set the phone back on the table. "Where were we? Oh yes, your life."

"Actually, I was just curious, Miranda. I'm quite happy with my life as it is. I was simply making polite conversation."

"Nonsense. You ring me up after ten years time because there is something going on. We both have art history degrees, but the difference, Gemma, is that I have spent the last decade *doing*. I've made a name for myself in the art world. And it's not a pretty world. Despite appearances, it's cut-throat in my circle. It's filled with children, fresh out of university, who are desperate and unforgiving. Really, they'd never let an old girl like you in." She paused to sip her wine, then added as an afterthought. "You could always run a till at a museum gift shop."

Gemma narrowed her eyes and pursed her lips.

"Darling!" Miranda exclaimed. "Don't take it like that. If I weren't already in, I'd be out myself. The face of the art world is getting younger by the day. You're ancient by thirty!" She laughed, then lowered her voice, leaned closer to Gemma, and reached across the table to touch her hand. "I'll let you in on a secret. It's no longer enough for an arts patron to be wealthy and eccentric. You have to be a businesswoman and know how to play in both the art and business courts. Miranda the arts patron would love to walk around in sandals and drawstring pants all day with a..." she waved her hand in a flourish to stimulate the brain, "straw hat and no makeup. But Miranda the businesswoman is..." she dropped her voice to a low whisper, "scheduled for a teensy-weensy procedure next week."

"Really?" Gemma said. "Oooh," she cooed and pulled an extremely sympathetic face. "A chin-tuck, I suppose. Or maybe liposuction?"

February

Chapter Sixteen

"SIMONA," HAL SAID, "I found you a table." He unfolded the legs of a card table and set it up next to Simona's box of supplies, which he then lifted onto the table for her. "You shouldn't do all that bending."

"In my condition, you mean?" She smiled.

"In your condition, yes."

"Thank you, Hal."

"Your mural's really coming along. Who are you painting today?"

Simona had finished Alma and Flora Blanca's portraits and moved on to a figure of her imagination. She tilted her head toward the charcoal sketch taped to the wall of a black-clad girl in combat boots. "She's young, urban, a punk."

"I think I rode the light rail with her this morning. She gave up her seat for a priest," he added.

"That's our girl, then. On the fringe of society, artistically misunderstood, but behind the black eyeliner and body piercings, she's really a sweet girl."

Hal nodded again. "These women you're painting, I feel like I know them, like I can see their whole lives in their faces."

Simona put a hand on Hal's arm. "Thank you. That's the best compliment I've ever received."

"No, it's not."

"Yes."

"I hope the table helps," he said with a friendly nod and left her to work.

Simona opened her can of Ivory Black and plopped a large blob of the paint onto her palette. She spent the afternoon painting her punk girl into the first row of women. She wore steel-toed boots over fishnet stockings, a black vinyl mini, a white tank top with a skull and crossbones printed on the chest, and she held a black leather jacket over her shoulder. Her shaggy black hair had a shock of neon red at the front, which she held out of her eyes with plastic teddybear barrettes.

As she worked on Punk Girl, the details of her life came to Simona, drifting through her mind as each element was added to the portrait. The girl was too thin—not anorexic, but hungry. Her eyes were dark and sleep deprived. She was no suburban kid who put on a costume for weekend clubbing. This girl had it hard. Punk Girl had been kicked out of her parents house, was squatting with her boyfriend and a bunch of kids. Drugs? Some who saw this portrait would be certain of it. Simona saw her as an escapist not opposed to tripping with her friends or getting wasted on Mad Dog, but she wasn't hard-core. Not yet.

It was tiring, this act of creation. Simona had a knot in her shoulder and a cramp in her hand. Her eyes ached and her mind was singular in its attention. With each choice of color, each dab of the brush, each detail to be completed, she felt a tenderness for this nonexistent girl who could be so many girls.

She spent hours giving her punk girl hoops and barbells of surgical steel and a tattoo. It was a street-job, the sideways figure 8 for infinity sat on her chest in an almost black ink, between her clavicle and her heart. Simona carefully painted on heavy black eyeliner with a fine sable brush. Then she added a chain belt with a padlock for a buckle. As a last stroke of inspiration came to her, Simona painted a large tear in the girl's spandex skirt with a number of safety pins spanning the rip along her thigh.

Hal was long gone when she finished Punk Girl and ran across the lobby and downstairs to the bathroom, about to burst.

She climbed the short flight of stairs, relieved and excited to see the newest portrait from afar, to approach it with the perspective of one coming upon it for the first time. She rounded the top of the stairs and startled. Finding a visitor waiting for her return was not unusual at this point, but she'd been so singularly focused on her work that she'd forgotten to expect it. Alma sat in the camp chair with her arms crossed against her chest, knees clamped together and shins perfectly parallel to each other.

"I never did like living in the city," Alma announced when Simona was a few steps away. "Filth everywhere. And all those automobiles scare me. Too many of them jamming up the streets." She smoothed the placket over her bosom. "You know my children moved me here when I got too feeble to look after my big house. Nobody would dream of moving home, so they set me up in that dirty little apartment so I could be looked after."

Alma looked crossly over her shoulder at the mural. "Clarice!" she bellowed. "Clarice, get on out here!"

A ripple moved through the painting and Clarice pushed her way out of the wall, arriving at her mother's side in a matter of seconds.

"Yes, Mama? I hope you didn't call me out here just to complain about the apartment."

"No, Clarice, though I always did despise that place. I want you to introduce me to your friend." Alma smiled at Simona with a plastic politeness.

"Mama, I would like you to meet Simona Casale. Simona, this is my mama. Mama believes in being properly introduced."

"It's the only way for civilized people to meet." Alma turned to Simona. "Alma Mae Roberts. Pleased to meet you."

Simona shook her hand.

"I'd like to thank you for dressing me so smartly," Alma said, smoothing a non-existent wrinkle from her skirt. "Well now. I just wanted to meet you. I expect you've got plans this evening. Come along,

Clarice, we mustn't overstay our welcome."

"Mrs. Roberts," Simona said, "I don't have anything planned. In fact, I would enjoy your company."

Alma nodded. "Then I will visit with you tonight."

"I'd like that."

Simona painted for hours. Clarice, Rosa, and now Alma were with her, and she hardly registered the passing of time. She felt a warm belonging, though she would have been unable to explain it, and when she was away from the Center she missed them. It was not like the growing love she had felt for Peter. It was something even he could not provide, if he would provide anything at all. It was, she finally decided, unconditional love. It was the same love she would give her baby. Simona began working nights at the Center, when Hal was gone and the building was quiet, to ensure she would not go a single day without that feeling.

Chapter Seventeen

SHE WANTED TO PASS a hand through the window and touch each of the blooms: the convoluted cockscomb, alien-looking veined sarracenia, round puffed protea, and tall stalks of liatris. The arrangement was filled out with leatherleaf and branches of pepper berries, all emerging from a fluted amber-colored glass vase. Gemma stood staring for several seconds, unconsciously leaning closer and closer to the glass. The arrangement was entirely done in dark, intriguing shades of red. When she could resist no longer, Gemma stepped into the shop so that she could inspect the window display up close.

"Good afternoon." A woman called from the back. She gave Gemma a friendly nod of her head, then returned her gaze to her books and placed the end of a stubby pencil between her teeth.

Gemma admired the arrangement so closely that she didn't notice the shopkeeper approach. Just as she was about to run a finger over the cockscomb, the woman spoke, "It's a very feminine piece, I think."

Gemma startled and spun to face the woman. "Yes. It's lovely."

"I'm sorry I startled you." The woman's gray hair hung to her waist in a thin plait. Large silver hoop earrings framed her face and some sort of crystal pendant dangled on a long chain. In her brown tunic and straight skirt, she resembled a walking stick insect. The woman smiled warmly, deepening the creases that radiated out from the corners of her eyes.

"Can I help you find something?" she asked.

"I only came in to admire this arrangement up close."

"Thank you. I enjoyed making that one—it has wonderful texture." The shopkeeper clasped her hands together modestly and Gemma saw, besides a number of large silver rings, that they were dotted with light brown age spots, giving away years that didn't show in her posture. *These hands haven't been idle a day in their life,* Gemma thought.

"Come along," she said, "I'll show you something else."

The shop was crowded with displays of flowers heaped into tin buckets. Trellises sprung up throughout the store, joining displays, arching over walkways, overgrown with flowering vines. At first, it appeared all a jumble, but Gemma became aware that the displays had been orchestrated so that the size, color, and texture of dozens of varieties flowed together in visual harmony. She paused to smell a stargazer lily. A clear drop of nectar clung to one of the yellow powdered stamens, and she touched her finger to it and stuck it in her mouth. The sticky sweet drop on her tongue flooded her with an inexplicable mixture of sadness and relief, as though a very ill friend had just passed away. Gemma blushed when she realized the shopkeeper was watching her.

"Here it is, dear," the woman said, having arrived at a cooler filled with fresh arrangements. She brought out a small black rectangular dish with three birds of paradise sitting at graduated heights in a bed of thick, dark green leaves. "This one suits you."

Gemma had let the mess remain, the remnants of the meal still scattered over the table in half-emptied serving dishes, with cloth napkins mounded beside the good china. Despite her insistence that Nikolai was only an old friend, having him over for supper, on the good china, with wine, was something that could not be strictly innocent, no matter how one turned it in the light. Gemma wore a skirt with a provocative slit up the thigh. She also wore dark red lipstick and perfume. That was condemnation enough.

While Nikolai poured them cognac at the sideboard—something Peter had done hundreds of times—Gemma turned on the gas fireplace. They sat together and she stared at the flowers on her coffee table, waiting for the conversation to resume. The birds of paradise looked as fresh as they had in the flower shop two days ago. The vibrant orange-yellow petals were exotic and sturdy. "The woman said these flowers suit me," she said.

"They do."

"How so?" Gemma's surprise came through in her voice.

"You're bright. You're strong." Nikolai paused to tilt his head and study the flowers. "There's an energy to you both, a lively one."

"I haven't felt lively for years."

"But Gem, I've never known you to be otherwise."

"Things change, don't they?" Gemma fell quiet. She was afraid to spoil their evening with her troubles, yet she suddenly longed to tell Nikolai everything, to trust somebody with the whole truth. She was debating whether or not to begin and hadn't quite decided, when she sat up straight and faced him. "Peter and I can't seem to have a child and I have no one to talk with about it, outside of my therapist, but I mean I don't have a friend to talk with. Really, I'm a terrible mess." She stopped and worked her mouth into the crooked half-smile of an apology.

"Gemma, we're old friends, aren't we? You can talk to me."

It was what she wanted to hear, to know she hadn't made a fool of herself. The words came pushing from her mouth, an oral history that needed to be passed on, a risk that had to be taken. Gemma told him of her two miscarriages and the anencephalic baby, the one without a brain that was stillborn, purging with a newfound freedom. "You can't imagine how hard it was," she said, "delivering that baby." There she stopped and caught her breath. And Nikolai only nodded, his dark eyes filled with sympathy. Gemma refilled her glass and drank as if it would finish the story for her, if only she had enough. Nikolai sat patiently, sipping from his own glass. Finally, Gemma set hers down and looked

Nikolai in the eye so that she could watch his face for signs she was going too far.

"Even Mum and Molly don't know about the last pregnancy," she said. "They think I had another miscarriage." Gemma stopped to catch her breath. She'd told him so much already, all of it raw and true. If she left the last chapter untold, there would be that withholding between them, getting in the way of whatever might become. "Last November, I went in for a twelve-week check-up and when they couldn't find a heartbeat, I thought the baby had died, just like the one before." She paused to take a sip of cognac and look at the flowers. "I was never pregnant," she said at last, exposing her rawest nerve.

"I don't understand," he said.

She looked up and whispered, "It was a phantom pregnancy."

Nikolai sat perfectly still, seemingly hung in that moment between the delivery of news and one's response, that uncomfortable pause given to deciding how to tactfully handle a situation. Gemma held her breath, waiting. "Oh Gem, my little Gem," he said at last and reached out, pulling her to his chest, securing her with strong arms that smelled like the Mediterranean.

Gemma let go of herself and cried like a child, her tears wetting Nikolai's shirtfront. He stroked her hair and let her be weak and hurt until the tears stopped on their own. "Do you know," Gemma said, drying her cheeks, "after the stillbirth, when they released me from hospital, I didn't want to come home. I was exhausted...and sad...and so we went to a film. There was some stupid horror film playing. It was that, or this very depressing drama. See, I didn't want to wait for another one. I just wanted to go inside and sit in the dark. In the very beginning, this girl is hung up in a tree and eviscerated, her guts spilled all over the ground. It was horrid, and I thought, that's just how I feel..." Gemma fell silent.

Nikolai kissed her forehead. "I should have taken you to Greece."

Nikolai had matured into a lover of women. No longer the college student eager to satisfy his own particular urges, he was slow and tender, exploring her body and responding to her cues. Gemma felt like the same inexperienced girl she had been in college, unsure of everything and both eager and afraid to please. She wasn't that way with Peter, but they had their routine. Their boring old routine. After they had both climaxed, separately, Gemma lay in Nikolai's arms and felt dreamily content for the first time in ages.

They drank a morning coffee at the kitchen table, smiling fondly at each other the way couples do. Gemma could not believe how at ease Nikolai was, as though he belonged in her kitchen, as though it was their own kitchen. He brought up Gemma's birthday and offered to take her out to dinner. She was delighted he had remembered and quickly agreed. He left early and discretely.

A package from America arrived in the morning post. Gemma set it on the kitchen table and sliced through the tape. Atop a lot of packing foam sat a lavender envelope. Gemma put the card aside and dug through the foam. She found a package of Minnesota-grown wild rice, a jar of local honey, and a coffee table book about the Twin Cities. She flipped through the book without paying any attention to it, then dug deeper into the box. A small velvet jewelry pouch produced a pendant, handmade by some Minneapolis artisan. The silver pendant had a bevel set amethyst, deep purple and clear, her birthstone. Gemma looked at the pendant, turning it over in her fingers. *Here I am turning thirty-three*, she thought, *and my husband is out of the country*. She imagined the sort of things he could be doing on his own. The sort of women he could meet. She stared at the contents of the box, now spread over her kitchen table—the local wares, the unopened card, and the velvet pouch. It seemed to Gemma that Peter was on the other side of the world with no one to hold him accountable for anything. And what about her?

She dropped the pendant back into its pouch and left Peter's presents there on the kitchen table, unceremoniously spread out like something waiting to be cleaned up.

The London sky was dark, but the city itself moved with artificial light that glowed and pulsed from every building front, blocking out the stars. Gemma felt nineteen again and free. Her wedding set lay on her dressing table—nothing but cold metal without her blood to warm it. Her hand fit into Nikolai's, palms touching, fingers laced together, and it occurred to her that whatever their true lives held in wait, to anyone who took notice of them tonight they belonged together. It had been obvious when she laughed at his remark in the restaurant, her eyes twinkling. When, just moments later, they fell silent and he reached across the table to rest his hand on hers. When they sat through the entire concert with his arm around her shoulder. And now, holding hands on the street, as though they couldn't possibly run into one of Peter's acquaintances, or a friend of Gemma's from the gardening society. It had been so long since she'd seen anyone, so long since anyone had wanted to see her, who would recognize her? Who would believe it? She had something special planned, a birthday present to herself. And after her present was opened, she was going to ask Nikolai if he meant what he'd said about taking her to Greece.

Nikolai leaned over and nuzzled in her hair, next to her ear. "You smell fantastic," he said. "And that thing you're wearing!"

Gemma smiled at his attentions. She had taken careful consideration in dressing: black trousers, heeled boots, and a plum-colored velvet body suit with a thong back and scooped neckline under a short, black leather jacket. She knew, with his face next to hers, he was peering into her cleavage. His admiration pleased her and confirmed that her plans were well-made.

They came to The Dormansly Hotel and Gemma stopped Nikolai

with a gentle pressure on his arm. "Let's stop in here. Just for a minute...or more," she urged him coyly. They turned up the stone steps and a doorman greeted them as they entered the lobby. Her stomach fluttered as she thought of the room key lying in her handbag. The old hotel had an elegant lobby with a marble floor, deep sofas, lush potted trees, and a front desk with staff groomed for both appearance and manner. Nikolai was moving them toward the lounge, but she had a bottle of champagne already waiting in the room. Gemma pulled against his arm, turning him gently toward the main staircase.

"Nick!" somebody shouted from behind them. They kept moving. "Nick Mylanos!" The voice rang out and then the woman attached to it bounded after them. Gemma cringed to think that someone—especially a woman Nikolai knew—was intruding on her evening, and now of all times. They stopped their progress past the registration desk and turned. The woman wore a short black skirt and red sequined shell. Her platinum hair and red lipstick looked garish, designed to draw attention of a certain type. Gemma stood stunned, her arm linked through Nikolai's. He shifted uncomfortably and cleared his throat.

"Nick, I didn't realize you're staying here," she said.

"I'm not."

"You were very naughty," she scolded. "I expected a call from you yesterday. And who's this?" She stared at Gemma, wearing a smile that didn't veil her contempt in the least.

"Gemma, this is Marlena. A friend."

"Oh, Nick, you're too modest." Marlena wrapped herself around Nikolai's free arm. Gemma released his other side. "It's bad form to neglect a girl who shows you around town, Nicky."

Nikolai squirmed free of Marlena and shifted closer to Gemma. "I'll call you later this week. Perhaps we could all meet for a drink."

"Why don't you join Marlena in the lounge?" Gemma said, employing her party smile. "I'm sure she'd appreciate your company." Turning away from the pair, she started up the stairs.

"Excuse me, Marlena." Nikolai hurried after Gemma. "Gem.

Gemma." He took the stairs two at a time, something she could not do in heels, and grabbed at her arm.

Gemma shook him loose. "I've never been so humiliated."

"I find that hard to believe."

She stormed down the hallway without looking back, her shoulders held square and rigid. At the door she had to dig in her handbag for the key, and Nikolai caught up to her again.

"I'm sorry." He touched her elbow and she shrugged him off. "I didn't know, did I? It's only an unpleasant coincidence. It doesn't have to ruin our evening."

She faced him, the key in hand at last. "It already has."

"Oh, Gemma, isn't that a bit dramatic? Look, I had no idea—"

"That I'd planned something special? If you'd known, you wouldn't have slept with her, I suppose."

"No. No." Nikolai paused to smile and push a dark curl back from his brow. "Gemma, please, can't we at least...."

"Not likely." She swung the door open and stepped into the room.

"Gemma, wait! I don't understand why you're so mad. We aren't dating, are we? We're just two old school chums having a reunion, a bit of fun. You're married, remember?"

"What were you doing with a cow like that for anyway?"

"She was a bit handy," he shrugged.

"That's disgusting."

"Now you're taking her side, are you? Is it any more disgusting than a married woman booking a hotel room?"

"Sod off, Nicky." She shut the door and locked it.

"I'm sorry, Gem," he called through the door. "Please, let's talk about this."

Gemma curled her shoulders forward and sighed into her hands. She stayed there against the door until well after she'd heard Nikolai walk away from the other side. She had never been so humiliated in her life, that much was true. But it wasn't the fact that Nikolai had slept with some *handy* woman. Gemma rubbed her ring finger where her wedding set should have been. It was unbearable, the things she'd done: spent two hours in a lingerie boutique squeezing herself into all sorts of stretchy lace things, booked The Dormansly...and now. It brought her to tears. Gemma had rushed over after lunch with a bottle of champagne and box of chocolates, her toiletries and even a toothbrush for him, and the new lingerie. There it was, laid out suggestively on the four-poster bed, an ivory silk gown with ribbon straps, a slit up the thigh and pearl-beads decorating the bust line. It came with matching panties and a matching dressing gown. At the shop, she couldn't bring herself to choose between the classic gown and a more risqué black lace teddy. So she bought them both, even though they were quite dear, arguing logically that a proper affair would require more than one sexy nightie. And what would Peter say when he saw the report from the credit company showing her day's expenditures? The hotel room alone was over £300.

Gemma turned on the tap to run a hot bath and went into the main room where her champagne waited on ice. The bottle opened with a celebratory *pop* and she filled both glasses.

She clinked the glasses together. "Happy birthday, Gemma."

Chapter Eighteen

THE PORTRAIT WAS OF a ragged woman with a dirt-encrusted face and torn clothes. The woman had white hair, bleached by hard years, and a permanent squint to her eyes. She was younger than she looked and older than she needed to be. With a filthy cracked hand, she tugged on a lock of hair, pulled the thin section of scraggly strands so taut it stretched across the eye, along the nose, and past the purplish lips, threatening to break free from her scalp. The dismal eyes were vacant and the scarf that circled her neck full of holes. This one she called Medusa.

Simona sang the "Itsy Bitsy Spider" as she worked.

It wasn't long before the mural seemed to move, as though someone had tossed a rock into a pond. The ripple originated over Marguerite's heart. The waves spread and grew as they moved outward and dissipated into the far corners of the wall. Simona watched as Marguerite's hands flexed, one then the other. She seemed to stretch the wall itself, pushing against it, until a limb emerged and Marguerite stepped free of her confines. She stood in front of her portrait and struck her hands together, brushing off dust, then turned to face the wall.

"Flora Blanca," she commanded, reaching for her granddaughter. Flora Blanca joined her outside the mural, her arms wrapped tightly around Marguerite's waist.

"I always sang to my babies, too, especially while I was cooking,"

Marguerite said, stroking Flora Blanca's head. "This is Flora Blanca, but I suppose you already know who we are."

Simona nodded.

"Why did you paint me holding dirt?"

"It's symbolic. It means that you know what's yours and you hold onto it."

Marguerite nodded, satisfied.

Simona noticed that Marguerite spoke without an accent, unlike Rosa. Marguerite took Flora Blanca's hand and led her to Rosa's portrait. Flora Blanca pointed, "Mama," she said.

"Rosa was the most difficult of all my children. Right from the start. She was hard coming into the world and every day thereafter." Marguerite turned to look at Simona. "I'm going to tell you something. Rosa met her husband, Juan, at her *Quincañera*. He was not invited. He came with his cousin who was a neighbor of ours. Juan was eighteen, good looking, and had already done some traveling about. He seemed quite worldly to my little Rosa. She was a beauty—before he took that away. Now she is fat and does not take care of herself." Simona was surprised by the accusatory tone in Marguerite's voice. "When I realized he was out to possess her, I forbid her to see that boy. Rosa was so willful that she ran away with him. They got married in secret and when they came back, I disowned her."

"Mama?" Flora Blanca looked up suddenly. Marguerite patted Flora Blanca's shoulder and smoothed her hair with a firm hand before continuing.

"It was three years before I saw Rosa again. She came home begging forgiveness. She told me Juan beat her and she was four months pregnant. She was terrified for the child."

"What did you do?"

"I am her mother." Marguerite shrugged. "When the child was a month old, Juan turned up. He had heard from his cousin that Rosa had his baby. He told Rosa he missed her and promised he had changed. I warned her against letting him back in her life, but she decided to give him one day to prove himself. They were supposed to go on a picnic. I did not see Rosa or the baby for two weeks.

"Finally she made it home, but Juan was with her. She didn't even come inside. Her face was bruised and her lip cut. She handed me the baby..."

"Baby!" Flora Blanca echoed.

"And she left. A week later I received a letter, but by then I had a good idea what had happened. Juan took the baby and put a knife to her, saying that if Rosa didn't go with him, he'd kill the baby. Once he had them away from home, he was very sweet for about a week. Then he slipped back to his old ways. He only hurt Rosa at first, until one day, the baby had a fever and Rosa couldn't stop her crying. Juan was drunk. He snatched her up..."

"Snatch, snatch, snatch," Flora Blanca repeated.

"...and shook her." Marguerite held her hands out, as though around a tiny body and shook them back and forth violently. Flora Blanca held her hands out, mimicking her grandmother, laughing. "Her little brain broke apart."

Simona gasped, a hand quivering over her belly.

"He broke Flora Blanca and Rosa both that day," Marguerite said. "Somehow she convinced him to give me the child. I don't think he wanted a daughter anyway."

"Why didn't Rosa leave him?"

"He said if she did he would come straight to my farm and kill both me and the child."

"Look." Flora Blanca reached into her pocket and held out a shiny American quarter. "From Mama. For Flora Blanca's *Quincañera.*"

"It's so shiny," Simona said. "What a great present."

Flora Blanca smiled, her crooked front teeth accenting her innocence as she held the coin to her chest and rocked herself, twisting side to side.

"I can tell you need your sleep. You should go home now."

"Marguerite," Simona said, as the woman was turning to go. "Why did you tell me this?"

She looked at Simona, her posture rigid, her dress modest, her strength obvious. "Because," she said at last, "it is the truth."

The old woman guided Flora Blanca back inside the painting, then reentered it herself. Simona stood in the empty lobby, alone again with the stony silence. The gravity of Marguerite's story, Rosa's truth, the sadness of Flora Blanca's beginning, atop Peter's sudden absence, left Simona exhausted. Marguerite was right, she needed to sleep, but there was something she wanted to try first.

Simona followed in Marguerite's footsteps. When she reached the wall, she carefully lifted her foot toward it, her eyes closed, expecting to find foothold inside the painting. The wall behaved properly, refused to exhibit any magical qualities, and the toe of her shoe left a smudge where it hit the wall. Off-balance, Simona wobbled, catching herself against the wall. She realized she had actually expected it to work and stood staring stupidly at the mark she'd made. Tomorrow she would have to clean and repair the painting.

Leaning in closer, she studied Marguerite and found she was just a flat image. The Marguerite who had spoken to her moments before had a shine in her eyes and a texture to her skin that could not be reproduced in any painting. Simona raised a hand to touch Marguerite's face and gently laid a finger on her cheek. There was no reaction whatsoever.

Chapter Nineteen

GEMMA SAT COMFORTABLY SLOUCHED into the back of a taxi, playing with the fringe on her wrap. She had stayed at Anna and Nathan's party far longer than planned and had a much better time than anticipated. It was the first time she'd seen the old crowd since the stillbirth, and she was still amazed Anna had thought to invite her. She replayed the billiard's game in her head, visualized how she had looked leaning over the table, then smoking the cigar. She saw the seductive line of her neck as the grayish smoke curled from her lips in slow plumes. Her imagination's eye traveled the room, capturing the expressions on the men's faces—the *one* expression on the many faces: want. All those old chums had wanted her to a one. She never would have guessed how much fun it would be to go solo, so used after years of marriage to being part of a whole. Gemma regained her confidence in that billiards room. She had at last touched on those dead traits, sparked something she had believed lost. A certain social grace she'd been fumbling after for ages returned to her in the unlikeliest of places, and if she could hold onto it, she might just become herself again.

The taxi wound through Hampstead's sleeping streets. Old houses nestled close together secured their dreaming families, their artists and politicians, Gemma's neighbors, so few of whom she actually knew. Droplets of water clung to the windows of the cab, adding another dimension to the chill gray scene. She was suddenly tired, ready for her own bed, and leaned her head against the cold glass. With a gasp, she inhaled the dry heated air of the cab and jerked upright, her spine a lightning rod shocked by a bolt of electricity. The ammonia smell filled her so that her nostrils burned and her temples throbbed.

"I'm going to be sick," she said.

The cabbie sped up with a worried glance over his shoulder. They turned onto her street with a rather violent lurch and Gemma swooned. She had only moments to get inside before she'd slip away. The taxi stopped in front of her house and Gemma thrust a note at the driver over the back of his seat and hurried out of the cab without waiting for change. The pounding in her head was unbearable. Her fingers felt thick and clumsy as she fumbled with the lock, dropping her keys on the stoop. "Oh blast and damn-it!" she cursed as she bent to pick them up. When she straightened, she swooned again, dizzy, and broke a nail reaching for support.

Inside, Gemma collapsed onto her sofa, both hands clutching her temples. It was a relief to let go, so much less painful once she gave in to it. Her breathing slowed and her muscles relaxed as the darkness swirled around her. She was gone, once again a visitor in somebody else's body.

An elderly Mexican woman stood before her, a handful of dirt silently slipping through her fingers onto the marble floor. A girl, with long black plaits in pretty ribbons, clung to her. The woman introduced them as Marguerite and her granddaughter, Flora Blanca. She took the girl to look at the portrait of Rosa, the missing generation.

Marguerite sat and told them her daughter's secret, the thing Rosa had been unable to speak. Gemma listened attentively, as did her host, for there were no sketches made this time. Marguerite held her hands out, as though around a tiny body, and shook them back and forth violently. Flora Blanca held her own hands out and mimicked her grandmother, a wide grin spread across her simple face. "He broke both Flora Blanca and Rosa that day," Marguerite said without a sentimental note. Her words resounded, echoing in Gemma's head. A broken baby, broken by a single evil act.

Gemma awoke with the image of a small brown hand, held out with a shiny American quarter centered on its palm burned into her memory. The evening's exhilaration was gone and her cheeks were wet with tears that she didn't remember crying. They were not sorrowful tears, for Gemma did not feel sad. Her chest was constricted and she was hot, burning with rage at a man whom she didn't know existed for certain.

Wherever these visions came from, they no longer scared Gemma. Though she did not fancy their unpredictability and the smell or headaches that preceded them, she was beginning to think of the visitors as friends. Perhaps as eccentric, companionable aunts. The Artist, however, was something else to Gemma. Her proxy? Her double? She did not quite know how to feel about the Artist.

Gemma stopped at the same flower shop window to view the current arrangement on display, then looked for a name over the door: The Enchanted Garden. The warm air and scent of a mixed bouquet enveloped Gemma as she stepped inside, sliding the chill of the damp morning from her body.

Besides the flowering vines that hung off latticework, the ceiling was strung with white lights that gave the place a fairyland feel. Gemma let her eyes travel around the shop, taking in the purples and pinks, blues and reds, so many shades and textures had been carefully arranged so that they flowed like a wandering color wheel. Gemma followed the colors, ivory, butter, yellow, gold...delighted by their clear order, and allowed herself the pleasure of this rich sensory experience.

The shopkeeper came out of the back room and her face expanded into a warm smile when she saw Gemma. "I knew you'd be back. Please," she motioned Gemma toward her with both hands. Her hair sat folded on top of her head, hair sticks adorned with glittering baubles crisscrossed through it.

"Thank you for the flowers," Gemma said. "I enjoyed them immensely."

"Would you like some tea?" She parted a beaded curtain behind the counter and motioned Gemma through.

The back room consisted of a small table with two chairs, a work counter with a sink, storage cabinets, and a hot plate. There was also a door to a lavatory, one to the back garden, and a flight of stairs leading up, Gemma assumed to the woman's flat above. The room reminded Gemma of her mother's kitchen—shabby, but cozy and functional.

"I'm Letitia," the shopkeeper said. "You can call me Leti."

Gemma introduced herself and took off her jacket, realizing she'd been invited to tea before that slightest formality of exchanging names. Leti dropped tea bags into two mismatched mugs and poured steaming water over them. She put the kettle back on the hot-plate, then stooped to open a lower cabinet. The door was labeled "tall vases," but she removed a short round tin of biscuits, which she slid onto the table in front of Gemma. Leti set a mug before her, then sat down and plunged her tea bag up and down in her own mug, smiling all the while.

"Thank you for the flowers," Gemma said again, feeling awkward in this strange woman's back room.

"As soon as you walked in I knew we'd get along famously." Leti tossed her tea bag into the sink a few feet away, and missed. It stuck on the edge of the counter for a second, then slipped to the floor. "Go on," she said. "I bet you've never thrown a tea bag in your life." Gemma took hold of the string and flung her bag at the sink. She overshot and it splatted against the wall behind the counter. She and Leti both giggled. "A bit of silliness never hurts, I say."

"I don't mean to be rude, but when I first saw you, I didn't think we'd become friends."

"No," Leti said. "I'm not surprised, but here you are all the same."

"Your shop is very appealing. I find it soothing."

"We all need a place to go, somewhere comforting, where we can be ourselves without all the trappings we've piled on, or had piled on us by others."

"But how do you know," Gemma asked, "which trappings you put on yourself, for comfort or protection, and which things others force onto you?"

"Nobody can force you, dear. You can shrug them off, strip them away, or allow them to hang in place. Ultimately, you have to decide what you need and what you don't."

"These days I can't even find myself under all the layers." She laughed, and it sounded forced to her own ear. Gemma hoped Leti wouldn't think her phony.

"That happens more often than you would think. Just start with one layer at a time till you reach skin. Then start over with yourself, wear only the things that really suit you."

"How does one go about stripping away these layers?"

"With kindness, dear."

"But it's not that easy...." Why was she having this conversation? She hadn't revealed so much to Dr. Hamilton in months of therapy. What was it about this woman?

"It's not easy, but it is necessary." Leti sipped from her steaming mug. "Now, tell me how you came across my little shop."

The women talked for a good half-hour, mostly casual pleasantries after that strange initial exchange. When they stood, Leti linked her arm through Gemma's and they stepped back into the quiet shop. "I need someone to help me run this place, and I think you'll do quite well."

Gemma faced Leti, searching for some joke, but found only Leti's generous eyes. She nodded.

"Good. I'll see you Monday." Leti embraced Gemma and sent her out the door.

March

Chapter Twenty

IT WAS THE UGLY time of year and everyone welcomed it. Snow banks were black with sand and exhaust. Run-off filled storm sewers. Dark and barren trees pressed against the gray sky. Snowplows sat quietly in out-buildings, slipping into their dormant season. If more snow came it would be light and disappear quickly. Meteorologists were no longer talking blizzards; their attention had turned to the prediction of a wet spring and the threat of flooding. People went about with coats unzipped, scarves and gloves abandoned, slush and slop ruining shoes daily. The ugly didn't matter because it was the cusp between seasons, the verge of spring.

Simona survived the changing seasons without Peter by spending as much time as possible painting. If she was working, she couldn't think about him. She didn't allow herself the time to wonder why he'd left or why it mattered so much. She was too proud to call him and ask why he was running from her. One day she made up her mind that he loved Gemma, the next she decided he was scared, and the following that he wanted the baby, but not her, or vice versa, or loved her but couldn't face all the complications. Whichever it was, however he was motivated, she would never ask. All that remained was for her to wait until time had cleared him from her thoughts. Of course, time never cleared the past away completely. She still thought about her mother, whom she never knew. And her father, who never loved her. These thoughts remained painful, but were tolerably infrequent. Someday thoughts of Peter would consume her less, and then one day she wouldn't think of him at all. Eventually she would be able to go weeks on end without thinking about him. She only hoped these few months would hurry along so she could know he was back in England and would not have to worry about bumping into him at the park or the cafe.

Simona went to the Center in the evenings, arriving as Hal left. It was good to see Hal, for someone to know she was on site each day. In the still darkness of night, the chandeliers cast a sparkling light that seemed to soften the old floor boards. Simona fixed clamp-lamps onto the legs of her scaffold for more direct light where she worked. And she worked. Her crowd of women grew at an accelerated pace and she made them all rich in expression and detail.

Her five spirit friends came in turns, in pairs, all at once. It was up to them—welcome friends arriving unannounced. Often they all came together and sat on the old blanket Simona had brought from home, as though having a picnic. She painted and listened to the women, memorizing their voices and their mannerisms.

Clarice took on an almost Southern note when she was agitated with Alma. Alma's voice grew strict and tight when she was angry—something that happened when she felt patronized because of her age. Marguerite spoke formally in her native Spanish, while Rosa's English was broken and accented. But when mother and daughter spoke directly to each other, Rosa reverted to Spanish and the words flew, perfect English to Simona's ear in the magic hours. Flora Blanca spoke very little, but when she did, it was in the sweet voice of a child. Mostly she climbed the scaffold and sat up high in her party dress. Her legs dangled over the side and she swung them, tapping her heels against the steel supports in an even rhythm, keeping beat with the conversation below.

Simona stood in the lobby, her back to the wall, a dry paintbrush in her hands. She closed her eyes. *I'm ready,* she thought, as a smile spread across her face.

"See-ma!" Flora Blanca cried. "Sima, Sima!"

She spun on her heels and held her arms wide, the paintbrush sticking out like an extension of her hand. Flora Blanca rushed forward clumsily and crashed into her. Simona caught her up and squeezed tight. "Hey, sweetie." Smoothing stray hairs from Flora Blanca's face, she looked into the child's sparkling dark eyes. She was fair skinned, but when excited her cheeks flushed a reddish brown reminiscent of her mother.

"Child, what did I tell you about crushing Simona's baby?"

Flora Blanca turned around to face her grandmother.

"It's all right, Marguerite," Simona said.

Rosa, Clarice, and Alma stood beside Marguerite, who rubbed her fingers against her palm, sprinkling what was left of her handful of dirt onto the floor.

"Hey, baby." Clarice kissed Simona on the cheek, then sat on the blanket with a huff of breath. "These old joints ain't what they used to be."

"You young people don't know how to take care of yourselves, is all," Alma said, sounding typically cross. "I am seventy-three and, apart from a touch of arthritis, I am fit as a fiddle." Smiling to herself, Simona noted how Alma constantly contradicted Clarice, as though mother and daughter were in a competition.

"*Hola, mija.*" Rosa touched Simona's elbow, then took Flora Blanca's hand and led her to the blanket. "Come, my flower. I'll fix your hair." On the blanket, Rosa undid Flora Blanca's braids and combed the long shining hair with her fingers.

Marguerite was the last to sit in the semi-circle facing the mural. She knelt next to Alma, then sat sideways so her knees and feet were tucked modestly underneath her skirt. Alma, however, always sat with her legs straight out in front of her, touching at the knees and ankles with her dress laid carefully over them, the pleats fanned out smoothly at the hem in a half-circle and her back held straight as a rod. She looked at Clarice who had plunked her sizable-self down with her ankles crossed and her knees splayed. "Well it's no wonder your joints are shot to hell, the way you sit. Look at your back, girl. It's bent all out of shape."

"Oh Mama! Not all of us was born with a stick up our butt."

"Clarice Abigail...!"

"*Mija*," Rosa interrupted the brewing argument. "What are you painting tonight?"

Simona was busily laying out her supplies. The crowd of women was almost complete, filling the lower third of the wall. Only the first two rows of women were full-bodied portraits. Behind them, she had worked in torsos, heads and shoulders, sometimes filling a gap lower on the wall with some small body part, like an elbow or knee peeking through the crowd. She had been walking the city streets for as long as she could remember and was careful to represent the people she found there: Hmong, Indian, and Somali immigrants were among those in the urban mix, as well as Native, African, Mexican, and European Americans. Her gathering followed a loose chronology with the period of the subjects receding further and further into history toward the back of the group.

The viewer could trace time, weaving through the rows, following a different trail of characters with every visit, from Lakota native, to prairie settler, to Victorian lady, to flapper, to war-era factory worker, to 1950s housewife, to hippie, to disco queen.... The women outside the realm of Minnesota history were at the back of the crowd, acknowledged by the tops of heads: bonnets, powdered curls, simple veils. Though practically invisible, Simona acknowledged them as critical links to the beginning and the magnitude of this maternal base upon which each woman thereafter claimed her life.

There were no mythical or historical figures in the painting, save one: the one Simona was about to sketch. She ascended the scaffold and picked up a new stick of charcoal, the last in a box of broken pieces, tiny nubs laying carelessly in their black-smudged paper box. She liked the feel of a new stick in her fingers, liked the sense of its potential, the power of beginning. The fresh square end rested against the wall for a brief moment, then Simona moved her hand and creation was begun.

Tiny flecks of black dust fell away from the charcoal stick and floated down along the face of her painting.

Her vision was clear and the sketch did not take long. Simona prepared her palette and climbed the scaffold again. On this day, although everyone had come out, Simona barely heard them. The humming, their constant companion, was long forgotten and their conversation likewise tuned out, with only the briefest snippets registering in her consciousness. Simona dipped her brush in a rich sepia color and began painting Eve.

Eve stood above the other figures, looking forward over the heads of all those who had come after her. Her arms were held simply and modestly at her sides, not spread, not drawing attention to all she'd born. Her ribs showed above the heads of her daughters and her breasts were large and round and bare. A drop of milk glistened wet on one nipple. Long kinky black hair hung behind her shoulders, which were held square. A slight smile played on her lips and her eyes were open, taking in all of the history before her. Simona's Eve was not the image of a fallen woman. She was the Original Mother.

Simona worked hard, forming kinks in her neck and putting a cramp in her arm from holding it raised for so long. The conversation below came back to her and she was soothed by the familiar note of each voice rising up the scaffold. The sound sustained her while she painted. When at last Eve was finished but for some fine detail work, Simona came down and stood back from the wall. The women had fallen silent and come to stand beside her and stare at the new portrait.

"Fantastic," Marguerite said.

After remaining in silence for some time, Clarice took Simona's brushes and palette from her hand. "Sit and rest," she said, then ambled off to the janitor's closet to wash them. Simona stretched, exhausted, but pleased with the night's work.

"Simona," Alma said, "who will go in that space?" She pointed to a gap in the crowd of women at the center front, where a figure's empty silhouette stood outlined in charcoal.

This central figure would have a marked significance being at the head of womankind, just as Eve stood at the foot. She would be the only figure whose entire body was visible, further emphasizing her importance. Everyone else, including Clarice, had at least an elbow or the edge of her skirt tucked behind a neighbor with her frame turned slightly toward the center and the unknown woman.

"I don't know yet," Simona answered. "I'm saving her for last."

"Will it be a problem, painting the first person last?" Rosa asked.

"No. I can cover over some of the other figures or fill in around the edges, whichever I need to do." She gestured at the space, pointing.

Flora Blanca jumped to her feet while Simona talked and ran up to the wall. She turned, her face aglow, and pressed her back into the blank.

"Flora Blanca!" Rosa snapped.

"She's fine." Simona smiled.

"Paint Flora Blanca!" Her palms were laid flat against the plaster, her fingers spread evenly. She swayed, her hips and shoulders brushing gently against the wall in her excitement.

Rosa's face lit up suddenly with some mischief as she took a large brush from Simona's toolbox. She approached her daughter, holding the brush out at arm's length. "Look at that pretty little flower. I think I will paint it." Flora Blanca squealed as Rosa tickled her cheek with the brush. She giggled and her eyes shone with simple joy. Flora Blanca pulled herself away from the wall and ran with long awkward strides, her arms held high with her elbows cocked out to the sides. Rosa chased after her, crying, "Come back, little flower. I need to paint you!"

Flora Blanca lurched forward, landing heavily on her knees and, like a toddler who hasn't learned to reach out with her hands, crashed forward, bloodying her nose and bruising her chin on the hard wood floor. Rosa dropped to her knees beside her daughter. A wail of pain came from Flora Blanca as she struggled to her feet. Rosa took hold of her to draw her into an embrace, but the girl twisted away. She cried, "*Ambu!*" as she stumbled onto the blanket and threw herself into her *ambuela's* arms.

Rosa remained on the floor. Her face fell into a look of anguish, her lips pressed into a thin down-turned line, as though setting them so was the only way to contain her own cry of pain.

The grandmother rocked and whispered into Flora Blanca's ear. The girl whimpered and settled her head against Marguerite's lap, who looked at Rosa now. "You know the child is not coordinated, Rosa. See now what such foolishness gets you?" There was a spot of blood on Marguerite's shoulder from Flora Blanca's nosebleed.

"That's all right." Clarice went to Rosa and squeezed her shoulder with one hand. "It was fun while it lasted. Wasn't it, Flora Blanca?"

Flora Blanca responded to Clarice's soothing mama-voice and raised her head to smile and nod.

With the mood spoiled, the ladies decided they were tired, or that Simona was. Simona watched as Rosa, taking Flora Blanca's hand out of Marguerite's, led her to the mural and helped her into place. Marguerite called a general goodnight and Rosa did not respond. Alma went next, then Rosa. Clarice gave Simona a hug, said that Eve was beautiful, and instructed her to get some rest. Simona called a cab for her own departure, then waited outside on the quiet sidewalk, watching the sky turn pink.

At home she sat on her couch, watching her discus swim about the tank. Red George, the pigeon blood, darted amongst the unnamed blues, appearing, disappearing, reappearing in flashes of color. Though the fish generally seemed content in their habitat, Red George had periodic nervous fits, as though he realized there was nowhere for him to hide amongst the blue foil-backed tank, blue rocks, blue fish, and plants that while not blue, were not red either. Whatever synapses fired in that tiny fish-brain, Simona recognized these moments of anxiety. She should buy a little red barn with open doors, some tall and narrow entrance for her flat fish to hide in, but she sensed that the blues would take it over, enjoy it too much, and poor Red George, perverse little creature, would be no better off for the addition of red to his habitat.

While she watched Red George, Simona thought about all the forms of heartache a mother must endure. Alma and Clarice had buried children. Rosa was separated from her daughter. She wondered what motherhood would bring her as she rubbed her growing belly, registering each of the baby's kicks, punches, and rolls. Simona imagined her daughter, skinny and naked, safely curled inside her womb. She was proud that her body was capable of such a feat. She told herself that Peter didn't matter, and that if she had the baby, then Gemma could have the man. She smirked at the thought that Peter was a consolation prize while she carried the real prize inside her. Of course, it was bull. She still longed for Peter to come back and choose her.

Eventually Simona slept. She rose in the late afternoon to eat a bowl of chocolate Malt-O-Meal. Once dressed, she returned to the Center, passing another day without any real human contact.

Simona left the Center for Women later than usual the next morning, with little time to spare before Hal arrived for the day. Her work had absorbed her so intently that she hadn't even noticed the silence, the quiet that settled in the lobby when her companions returned to the mural and the tuneless hum ceased. Reflecting on their quiet disappearance while cleaning her brushes, Simona realized the women must have two ways, at least, of entering the mural. She would have noticed the five women passing back through the wall while she painted, no matter how engrossed she'd been.

It was after seven in the morning when she stepped outside and pulled the heavy door shut behind her. Simona pivoted on her heels to face the street, the sun, and the morning commuters on the sidewalk. The spring air was chilled and damp and she filled herself deeply. As she exhaled, Simona patted her baby with both hands, and that was when she saw him.

Peter had parked directly in front of the double doors and now he stood outside the car, his arm resting on the roof, his face twisted into a nervous grimace. "Simona," he called across the sidewalk.

She stood, her hands still holding her baby, and realized that her mouth had fallen open in surprise. Simona came down the stairs to the sidewalk and turned toward home. She took long, don't-follow-me strides. She heard the car door slam, and he called her name again.

Trotting, she gained speed and passed other pedestrians, but it wasn't enough and Peter caught up to her after only a block. He grabbed her arm. "Simona, please."

She didn't answer.

"Please let me talk to you."

Simona allowed herself to be led back down the street to his car. Peter held her wrist, loosely cuffed by his index finger and thumb. She could break away, but he owed her something and in order to get it, she had to give him the chance to speak. She was afraid to speak herself, certain that if she opened her mouth she would either scream or cry. They got into the car and Peter started the engine.

"No," Simona said. "I don't want to go anywhere with you."

"But...we could get breakfast."

"No. Just tell me why you're here."

"Simona..." He sighed. He rubbed his hands on his jeans, then wrapped them around the steering wheel. "I made a mistake. I got scared and I made a mistake."

"Why?" She stared straight ahead at the street.

"I feel guilty about leaving Gemma. She's not been well for ages now. She's battling depression."

"I don't want to hear about her," Simona said. "You either want me and this baby or you don't. And you can't have just one of us. It's us or her." She faced him now, her hands clenched in her lap. "I'd given up on you coming back." She had to stop herself speaking before her voice and her whole body gave in, cracked, and released the hurt she'd pushed down for so many days.

"I'm sorry. I needed time to sort through my feelings. Please, Simona, give me one last chance." He looked at her beseechingly.

"I need to sort through my feelings." Simona pushed open the car door. She stepped onto the sidewalk and slammed it, leaving Peter behind again. She walked with her back as tall and straight as she could make it. Peter's eyes were on her; she felt them watching, struck dumb, hurt, lost. As the distance between them grew, she wanted him to follow her and she was glad that he didn't. As the knot in her chest enlarged, she wanted to change direction and reenter the Center, sit with Clarice and the others and share her troubles. The pull was strong, but Hal would be at work soon, making a return futile. So, she continued to walk away from Peter as the sun lifted itself over the tall buildings and began to dry the dampness that hung in the morning air.

Turning the corner at the end of the block, Simona leaned against a brick wall, pressed herself into it, touched her baby again through all those layers of dressing, external and internal. She needed to talk to someone.

Hannah opened her door in a bathrobe with a mug of coffee steaming in her hand.

"Oh good," Simona said. "I was afraid you'd already be at work."

"It's Saturday."

"Oh." Simona stopped in Hannah's doorway for a moment to consider her loss of time and the fact that Hal would not be at the Center.

"Want coffee? I have decaf."

"Sure." Simona followed Hannah into the kitchen and stooped to pet Riley, the blue-eyed calico. Hannah had bought a house in a questionable neighborhood before the real estate market crashed. Lots of people who'd bought houses around the disreputable park, intending to fix and flip, found themselves unable to recoup their renovation costs. The urban renewal movement she'd been a part of ground to a halt and her neighborhood remained an unfortunate choice. Her house, however, was a beautiful Edwardian with hand-turned woodwork and leaded glass windows. With a privacy fence and alarm system, she was prepared to wait out the recession.

The women sat on the couch in the living room, legs tucked up, mugs in hands, bodies mutually, comfortably, turned toward each other. Sunlight poured through the leaded glass window above the fireplace mantel and made a dance of light on the maple floor.

"Peter wants to come back," Simona said.

"Come back? I didn't know he'd gone. I thought the reason I hadn't heard from you in nearly a month was because you were busy doing the new couple thing with Peter."

Simona told Hannah about falling in love, his wife whose name she now knew, and his sudden exit followed by this morning's entrance.

"I can't believe you didn't tell me sooner. I had no idea."

"I know, I know. I just threw myself into my work. I spend all my time painting. I can forget about him when I'm with them."

"With them?" Hannah's voice held a note of doubt and concern.

"My work. I just meant the portraits I'm painting."

The morning sun filled Hannah's living room, loving her stands of potted plants that all leaned slightly, subtly toward the window. Their cells worked in concert to consume that invisible, intangible nourishment. Riley padded softly, called by the radiance, across the room and sat, looked about with quiet turns of his head, then leapt through floating dust particles and yellow light to the windowsill. He laid himself out along the narrow ledge, one hind paw draping the sill, and yawned.

"Hal said you only work at night. Should we be worried about you."

"It's the pregnancy. My clock's backwards," She chuckled. "I sleep best at noon and work at midnight. I swear."

"You should take a break from work. A week, just to sleep and sort out this thing with Peter."

"Which is why I came here. Peter." Simona steered the conversation away from her odd schedule.

Hannah sighed, dropping the subject. "So, Peter. Do you want him in your life?"

"Yes." It was a confession, something she wouldn't have admitted anywhere else, but Hannah knew her too well to hide anything.

"But you don't trust him."

Simona put her thumb over a spot on Hannah's couch cushion. A drop of red wine that had fallen onto the sage fabric and soaked in, spread through the fibers, thinning and broadening as it set. A stain that was not caught in time. Her friend had worried over it, spot treating with a dozen products guaranteed to work. The burgundy stain faded to a dull brown. Simona had no trouble finding the subtle spot because she had caused it.

"What are you afraid of?"

Simona took her time to answer, as though pondering, formulating a response, but the answer had been ready before Hannah finished asking her question. The answer was difficult. It was something Simona held in her walnut-shell-heart. Cracking that shell to reveal the meat, even to herself, was the difficult thing. Hannah sat with her legs curled, her robe cinched around her waist, her coffee no longer steaming, as patient as the cat.

"I am afraid that things won't work. That my daughter will grow up without one of her parents and I'll do no better than Gilberto did. If I let him go, she'll hate me because she never got to know him, and if I take him back, we'll be miserable together and she'll hate me anyway."

Hannah was a pragmatist and not overly prone to talking. Simona's admission sat between the pillar candles and the magazines piled on the coffee table while both women considered it, thoughtfully inspecting its size and shape. Finally, Hannah offered a question with the calm rationale of a scientist. "What if you weren't pregnant?"

"I'd kick his ass for leaving me hanging."

"Would you be in love with him if he weren't the father of your baby?"

Simona turned Peter over in her mind, poked at his underbelly and big toes. Would she want him still? "Yes."

"There. Give him another chance."

"But..."

"Simona, he's not Gilberto. I know you don't trust men because your father was an ass, but if you really love Peter, you need to give him a chance to make it up to you."

Speakers mounted in every corner of the studio filled it with Lucinda Williams singing "Lonely Girls," a befitting melody for Simona's mood. Hannah's encouragement and reassurances had bolstered her through much of the day, a day they spent together. After they parted company, Simona came home to her studio, her fish, her empty bed, and the doubts and incriminations came back. So, she had filled the bath and put on music.

Reclining in the tub, she poked a finger into her shallow navel, then traced circles around it. The baby woke in the stillness and began somersaulting, pushing, and punching. She laid her hands on her abdomen and felt those undisclosed protrusions—foot, fist, elbow, knee—rolling along the inside of her body. She wondered if her mother had done this with her. She'd never given it thought before: that a child could be loved deeply even before it could be seen and held, that perhaps she and her mother had some time together after all.

As a seven-year-old girl with long black hair that was snarled into a sort of loose Afro because her father didn't and she couldn't comb it through, she stood in the corner next to the garbage can that smelled of spoiled tuna salad and cried. Gilberto yelled while refilling his glass with Chianti. "You do not jump rope in the house! Now the lamp is broken. You see what a stupid girl you are? *Comment se stupida ragazza!* Carina..." He invoked his dead wife's name, as he always did when upset with Simona. "If only you were here to teach this child. If only she hadn't killed you even while you gave her life." Perhaps he didn't mean it. Gilberto Casale was drunk and mean things often came out of him. But those words filled her with a pain and a guilt that weighed her body down and led her to repent with all the devotion and fear of a seven-year-old murderess.

That night, as soon as she was released from the corner with the smell of rotting mayonnaise still heavy in her nostrils, Simona created a shrine. White pillar candles, a statuette of Mary, one snapshot of her mother in a hat, and her mother's rosary stood up on a small table draped in a red cloth. White for innocence and heaven, red for love and devotion. She knelt before the shrine and prayed to *Mother*—Carina, mother of Simona, and Mary, mother of God. They became one in her mind and in her prayers. Thus she began her penance, begging for a sign of love and forgiveness. A message that it was not her fault and she was not entirely alone.

Simona pressed her palms together and aligned each finger in perfect symmetry, because symmetry was pleasing to God. She knelt and rested her elbows on the edge of the low table so that her forearms and pressed hands reminded her of a church steeple. She bowed her head in formal supplication and prayed until her palms stuck together and her vertebrae kinked into a position of servitude.

"Mother, forgive me my sin." She could not have brought herself to name her sin, even if it were necessary. Simona prayed every night until she was so weary her elbows slipped from the table's edge, her candles had burnt themselves out, and her head bobbed with sleep.

The Original Sin. It was the burden she had not chosen, that had been laid upon her head at the moment of her birth. The priest spoke of it often, and it was clearly her fault. The other girls at school seemed untroubled, oblivious even, to this burden. But then, they had mothers, while Simona had killed hers.

Over the years, Simona's devotion to the shrine wavered with the phases of her youth, but whether she was praying or not, the shrine stood erect. Candles sometimes lasted days, sometimes months, depending on the season. Until she turned fifteen and met some kids who were different: artsy, rebellious, dark, and irreverent. She adopted their black uniform and attitude. Her faith in Mother was packed up along with the half-burnt candles, statuette, and rosary in a Doctor Marten boot box and sealed with duct tape, crisscrossed in layers until the box had the slightly spongy feel of a roll of the stuff. It had become a testament to Simona's bitter rebellion, her absolute certainly that her father, the Church, and God Himself had nothing to offer her.

After toweling off and putting on pajamas, Simona opened her closet doors and got down on the floor. She reached over shoes and under hanging clothes to the deepest recesses of her closet. Shoved in a corner, beneath a haphazard pile of old shoes, Simona found the box, recognized by the smooth thickness of the layers of tape, and dragged it out of the closet.

With a utility knife, she slit the tape that encircled the box and there, leaning against her bed, Simona unpacked her childhood shrine, unwrapping parcels of newspaper dated 1994. The largest parcel contained the statuette of Mary. The figure emerged from a sheet of newsprint on which Down in the Valley record store was featuring albums by Nine Inch Nails, Blink 182, Green Day, and Red Hot Chili Peppers.

Mary stood upon a hillock with her bare foot upon the serpent. The snake was painted green and brown with red pin-dots for eyes. The Mother of God gazed serenely toward Heaven with her sorrowful face and her empty hands held out from her body, palms up. As a young girl, Simona asked if Mary hadn't been afraid the snake would bite her foot. And, she reasoned, wasn't it unkind to stand upon another of God's creatures? Were not the priest and a string of nuns that stretched back through her memory constantly asking children, "How would you like it if that was done to you?" She would not enjoy being stood upon. Young Simona was informed that the snake was the Devil in disguise, and Mary, as God's chosen one, was not afraid of being bitten on the foot. The plaster statuette had chipped over the years, the chalky white material showing wherever the painted surface had broken away. Simona shifted it from hand to hand, examining it closely. Those years spent kneeling and praying had never provided any answers. Or any solace.

Simona fingered her mother's rosary, the smooth ivory beads, and then coiled it into the jewelry box with the photo of her parents. "So much for original sin," she said to the statue and dropped it into the trash.

Chapter Twenty-One

GEMMA STOOD IN THE open doorway of a log cabin. The single room opened before her with a fire blazing in the hearth. In the center of the room, a group of women sat at a large table. Their heads were bent forward, their hands moving, and Gemma realized it was not a table, but a quilting frame. These women moved their hands over the invisible surface of the quilt, pulling invisible thread with invisible needles.

A chair sat empty, the sixth chair, and Gemma filled it. When she sat, the group looked up from their work, and Gemma recognized Clarice, Alma, Rosa, and Marguerite. Next to her sat a woman with long black hair that fell in curls over her shoulders. She had lovely dark eyes, and she smiled at Gemma. Her hands were moving constantly over the surface of the quilt. The crescents of the short, unvarnished nails were tinted with various shades of paint. It was the Artist.

Simona smiled at the woman who joined them now, welcoming her. She did not know who this woman was, but she was welcome as was all her family.

This woman took up her invisible needle and joined her in this work of *women. An act of creation, as all work of women is an act of creation.*

An easiness settled into Gemma. She felt herself among family.

Simona felt the baby kick and scooted back from the quilting frame. She placed her hands over her belly and smiled as her child moved within her.

When the Artist scooted back, Gemma saw that her belly was swollen with child. The Artist smiled at her, then took Gemma's hands in her own and placed them on her belly. Gemma felt a good thump against her palm and gasped. She looked at the Artist and they smiled at each other, sharing in that marvelous sensation of new life. Gemma was...happy.

At that moment, the quilt became visible. An apple tree with a twisted trunk filled the center. A single golden apple hung amongst its boughs.

Chapter Twenty-Two

GEMMA SHUFFLED THE CARDS with her eyes closed, meditating on her life, as Leti had instructed her to do. The cards were smooth and worn at the edges where the laminate had been rubbed off by years of handling. Here and there she felt a slight ridge where a card had been bent or torn. The act of shuffling the cards was soothing and facilitated the flow of her thoughts. She dwelled on her failure to produce a child only briefly, not nearly as long as she would have expected. Peter made his way into her thoughts: his absence, how she'd grown to enjoy quiet evenings at home, how, on occasion, she imagined him with another woman. Was it merely suspicion? Or wishful thinking? And she thought about the Artist. The dream she'd had the night before. The Artist was pregnant. The Artist...and Peter? She did not know what to do with that thought, so she put it aside and made herself think about Nikolai. What a fool she'd been to think he would take her to Greece and everything would be better. When Gemma's mind finally quieted, she laid the deck of cards on the old wood table in The Enchanted Garden's back room, halfway between herself and Leti.

They had closed shop and instead of putting the kettle on as usual, Leti retrieved a dusty green bottle from France, a Bordeaux specifically, and two small tumblers from a cabinet labeled "Floral Foams, Bases, Adhesives." They had barely finished their first glass when Leti made a comment about reading Tarot.

Leti took up the deck, her long fingers cradling the cards. Her right hand paused over the top card with her index finger crooked, adorned by a silver ring with a large blue topaz gem. The stone made Gemma think of a carnival fortuneteller, and for a moment, she fancied she saw a bejeweled turban on Leti's head.

"Ready, dear?"

Gemma erased the carnival image from her mind, feeling suddenly unkind, and nodded, noting the concern in Leti's expression.

Leti put on her reading glasses and turned over the first card, then another to the left and one to the right. She continued, making four more sets of three cards that surrounded the first grouping. All of the cards faced Leti, appearing upside-down to Gemma. Studying them, her hand passed over each cluster as she took in the spread.

Gemma gripped the edge of her seat with her hands partially tucked under her thighs and held her breath. It wasn't that she believed, only she wasn't in a position to disbelieve.

"Interesting."

"What is it?" Glancing over the cards, Gemma's gaze landed on the Ace of Wands, which sat to the left in one of the groupings. The red and yellow card stood out in the spread of blues and greens. It was fire and lightning, elemental power.

"Yes," Leti nodded. "See here. There are a large number of Cups in your spread—water, emotions, issues of love. Wands are fire and great energy. This ace represents a natural power waiting to be discovered."

Gemma wanted to ask what the power was, but instead waited while Leti concentrated on the spread of cards.

The Ace of Wands sat next to the Five of Swords, which had the word "defeat" printed across the bottom. On the other side of the Swords sat the Prince of Cups.

"These cards show the course your life will take if you don't change it," Leti said. "The Prince of Cups is an artist. He has a calm surface, but is pure passion underneath. This artist has a great power." She again touched the Ace of Wands and looked directly at Gemma. "But unless you change something, the artist will remain defeated, buried and undiscovered, along with this terrific passion." She paused. "The Five of Swords is a miserable card, dear. It represents the most painful separation."

"From what?"

"The cards don't give specific answers, but the Ace of Wands leads me to think it's something important."

Leti reached over the cards in the upper left. "This is your future if you do alter the present course. The Queen of Disks, dignified by the Three and Two of Cups. Here we have abundance and love without the trouble we see in your present situation. This queen is accompanied by the mountain goat: sure-footed and useful. She represents fertility and warmth. The Three of Cups also represents fertility. See how the lotus blossoms shower the cups to overflowing? Again, in the Two of Cups, we have a lotus blossom filling the cups, and it shows the union of male and female."

"Fertility?" Gemma said. "But, I'm not..."

"This is very encouraging, Gemma." Leti smiled, ignoring her protest. "It speaks of strength, harmony, and fulfillment."

Through everything the last several months, Gemma hadn't thought once of trying again. How could she, now that she knew of what she was capable? The phantom pregnancy had been such a horrid trick. Were these cards telling her to try again?

"What about these?" Gemma pointed to the other groupings.

"Change is inevitable, dear."

Change. Gemma glanced out the small paned window in the back door. Night had already fallen and the glass was a square of black. The back garden, small compared to Gemma's, was framed by high stone walls that had stood for over a century, been climbed by countless boys with scrapes on their knees. Leti fed the birds out there and let the plants grow wild. Gemma liked to sit outside on her lunch breaks. The unmanicured lawn and plantings were a relief after putting so much energy into the carefully orchestrated beauty inside.

"This last grouping represents influences outside your control," Leti continued, "your fate, so to speak."

The ammonia stink she was so used to filled Gemma's nose and penetrated her sinuses with sharp talons that stabbed at her olfactory. She turned her head away, her face contorted.

"Gemma?"

"Blast! Leti, I think..." Her hands gripped the edge of the table, her finger tips white from the pressure she exerted. "I think I'm going to have a sort of fainting spell, but you mustn't worry. I'll...I'll be fine."

Coming to stand beside her, Leti placed the back of her hand against Gemma's forehead. "You're warm, dear."

"It's not fever," she said with a strained voice. Her head ached from resisting the vision, but there wasn't time to get all the way home to Hampstead and she couldn't bring herself to let go of the table and relax. It was embarrassing, having a vision in front of a friend, and her employer at that.

"Come lie down upstairs."

Gemma couldn't answer. She couldn't make herself speak through the pain anymore, so she shook her head with her eyes squeezed shut and her hands clenching the table. A short ribbon of blood trickled from her nostril.

Muscles relaxed slowly and her head slumped over her shoulder. She was still for a minute, then her eyelids fluttered. Gemma sat up, opened her eyes, and crossed her legs under herself on the chair.

"Oh, thank goodness. Gemma, I was..." Leti stopped. Gemma was not present, though she appeared conscious. Mostly she looked down at her lap and listened, her head cocked, her expression changing with the flow of a conversation Leti could not hear.

Leti found a tissue and wiped the blood from Gemma's upper lip. As she did, she noticed Gemma's right hand shook. "How curious," she said aloud. The left hand was laid flat against Gemma's thigh and the right moved over her lap in quick strokes.

She gasped as she recognized Gemma's motions and hurried to a drawer across the room. Under old design books and catalogues, she found a sketchpad with large blank sheets. In another smaller drawer, Leti fumbled through an assortment of junk until she found a soft-lead pencil.

Her eyes wide with the excitement of discovery, she hurried back around the table. Leti placed the sketchpad on Gemma's lap and put her left hand atop it to keep it still. Then she firmly grasped Gemma's right wrist and slid the pencil into her waiting hand.

Pencil immediately found paper. Leti pulled her chair around to watch Gemma closely. Her hands were quick, her pencil strokes sure. Yet the image baffled Leti. It appeared to be a woman's face, but it seemed abstract and hollow. Then Gemma deftly turned back the page and started anew. All the while, her expression remained one of concentration, both on the sketch and the absent conversation. Leti watched Gemma look at the paper while cocking her head to listen, then smile. Occasionally her hand paused and she looked up from her work to focus on that other world.

The new sketch was easily recognizable as a woman's face, quite realistic this time and beautifully rendered. Though Gemma's gaze seemed focused on the work, it was an empty stare, as if the movements of the hands and face weren't really connected. Leti waved her own hand in front of Gemma's eyes. Nothing happened. She took a sheet of paper and held it flat above Gemma's hands. It didn't matter. The hands moved, the eyes focused. The paper, and Leti for that matter, might as well not have existed.

Leti poured herself more wine and sat back in her chair. She kicked off her clogs under the table and unpinned her plaits from the spiral atop her head so that they fell loose over her shoulders. A little pile of bobby pins sat on the table in front of her, next to the Tarot spread. Leti studied the spread with a new, intensified interest while keeping an eye on Gemma.

The wine bottle was empty before Gemma at last sat still. Her body relaxed again and the pencil and sketchpad slipped to the floor. She slumped in her chair. Leti rushed round the table, knelt and took hold of Gemma's hand. Patting it like a nervous mother, she spoke softly, "Gemma. Come back, Gemma."

Gemma stirred, rolled her head and drew in a deep breath. It took some minutes before she was aware of her surroundings, but finally she unfolded her legs and stood to stretch. "How long..?" she asked.

"About two hours. How do you feel?"

"Stiff. Tired." Gemma took a sip of her wine and made a sour face. "I think I'd like some water."

Leti brought her a glass.

"What's this?" Gemma picked the sketchpad off the floor.

"You did those."

"No." She sat again and stared at the sketch before her.

"Your hand was shaking, the right one. At first I didn't know what it was. Then I realized it wasn't shaking, it was drawing."

Gemma looked up and saw the interest sparking in Leti's eyes. "I drew this?" She flipped back through the pages to the first sketch. "What's this?"

"I thought it odd myself." She tore the page out of the pad and set it on the table. The two women stared, puzzling over its difference. "I know," Leti exclaimed. "This first one is only the second half of the picture. It looks so odd because it's the shading and detail without the foundation work."

"Brilliant."

"I didn't realize you're so talented."

"It's not me. It's the Artist. When I...go away like that, it's like I'm in her body. She's always drawing or painting, but I only get to see pieces of it at a time, like I'm looking through a tube. I've never done *that* before," Gemma pointed at the pictures.

"You could have, if you'd had the paper. These women you drew, were they there, talking to you?"

"No, I don't know them. But there were other women. The Artist listens to them talk while she works."

Leti nodded. "You looked as though you were listening."

"It wears me out."

"Of course, dear. You must be exhausted, but would you like to finish your reading tonight? You may find it interesting." Leti propped her reading glasses on the end of her nose and pointed. "This last group again—your fate."

This group of three was especially beautiful. A woodland maiden stood, pregnant and wearing a horned headdress. She radiated life. To one side: the Star with blue and purple swirls, a voluptuous woman bringing about a new age as she emptied a bowl over the earth. On the other side: the Hierophant, a wise man wearing an orange robe, sat surrounded by the cherubim, with a child positioned over his heart inside a pentagram.

"I was surprised by this grouping and unsure how to interpret it for you, until I saw you go into a magic-induced trance."

Gemma straightened up with surprise. "Magic-induced?" Her mouth held a string of questions she didn't know how to ask.

"Do you dabble in the occult arts, dear?"

She shook her head, her mind reeling at the possibility suddenly before her. Gemma had decided that the visions were no more than random dreams or a strange kind of ESP, but she had been afraid to investigate the possibilities, one of which she knew was a more mundane but frightening cause—something medical. "What's going on, Leti?"

"All I can tell you is what I see here." Leti paused, her fingertip resting gently on the edge of the card. Her face softened as she absorbed some vibration from the Tarot. "The Princess of Disks is a very earthy woman, beautiful, pregnant with life and possibility. Here, she seems to represent a friend, perhaps this Artist you visit."

Gemma leaned forward over the table, trying to see in the cards whatever Leti saw.

"The Star and Hierophant indicate a strong magical force at work in your life. It *seems* a benevolent force, a sort of spirit guide. The Star brings unexpected help and spiritual insight. The Hierophant represents divine wisdom, teaching, and also a mystical presence." Leti sat back and pushed her glasses up onto her head. She again examined the spread of cards, this time, there was something unsettled about her expression.

"I think I'll make that tea now." Gemma stood and poured hot water into their mugs. "These visions, I don't know where they come from, but when you said there is magic, or a spirit guide in my life...." She chuckled a raspy sound at the back of her throat. "It sounds crazy." As soon as Gemma said the word, she knew it didn't sound anything of the sort to Leti. She cleared her throat and explained. "I smell ammonia, then I get a terrible headache, then I sort of get knocked out. I wake up hours later."

"You had a nose-bleed."

"Did I?" She touched her nose. "That happens sometimes. I'm not sure why."

Leti reached across the table and put her hand on Gemma's, the blue stone in her ring shining under the bare bulb overhead. The simple gesture reminded Gemma that she was safe and, moreover, that Leti believed her. "Tell me more."

Gemma told her about all of the visions. As she spoke, the awkwardness of describing such silly, impossible events was worn away by Leti's sincere attention. Gemma found herself easily confessing her secrets, and one turned into another as she spoke of her dreams about Peter. "I've had that dream many times in the past months," she explained. "It's always the same. I'm walking through a beautiful apple orchard. The moon and the sun are rising together, arcing through the sky toward each other. When they both crest, there's an eclipse, and the orchard suddenly decays. I reach my hand out toward Peter, but he turns to ash and blows away..." Gemma stopped to consider for a moment. "My God," she said, "you haven't said a word. I've been rambling on and on about this, and you haven't said a word."

"I was listening, dear. Tell me something. How do you feel about the visions?"

"They used to frighten me. Now, I suppose I've grown accustomed."

Leti tapped the Princess of Disks. "Perhaps she is the source of your visions."

"Can you tell me what it means? With your gift?"

Chuckling softly, Leti stretched her arms. "I'm not psychic, only more intuitive and empathic than most." Leti took up her wine glass. "Now come over here and look at your spread the right way round. I always think it's good to meditate on a reading for a bit."

Gemma went around the table and sat in Leti's chair.

"I'm going up, dear. Stay as long as you like, and I'll see you tomorrow."

"Goodnight, and thank you, Leti." Gemma watched her disappear up the narrow back staircase, the old boards silent under her gentle step.

Gemma picked up the Princess of Disks from the center of the table. *So, you're the Artist.*

Chapter Twenty-Three

HOW DO YOU KNOW you're in love? Peter had believed himself in love with Gemma for years. And for years he had loved her. But then, over the years of trying and failing to have a baby, she had become someone else. Or he had. He only knew for certain that the more important a baby became to her, the less he wanted one. Obsessions were like that, he decided, consuming a person until she barely resembled who she'd been before. Poor Gemma.

He was busy giving Simona space. He thought it was what she wanted, if only to punish him for taking so long to come around. It was her turn to come around...or so he thought. Yet as the days passed, he started to think it was up to him again. He thought the ball was in her court, when instead he had fouled it and now he had to shoot again. He paused to consider whether his metaphor was mixed, and decided it didn't matter since he knew what he meant. It was difficult not having anyone to talk to about anything. In the States, he had Simona and business acquaintances, good for a pint after work once in a while, but nothing more. Back home he had Gemma and a few friends who, even if they would keep his secret, weren't the sort he'd want meddling in this business. More than once he considered calling Hannah, seeking her advice. But involving the best friend hardly seemed wise for this sort of thing.

Peter spent his evenings rambling around his flat, watching the television or reading. He drank to help pass the time and had Chinese food delivered to the flat. As he ate moo shoo pork or sesame chicken over the beige couch, he found himself thinking things like, *Once we're married, I'll have to go vegetarian, too. Might as well enjoy it while I can.* In the end, that was how he knew he had to be with Simona, because he believed in his heart that was how everything would sort out. Still, he let days pass until he was eating antacids between every meal. The thought of marrying Simona made him elated. The thought of divorcing Gemma gave him heartburn.

Peter barely knew what she was up to now. They hardly talked, as though the miles between them mattered. She had mentioned a flower shop, an art class, a new friend. Peter almost hoped the friend was a man. It was a selfish thought of course, and he knew it. If he returned to London to find her the same as he'd left her, only to ask for a divorce.... He did not want to crush Gemma, but he did want a life with Simona and their daughter. He only hoped she could forgive him.

Finally, Peter started asking his business acquaintances for recommendations, hoping none of them remembered that the last time he was in the States he had worn a wedding band.

April

Chapter Twenty-Four

GEMMA STOOD BEFORE *The Self Less Mother*, studying the painting yet again. She wondered about the Princess of Disks and the dream in which she'd met the Artist, had even touched her pregnant belly. Gemma touched the canvas, put her fingertip over the Artist's head. She half expected to feel those long curls of hair, but of course it was only paint.

Peter had bought this painting.

Gemma felt certain he was the father of the Artist's baby. She had nothing to confirm her suspicion, other than this painting, which had become dear to her over the past months. She was not crushed or angry. She felt, instead, a degree of relief. Peter would not come back to her. They would not continue as they had been. Nothing would ever be the same again. Gemma drew in a deep breath and sighed. "Oh, thank God," she said to herself. The realization that he was no longer hers filled her with a new resolve.

Gemma stopped in her hallway, a laundry basket perched on her hip. It was time at last. She pushed open the door and entered the room for the first time since the stillbirth. The room was just as she'd left it. A garbage can overflowed with scraps of wallpaper she'd torn down. Decorator samples of paint, fabric, and paper lay on the floor, grouped by color. The unassembled crib, still wrapped in plastic sheeting, leaned against the far wall. Gemma stood just inside the door and surveyed the physical record of her failure. She knew then that she had created her ruin by refusing to be anything other than what she could not be and putting her all into one unattainable goal. She dropped to her knees in the middle of the floor and scooped up a spread of samples in blue. She dropped them in the laundry basket, then went after the greens, the yellows, the ivories. When the floor was clean, Gemma looked at the bureau.

Over her four partial pregnancies, Gemma had acquired an array of clothing for both a boy and a girl. Piles of fresh white undershirts with their tiny snaps lay untouched. Sleepers with bunnies and trains and teddies and polka dots were carefully folded. Fluffy booties and a matching bonnet, hand knit with angora yarn, were lovingly tucked away inside tissue paper. All these things had to go.

One by one, Gemma pulled out the drawers and overturned them, dumping their contents into her laundry basket. One drawer contained a number of congratulatory cards and letters, and a baby book in which she'd documented the first two trimesters of her nearly successful third pregnancy. It had been doomed from the start, but it had felt like a success for six whole months. Refusing prenatal tests had given her that long to convince herself her turn for happiness had at last come.

When the basket was overflowing, Gemma lugged it downstairs and straight into the back garden. The evening sun shone warmly. Her rose bushes had grown unruly and there were bear patches where the annuals had not been replanted, soon to be overrun by weeds. Gemma set her load on the pavement and rolled the grill away from the side of the house. She found a bag of briquettes in the gardening shed and poured a mound of the black nuggets into the Bar-B-Q. Lighter fluid and a match started her funeral pyre ablaze with hot orange flames that teased the eaves of her house. Staring into the fire, Gemma watched the flames dance. She felt her heart harden with resolve.

Plucking a tiny yellow dress from the basket, Gemma began by placing it carefully on the briquettes. She watched it smolder, the lace caught first and glowed red, then melted away as the fire consumed the delicate trim. The bodice caught in the middle and the hole grew with its crumbling edges. Small flames stood up here and there, hastening the destruction. Next, Gemma laid on a dainty sleeping gown.

It was a long, slow burn. She wished she could simply heap it all into her fireplace and set it ablaze with a great whoosh and high flames that blackened the mantle, but it had been converted to gas when wood fires became outlawed in London. So the grill would have to do. She hoped briefly that none of the neighbors would see her blaze and call the fire department. That thought left as quickly as it came and she was consumed by the task she had begun. As baby things turned to ash, Gemma sat and wept. All the pain, pity, and loathing she'd been storing up came out. Large sloppy tears rolled down her cheeks, then dried up to mere sniveling, then began again flowing fresh.

As her pile of baby things shrunk away, the sun went lower in the sky, eventually tucking behind her neighbor's house. The garden looked soft and pale in the gloaming. Her fire had grown somber, dutifully eating away at the last of the white undershirts. She had saved the paper things for the end. Gemma set the cards on the embers and watched them catch, the flames climbing and dissolving them like miniature houses burning to the ground. Lastly, the memory book, that memento for the baby that was not to be. Gemma stoked the coals with a stick and set it on as the sun set, her eyes at last dry.

A bottle of wine and a Billie Holliday album kept her company as she worked through the night. Gemma filled a large bag with things that would not burn, including a lamp and porcelain music box. The remaining strips of wallpaper were removed and the walls washed. Despite her exhaustion, she was driven to finish the clearing-out in one go. She switched from wine to coffee around two o'clock. When her eyes began burning, she found some eye drops in the medicine cabinet and kept going. After the room was emptied and cleaned, Gemma dragged odd pieces of furniture from around the house to refurnish it, and when the sun colored the horizon pink, she had a room of her own.

Gemma took one last bag of rubbish outside to the bin and stopped on her way back. The crisp morning air chilled her arms, but she lingered and lifted the cover from the grill. She took up a handful of ash and rubbed it between her palms. A shred of fabric, burnt and reduced beyond recognition, rolled between her hands. *My own private crematorium,* she thought, *for the babies who died and the one that never was.* Probably it was the lack of sleep, or maybe it was the rush of relief that her period of mourning had come to an end, that made her rub her hands on her cheeks, blackening them.

She had seen a documentary about some African tribe years before. When a child died, the mother went crazy. She screamed and cried and moaned and tore out her hair for days. She had nothing to eat or drink, and if she collapsed from exhaustion, the village women woke her up and physically supported her so that she could continue to grieve. The more hair she pulled out, the more she loved her lost child. The mother—to prove her love and measure her sorrow—was completely bald when it was done.

Grabbing up fistfuls of ash, Gemma rubbed it into her hair, bathing herself in soot. It felt good in her hands, soft and dry. She stood in the middle of her garden, where the morning sun found purchase, the first of the yard to escape night's shade, and let the ash fall from her fingers and float away on the breeze. Gemma ran to the grill, made a scoop of her cupped hands and let her grief pour out.

"Be gone," she said.

She filled her hands again.

"Be gone," a command to dispel years of heartache.

"Be gone!" She did not know what would come of this release. She had no delusions of instant wholeness.

For now it was enough to let go.

"Be gone!" Gemma carried ash to her flower beds and let it pour down on the roses and on the peonies and on the tangle of weeds.

As Gemma made her way to Dr. Hamilton's, all the things she hadn't noticed before surprised her. The cherry tree with its blossom-laden branches arching over the walkway, the collection of garden statuary on the neighbor's lawn, the butterfly etched on the brass nameplate after Dr. E. Hamilton, but before Please use side entrance. Gemma strode along the crazy paving, the breeze ruffling her hair. She'd come straight from the salon and still smelled of coloring solution. The stylist had been somewhat daring and the shade was bordering on auburn. Gemma liked the feel of her hair brushing across her cheek when the wind picked up. She liked the color, too. She liked her new dark sunglasses with the tortoise-shell frames. She felt young again.

The door opened and a man with a shaved head and goatee stepped out. He paused to look at Gemma through thick-rimmed glasses. Gemma saw how his eyes caught on her glossy lips, and she knew he was distracted by them. They curled into a slight, amused grin.

"Gemma, you're looking quite sharp today. Fantastic new hair do," Dr. Hamilton said as Gemma made her way inside. "Is that what they call a pageboy?"

"Thank you," Gemma said. "I believe so."

The women sat in their usual spots by the fireplace. Gemma crossed her legs under a long red skirt.

"Tell me the latest."

"Peter has extended his stay in America. It'll be three or four more months before he returns."

"Why did he do that?"

"He said there are details he has to sort out."

"How do you feel about that?"

"Fine. I have my own details to sort out. I think I'll take another art class. Only not painting this time. I'm bored with fruit bowls and vases. Maybe I'll try basket weaving or pottery."

"Something to fill the time?"

"Something I can get my hands into." Gemma looked at her doctor and smiled at the thought of dirty useful hands.

"You don't miss Peter then?"

Gemma shook her head.

"You aren't lonely?"

"No."

"What prompted the new hair style?"

"I've decided to start over." Gemma glanced at the fireplace, undecided whether she would tell the doctor about her mourning ritual. "In fact," she said, "I'd like to end our sessions, Dr. Hamilton."

"That's your choice, Gemma, but I'd like to make sure it's a good idea first. Could you tell me about that panic attack you had in the painting class?"

"All right." Gemma recounted the evening over the summer, when Peter was in the States the first time. She had been at her easel, working on a still life. The woman the next easel over was visibly pregnant. Every time the baby moved, she jumped and giggled as though she'd just been tickled by some unseen hand. It was more than Gemma could bare. She made a fool of herself, jumping up and rushing outside to hyperventilate in her car. She left her materials in the classroom and never went back for them. As she spoke, she was aware of Dr. Hamilton watching her, taking notes. She didn't mind anymore.

"I am impressed, Gemma," Dr. Hamilton said when Gemma finished her story. "You did not flush or stammer, you did not seem uncomfortable at all telling me that story."

"I feel like I'm past it, Doctor. Everything is all right now."

"Why do you think everything is all right now?"

Gemma shrugged. "I think...I think," she started again, "that I've realized I can be something else. I don't have to keep trying to be someone's mother. And that's all right. I can be something new, something I choose."

Dr. Hamilton gave Gemma her blessing and a lengthy warning about something like emotional relapses, then bid her to call if she ever felt a return of her unease. The women shook hands and Gemma left, pausing on the crazy paving so she could listen to that door closing behind her.

Chapter Twenty-Five

SIMONA STOOD ON THE scaffold, paintbrush touching the wall. Her back ached from standing for so many hours. It wasn't just the standing, it was the reaching overhead, sometimes on tiptoe. She knew almost no one would see the mural up here at eye level. It would be fine to suggest details with broad strokes. The eye, on the ground, would see what was there and the imagination would fill in the specifics. Just like a tree at a distance is something of a green blob, but the viewer understands the idea of branches and leaves and so understands the tree. She *could* paint in broad strokes, but she could not. This was to be her masterpiece, and even as she scolded herself for supposing greatness, she imagined accolades, her mural photographed and put in books, future commissions....

Someone banged on the door.

Simona startled, dropping her paintbrush on the scaffold's platform. "Shit." She leaned over the railing to look at Clarice, Rosa, Alma, Marguerite, and Flora Blanca. They were in various poses, sitting or laying on the blanket. They looked up at her, their quizzical expressions asking *are you expecting someone?* Simona shrugged and climbed down the scaffold as the banging resumed. When she passed the women, Clarice reached up and caught Simona's hand to give it a reassuring squeeze, so warm and firm against her own.

At the door, she found Peter standing on the steps, looking out over the street. He turned to face her. He looked pale and weary, but maybe that was only the effect of the street lights. It was not quite dawn and the city was at its most peaceful.

"What took you so long?" she asked.

Peter shrugged, then came to the door and took Simona's hands in his. He leaned in to kiss her hello.

She offered him her cheek.

"Well. How are you then?"

"Come inside, Peter." Simona stepped aside so he could enter the lobby.

He looked for the work, naturally, and went toward it as though drawn impulsively. It was not the way Simona had planned to unveil her mural, especially being so far from complete, but what ever happened according to plan? She watched Peter walk toward her mural.

"Simona..." he glanced over his shoulder at her, his eyes wide in an expression of admiration, awe even.

Clarice and the others had not moved from the floor, but he had not seen them, could not or he would have said something. Simona stood next to them and Clarice rose to put an arm around Simona's waist. They watched Peter as he studied the wall, taking it in from one side to the other, from the bottom to the top. He turned, "It's fantastic. I knew you're brilliant, but I didn't have any idea what you've been up to here."

"Well," she smiled, "now you know."

Clarice's arm tightened about her waist.

Peter embraced her. For an instant she felt both Clarice's and his arms on her body, their solidity and warmth equal, but only briefly, then the spirit's were gone and she was standing in the Center for Women, under her mural, hugging Peter. He squeezed her tighter against his chest. After he let go, he bent to her belly. "Baby," he said, "your mum is a highly talented woman." He kissed Simona again. "Come on, then. Give me the tour."

Simona took him closer to the wall and showed him the portraits, explaining the genesis of the mural, how the idea of the quilt background came to her in a dream, and how close she was to finishing. She stressed the importance of her work and how she intended to finish before the baby came. She needed Peter to understand that she did not want any overlap between her mural and their child's first weeks. Peter's response was, "Darling, if you need extra time after the baby comes, I'm sure Hannah could arrange it for you." Simona could not explain why it was so important to her that the two events be separate, but she felt it mattered immensely. When she finished describing her work, Peter pointed at the vacant central figure. "Who's that going to be?"

Simona wanted to tell Peter, but some doubt suggested if she told him, or anyone, what it was she wanted more than anything else in this world, she would not receive it. So she told him she had not yet decided who to place at the head of the mural.

Peter's arm remained around her and it felt like something she had been missing for a long time. He took her hand. "Come with me. I have something to show you."

"What?"

"It's a surprise, of course."

Peter helped her clean her brushes and store her supplies. While they worked, she caught him gazing at her work and flushed with the satisfaction of creating something that called a person's attention over and again.

When they left, Simona's bag over Peter's shoulder, she looked back at her spirits, expecting a nod of approval or the warmth of shared excitement. There was nothing.

They walked along the Mississippi River, past old flour mills that rose up along the river's edge. Two rowing skiffs went by, their narrow bows cutting through the calm waters. Simona pulled her jacket closed against the early chill, too big to zip it. Peter put his arm around her shoulder and nuzzled his nose in her hair. The sky lightened while they walked upriver, turning pink and then gold. By the time they reached the Stone Arch Bridge, the sun dazzled the waters of the Mississippi.

Peter stopped Simona midway across the bridge and stood facing her. It seemed they were going to talk there, over the water. Simona shivered, wanting to ask if they could hurry across to one of the cafes on River Place when Peter spoke.

"Simona, I love you." His smile lit his face. "And I love our baby." He leaned forward and opened her coat to kiss her belly, then laid the coat closed again. "I have made arrangements to be here through the birth of our child. Then I'll go back to London, *briefly*, and divorce...get a divorce. And then..." His smile broadened until his face could barely contain it. He wiped tears from her cheeks as they fell. "Oh, darling, don't cry. Please don't cry. I want to marry you."

"I know," Simona put her hands on his cheeks and kissed him. "I'm happy," she said, and kissed him again.

"You are? You are. God, I saw the tears and thought.... But wait. We have to do this over."

Before Simona could respond, Peter knelt. The wind picked up, sweeping along the river, and she shivered again, but this time she didn't care.

"Simona, my love," Peter took a jewelry box from his coat pocket, "will you marry me?" He opened the box to present an antique Edwardian ring, a square cut sapphire with white gold filigree vining around the stone. A blossom opened on either side of the gem. "I wanted something unique, a work of art."

"It's beautiful." Simona held out her left hand and Peter placed the ring on her finger. She admired it, viewing it from every angle. The dark blue stone shone when it caught the morning light. Simona wrapped her arms around his neck. "Yes, yes, and yes."

He had a weekend all planned for them in a secluded cabin on the shore of Lake Superior, where Simona allowed herself to, briefly, forget about the mural and the spirits.

Chapter Twenty-Six

THE PILE OF SKETCHES had been growing with each day. The visions mostly came in the early morning hours, and Gemma had stocked her house with sketchpads and pencils so that no matter where she was when a vision came, she'd be able to grab up a pad of paper and let the Artist move her. She had mused over the sketches for hours and eventually formed the conclusion that her body became a shadow puppet when she was in trance, with the Artist pulling the strings from that other world. After awakening, Gemma often sat through those quiet morning hours and looked at the sketches. Sometimes she made her own pictures, playing, riding the euphoria of creating. She made no claim to the copies she drew while in trance. They were like copies made when a scribe connected two pens by a rod, and while writing with one, the other repeated every scratching on a second sheet of paper. Gemma shadowed the Artist, made duplicates that left her with a tangible keepsake, proof that what happened was real. It also left her with a familiar desire, one that had been buried under the ash of disappointment for years, to create art. Gemma began practicing again. Her hand worked to rediscover form, shape, texture, line. Her work was not very good yet, but it was satisfying in a way that nothing else was.

And then the visions stopped. The migraines. The nosebleeds. The automatic drawings. All stopped for three full days. Gemma worried at first that something had happened to the Artist. Then she began to enjoy her day without the constant vigilance against the oncoming vision. Then she tried to reach Peter and couldn't. It was a weekend and Peter would not be working, so he should be easier to get hold of. The Artist wasn't painting and Peter wasn't answering his phone. Gemma thought of the Artist's swollen belly, the kick she had felt in her dream.

Gemma lifted *The Self Less Mother* from its hook and turned the heavy frame over. There, on the back paper, she found a small label from the Jasper Gallery in Minneapolis, Minnesota, USA. It had a website address.

Gemma stared unblinking as she enlarged and tracked her way through the Artist's work pixel by pixel, looking for something, something that spoke to her, that was recognizable. The work had passed through too many lenses before reaching her eyes and its vitality had been dimmed by the transfer from medium to medium—clearly not the way art was meant to be viewed, yet it was as thrilling as it was disappointing. Despite the limitations of the electronic medium, Gemma was moved by the work, impressed by the Artist's range, and approved on a new, deeper level the Artist's talent. The last image of the series, her most recent work, was titled *Anima*. Gemma clicked to enlarge the image, leaned in closer to her screen, and stared with dry eyes.

Finally, she pulled back and blinked, closed her eyes and took a moment to refocus. When she opened them again, she looked at the whole. A group of female figures resembling prehistoric idolatry stood en masse with protruding bellies and enlarged buttocks, pendulous breasts, and featureless faces. They all touched one another, shoulder to shoulder, hip to hip. The colors were those of the earth in autumn: rust, amber, sienna, olive. The background swirled about them in a formless movement of color that enclosed them in a cosmic nest, an earth-womb.

There was a link to the Artist's bio: "S. Casale lives with her fish. She doesn't own a TV. She prefers to watch fish. Hobbies: painting. Interests: art. Last food item consumed: coffee." There was a black and white photo of S. Casale on a swing, so high that the photographer got underneath the arc of the swing and took a shot of her legs, the swing, her hands on the ropes, curly black hair trailing behind the rest of her. The face, however, was hidden from view.

Now that there existed a real world, non-mystical link between her and the Artist, she could simply phone her up and say.... Even if she could get the number, or the gallery did pass on a message, what would she say? "You're sleeping with my husband." "That baby should be mine." Or, best yet, "Your spirits are talking to me, too. I see them through your eyes and I sketch your sketches while I'm in a trance." And yes, it all sounded crazy.

Dr. Hamilton had only recently released Gemma from therapy. She smiled to herself. Perhaps the craziest thing of all was that Gemma wasn't that upset about the baby or about Peter. She had not put her wedding ring back on after the night at the Dormansly Hotel. Even though Nikolai was gone from her life once again, she saw no reason to replace her ring. Here she was, with the knowledge that her husband was probably leaving her for the Artist who was carrying his baby, and she didn't seem to mind at all. Gemma laughed out loud. Perhaps she *would* buy the painting, *Anima*, and give it to Peter. On one of their joint credit cards so he would end up paying for it. The idea amused Gemma, but she had no desire to be spiteful after all.

The nursery was gone, all evidence burned away. The room sat vacant at the end of the hall with the door wide open. Gemma entered the room, considered the spare furnishings she had dragged in just so it wouldn't be empty, and stared out the window over the back garden. In a singular moment, Gemma knew what she wanted. The decision was made cleanly, plumply, and she went to the phone.

"I need a painter who can squeeze one little room into his schedule this week. The sooner the better."

Mrs. Ledbetter of Hampstead hired men for a premium fee and signed a check without hesitation because of her insistence that the job be done before next Sunday. It was the sort of thing she'd done throughout her marriage. The home was a woman's domain, an attitude passed down from her mother, and a woman can make it whatever sort of prison she chooses. She had discovered *that* on her own. By Sunday the spare room had been painted in two shades of aubergine with café au lait trim. Gemma stood in the middle of her room with the paint still tacky on the walls, the smell of it itching her nostrils, and knew she had just taken a wrecking ball to her prison. Already she could breathe again.

The art shop off High Street was pricey, naturally, but Gemma didn't care. She folded down the back seat of her Suburu before leaving home. When she returned, she had a drafting table, easel, and £300 worth of art supplies. The painters had installed a cork strip along the walls and Gemma tacked up each and every sketch she'd made in trance. She vowed to put up her own work as soon as she had something she liked well enough. Bookshelves, a comfortable chair, and *The Self Less Mother* completed the study. Peter was going to pay for her study, and as Peter was still legally her husband it was as it should be. The awareness that she might soon be living on a florist's income helped motivate Gemma to spend freely and buy all the materials she would not be able to afford after the assumed divorce.

Each night, Gemma sat in her study, gazing over the art on the walls, recording her visions in a journal, creating her own sketches, or once the visions returned, sitting in trance drawing someone else's pictures. With all the sketches pinned up, Gemma saw their scope and felt that she knew something more of the Artist. The study of Marguerite's hand spoke of love. The sketches of women to use in the mural were vast and varied, showing entire bodies in full costume, often with accessories like a handbag or a pram, when Gemma knew from her visions the Artist would only use the head and shoulders of most of them. The stories inherent in the work, told by each woman's posture, costume, the shape of her hands, and lines on her face intrigued Gemma.

Moving slowly from one to the next, she peered closely. There was a likeness between a number of portraits of different women that lingered with her. Long after she'd circled the room with eyes wandering from one sketch to the next, a question took shape, scratching at the back of her mind. From her drafting table where she sat doodling, Gemma kept looking over her shoulder and cross the room and back the other way from one picture to the another. All of the sketches had been dated on the back and pinned up chronologically—just as they'd been drawn by the Artist, just as they'd been drawn and torn from the sketch pad by Gemma.

Gemma hopped off the stool and took down each of the drawings that gnawed at her, teasing that there was something to be uncovered. Laying them out on the floor, she studied them side by side, and it struck her. The eyes first. The eyes were the same. Then the mouth. Gemma shuffled and reordered them chronologically, but this time not by when they were drawn, but by the subject's apparent age.

There was before her the distinct mapping of a life. The baby, the toddler, the girl—all so happy. The sketches were like snapshots, not posed, not contrived, simply capturing a moment. She watched the girl grow, with her long black hair changing from ribboned braids to a graying bun. The portraits took this child into old age and, even as the corners of the eyes sagged and the waist grew thick, there appeared in her expression a constant look of satisfaction.

One sketch called Gemma's attention over and over. The girl was teenaged and dressed all in white with a veil pinned to her black tresses. Her shoes were shiny white patent leather with a heel. Her figure belied her transforming youth, and her expression glowed with the unique pride of coming of age.

Gemma returned to the wall, unpinned another sketch and laid it on the floor. It was Flora Blanca on her *quincañera*. She had her hair in braids and wore the simple, ruffled party frock of a child. Her shoes were scuffed with dirt and she fed a burro corn from her hand. The eyes and mouth gave it away. The two pictures were of the same person at the same moment in life. Flora Blanca as she was, and as she should have been on her fifteenth birthday. The Artist's love of Flora Blanca and her despair over the girl's fate were obvious in the portraits she'd created, these snapshots of a life that never happened. And there was something else Gemma saw in the series: a question, bordering on accusation. Was Rosa a bad mother for allowing it to happen?

The Artist was afraid. Gemma had not understood before, but now she realized that the Artist's deepest fear was failing as a mother. Gemma had never worried that she would not be a good mother. In fact, she had always assumed she would be a wonderful mother, if only she had been given the chance.

Chapter Twenty-Seven

PETER LAY IN BED and watched Simona rubbing lotion into her hands, one gliding over the other, the fingers interlaced briefly, the palms pressing and sliding against each other. She picked up her engagement ring and slid it onto her finger.

"I love that," he said.

Simona looked at him in her dressing table mirror, her reflection beaming. "Me, too." She held her hand up to admire the ring. "Are you ready to meet your daughter?"

He lunged forward, over the top of the bed, and grabbed Simona about the middle. He pulled her back onto the bed with him. She squealed with surprise and giggled. He kissed her belly feverishly. "Yes, I'm ready to meet my daughter!" The kisses were comical, wet and noisy. She laughed and squirmed on the bed until Peter quieted the game, moved upwards from her belly to her breasts. Then her neck. Kisses everywhere. And her face. Her mouth. Her brow. They wrapped themselves together and kissed atop the still warm bed. It was lovely, but there wasn't time for anything more than kisses because they had an appointment to keep.

Plants filled the waiting room and a television mounted in the corner
played a talk show. Peter sat holding Simona's hand over the arms of their
chairs. The last time he'd been to a doctor's office, things had turned out
badly. He didn't realize he'd been tightening his grip on Simona until she
wriggled her hand out from his and opened and closed it a few times.
"Sorry," he whispered.

"Nervous?"

"A little." Peter had not told Simona everything and this was hardly
the time, so he forced a smile and prayed this baby was healthy.

Simona's OB, an older woman with fat little hands and short gray
hair, pressed the wand to Simona's jelly-covered stomach. She moved it
around while Simona and Peter watched the monitor with fascinated
expectation. The doctor froze the image on the screen and hit print.
"There she is," she said. Using a pen as a pointer, she showed them their
baby's head, face, and torso. The baby had one tiny hand pressed to her
chest.

When Peter saw those matchstick fingers he began to cry. He stroked
Simona's hair and bent to kiss her. It was the first time he'd ever seen a
miracle. Simona had never looked more beautiful than she did now, lying
there with her abdomen exposed and covered in goop. It was not really
that she looked different, but that he had never been more certain of his
future than he was now, here, with his fiancée. Peter kissed her again and
let his tears fall.

Chapter Twenty-Eight

SIMONA CARRIED THE SONOGRAM image in her bag. "Did you see those tiny fingers?" Peter had asked Simona three times as they left the OB's office, before insisting they both take the rest of the day off to celebrate. Simona could imagine Peter holding the shiny paper sonogram all day, wearing it out with his adoration, and decided to put it in a frame for him as soon as she could. Simona laughed as Peter went on, guessing how cute she was going to be, whose hair she was going to get. They drove out of the city to a shopping area where big box chains clustered around highway intersections.

"These places creep me out," Simona said.

Peter parked the car anyway. "I know what you mean, but it's one-stop shopping." He got out and came around, then swung the door wide with a bow and a flourish. The edge of his door struck the car parked next to his. "Shit."

Simona suppressed laughter, while he checked the other car for damage.

Inside the store, fluorescent lights cast their blue-white glow over everything, and Simona winced when they passed under the ceiling speakers, playing some Top 40 hit better suited to a dance party than shopping for babies. As though reading her mind, Peter squeezed her hand and leaned next to her ear. "Give me half an hour." He left her side to grab a cart and returned smiling broadly.

"You're too cute like this," Simona surrendered to his enthusiasm. "Lead the way."

Peter maneuvered the cart down one aisle after another, filling it with onesies, booties, sleepers, diapers, bottles, and bibs. Simona marveled at his efficiency. He picked up two styles of pacifiers, looked at the nipples, rejected one and grabbed three more of the other. "Wait!" Simona laughed. "Shouldn't we read about them? What if the other one is better?" He assured her it wasn't better, only different.

In the clothing aisle, Simona stopped to look at something that caught her eye. Peter had to turn the cart around and come back to her. She was touching a little dress of pale blue cotton gathered into a simple yoke. Three embroidered daisies and a bumble bee decorated the front. The same friendly bees flit over a matching diaper cover and bonnet. "Can you believe she'll be this small?"

Peter laid a hand on her belly. "She'd better be that small." He put the dress in the shopping cart.

They rounded the end of the aisle and turned toward the check-outs. Simona stopped in her tracks. A dozen or so rocking chairs sat idle before them. She left Peter's side to sit in one, oak with turned legs and a honey-colored finish. A hand-carved center panel had been painted with swans in flight over a lake. Simona leaned her head against the rest and smoothed the arms. It fit her perfectly. She closed her eyes and imagined rocking her baby to sleep in this chair. When she opened them, Peter gazed at her, his green eyes alight even through the lenses of his glasses. "Pretty picture?"

"The prettiest." He offered her his hand and she stood.

Simona looked at the tag and read, "Hand-carved and painted...made locally to order...oh! $2100. That's too much for a rocker."

"Are you sure?"

"I'll pick one up second-hand and paint it myself." She shrugged and walked away.

After a long weekend away from her work, Simona was glad to be back with her paints, even though the shone while she worked with only her thoughts for company. As five o'clock neared, she became anxious for Hal to finish his day and leave. He finally went, and the spirits gathered around Simona. She pulled from inside her shirt the sapphire ring, worn on a long chain so that she wouldn't get paint in the delicate filigree.

"Oh, baby, ain't that lovely," Clarice said. The others agreed and admired her ring, but it was not the celebration Simona had expected. She had wanted Clarice to be the first to know, but was now regretting that she didn't show it to Hannah immediately. Simona went back to painting.

"How much longer do you think this wall will take you?" Clarice asked.

Simona looked it over. She had a good start on the background, a quilt hanging off a clothesline, the edges curling in a breeze above the crowd of women. On the quilt was the tree of life, a gnarled old apple tree, rising up into a blue sky. She was painting it in exquisite detail, and she had more left to do than she cared to think about.

"You're going to have to finish this before that child is born."

"That is my plan." Simona had never felt the prickle of irritation before in the company of her spirits. It surprised her to feel anything but content in their circle.

"Now don't be like that," Alma said. "We are only concerned because it's important you finish before she comes."

"Why?" Simona asked.

"There are things a woman has got to know before becoming a mother," Clarice said, "and you don't know them all yet."

"Why don't you tell me now?"

"It does not work like that," Alma snapped. "That's all. It is not up to us to tell you in the end. You need to finish this painting of yours and then you'll find out."

"You mean...?" Simona pushed her hair back and looked at the mural, at the blank space in the center of the figures.

Clarice folded her arms across her chest. "Simona Maria Casale," she said without the sing-song in her voice. "How do you expect to finish this mural on time if you're always off with that man?"

"You mean my fiancé?"

"Your fiancé who is keeping a wife back in London."

"He's divorcing her, and you didn't answer."

"Since you don't have a mother here to set you straight, it falls to me to do the hard talking."

The mention of Simona's lack of a mother came as an unexpected sting, especially from Clarice.

"You cannot count a man as your own if he's got another woman counting on him. What's more, you got a contract here and he's taking you away from your responsibilities."

"The Center's not opening until mid-June. And I can ask Hannah for an extension."

Rosa stepped forward and put a calming hand on Clarice's arm. "Oh *mija*," she said to Simona, "this can't be fixed with extra time. The painting must be done before the baby comes and that is all there is to it."

"Why?" She looked from Rosa to Clarice, imploring each of them with her gaze.

"We can tell her," Rosa said and patted Clarice's arm.

"Oh, all right, then. But I need to sit down." Everyone settled onto the floor in their usual places, Flora Blanca nestling against Simona's belly. "Now," Clarice said, "what you got going on is the greatest act of creation imaginable. None of us would be possible if you didn't have that universe being born inside you. The energy that goes into creating a person is like the energy of ten atomic bombs. Think of all those cells multiplying, dividing, specializing, *becoming*. All that potential is stored up in one single microscopic cell. The sperm gets absorbed by the egg and you got a whole person's blueprint. From that blueprint the person builds herself. One cell becomes two. Two become four. Four become eight, and so on. Now ain't that something?"

Simona nodded. Her companions looked reverent, as though Clarice were reciting gospel, and in fact she was. She was reciting the gospel of new life.

"While this baby is getting busy making herself, the father doesn't do a thing. The mother goes about her day, all the while...." She pointed at Simona's belly. "I guess between *that* act of creation," she gestured toward the mural, "and *that* almighty act of creation," she pointed again at Simona's belly, "you got more miraculous creation going on than you can contain. And here we are."

Simona stroked Flora Blanca's head. The girl pressed her cheek against Simona's side and the baby kicked her. "Do you mean," Simona asked, still trying to absorb everything Clarice had said, "that the baby is the reason you're here?"

"*Si, mija!*" Rosa exclaimed. She threw her arms around Simona's neck and held her tightly. "Isn't it wonderful? We all get to be together because of that little baby girl."

"And once the baby is born, this won't happen anymore."

The spirits nodded.

"Clarice, what do I do?"

"Asking me that question is the first sensible thing you've done in weeks. This piece of art has to get done while that child is still in your belly. It's a contractual obligation. That just leaves your *fee-yon-say*. He will have to be understanding for a little while."

Simona considered what Clarice had said and what she didn't say but intimated. It seemed she had no choice but to get back to work, and, she thought as she studied the mural, work her ass off. Simona patted Flora Blanca's back and got ready to stand, extracting herself from the girl's embrace. She wiped her hands on her thighs and measured out how much work remained and how many weeks. Too much and not enough, she decided. She approached the scaffold and grabbed hold of the bars that framed her ladder.

"Good girl," Clarice said. The spirits watched Simona climb the scaffold, the same satisfied look on each of their faces.

While Simona worked, she thought about Peter and what he would say. She thought about the magic of creation occurring inside her body and how strange and miraculous it was. And she thought about Carina Casale. If Simona finished the mural before her daughter was born, would she get to meet her mother?

Peter arrived to take her to a late dinner after only a couple of hours. Simona let him in and he helped her clean up her things. The spirits remained seated on the floor, invisible to Peter. Simona watched as he stepped on Rosa's hand. She winced, but neither Peter nor Rosa reacted. When everything was ready for the next day, Simona took the ring off its chain and slid it onto her finger. Peter embraced her. "God, I love seeing that ring on your hand." Simona smiled and kissed him. Then Peter bent down to kiss her belly and whisper something to his daughter. As they left the Center for Women, their arms around each other, Simona looked back at the spirits and was met by Clarice's stern gaze.

"I don't like it," Peter said.

They sat under a silk painting of a tiger in a Thai restaurant. The spring rolls had just been delivered to the table, and Simona slid one onto each of their plates. "It's only six weeks or so, then we'll have the rest of our lives together."

"But they're damned important weeks, Simona. You're in the third trimester."

"And doing great."

"You should go easy now."

"Peter," Simona said his name with an implied *be reasonable* attached to it. "We both have unfinished business. I have the mural. In fact, I'm under contract to finish it. You have that wife in London."

A man at the next table glanced their direction. Simona caught him and returned his look. He turned back to his beer and his curry with a shake of his head.

"She can't prevent us seeing each other now," Peter said.

"Maybe she should. Why don't you go back now? It would be better if you were divorced before the baby is born. Don't you think?"

"I can't. I've already made arrangements with the company to be *here* now and *there* after the baby's born. I'm booked out."

"So you do understand contractual agreements."

"Simona...." Peter did not finish his sentence. Instead, he waved to their server and ordered a beer to go with his Pad Thai, though he hadn't drank in Simona's company since finding out she was pregnant. When the server left, Peter removed his glasses and rubbed the bridge of his nose. "Simona," he repeated.

"I know you and Gemma had a hard time. I know I don't know the half of it. But I need you to support me in this. Right now, this is just the way it is."

Peter sighed and pushed his glasses back into place. "All right," he said. "I can see there's no convincing you."

"Good. Now hold out your hand." She placed two keys on his palm.

Peter turned the keys over, considering them like a business man accepting a deal sweetener. "This," he said, closing his hand over the keys, "certainly helps."

Chapter Twenty-Nine

GEMMA GASPED AND WOKE with a start. She stared around the room with wide eyes. She was alone. She was home. She was all right. Gemma placed a hand on her forehead and wiped away the sweat, her heart still pounding. Peter.

Peter had been there. She had seen him come inside this safe sphere of women, his presence so glaringly masculine, so…threatening. She had also seen him kiss the Artist, only it was as though he was kissing her again, after all these months. But it was different—of course it was different. She could tell that he loved *her*. And then the ring. She had seen the ring sliding onto that finger with the short, unvarnished nail.

Gemma ran to the phone.

When Leti arrived, Gemma was in a state. She had been pacing furiously through the sitting room, then up and down her hall and around the kitchen. Her face had gone red and was streaked with tears. "Whatever is the matter?" Leti asked when Gemma opened the door. Gemma tried to answer, but her breath caught in her throat and she began sobbing again.

"Oh, dear. Oh, dear. Come along." Leti closed the door behind herself and removed her coat and boots. She patted Gemma's hands and led her through to the kitchen. Leti found the kettle and tea and a tin of biscuits. "There, there. We'll sort this all out. Tissues?"

Gemma pointed toward the water closet.

Leti disappeared briefly and returned to hand Gemma the box. "Now, we'll sit down here and talk this through." She poured water over their tea bags and set the cups on the table. Leti was just lowering herself into a chair when Gemma found her voice.

"Peter. Peter was there."

"Oh, dear." Leti stood again and went through to the dining room. She found the sideboard right where she would expect it to be and chose the brandy. She returned to the kitchen with the bottle and two glasses. "This will help."

Gemma paced beside the table while Leti poured.

"I'm afraid I'll need you to sit down. All of this pacing is difficult for me, dear."

Gemma sat and, at Leti's urging, had a sip of brandy. She waited as the liquor warmed her chest, enjoying the calming sensation of fluid warmth. "Peter was in my vision. I was in the Artist, painting, everything normal. Then Peter turned up." Gemma swallowed more brandy. "She's pregnant. I knew that. I dreamt it the other night. I even suspected him, but I hadn't any proof, you see?"

Leti nodded slowly, the baubles on her hair sticks catching the light as her head dipped forward. "The Artist is pregnant with Peter's baby," Leti said.

"Yes. He kissed her belly." Gemma stifled a wail and slapped the table, knocking her teacup. Tea sloshed over the rim and she rose quickly to snatch up a dish towel. She wiped up the tea while Leti watched her, the epitome of patience. When Gemma sat down again, she had another swallow of brandy and refilled her glass. Then she sat, twisting the towel into a spiral.

"There's more," Leti said.

Gemma lifted her gaze from the tortured towel in her hands and nodded. "She has a ring. He said he loves to see that ring on her hand."

"Oh, dear."

Gemma sighed heavily and released the towel. She unrolled it and picked at the hem instead. "I don't know why I'm so upset, Leti. I want to move on. I do." She caught Leti's eye, watching for confirmation of some kind. "I haven't worn my wedding band for weeks, so I shouldn't care if he's found someone else. Should I?"

Leti took up her own glass of brandy. "You can tell yourself what you should or should not feel all day long, but it will sting all the same. Until it doesn't."

At those kind words, Gemma attempted a smile for the sake of her friend. "I didn't expect this. Even with all of my suspicions, I couldn't imagine seeing it happen like that. He kissed her. Only I was there. It..." Gemma stopped to control her swelling emotions. "I was inside the Artist, looking through her eyes. It was like he was kissing me, only he wasn't. And it was different."

Leti put her hand atop Gemma's.

"He hasn't kissed me like that in ages. Maybe even years. Maybe never."

"Then it's definitely time to move on."

Gemma sniffed loudly and wiped her eyes. "Here's to moving on." She raised her glass, and Leti picked up hers. They drank to change and to the future. They sat together and sipped their brandies. Gemma was not shy with hers and was on her third by the time Leti neared the bottom of her first. They did not talk much, but it helped having someone with her. It was better than being alone.

"Gemma," Leti said, "there is something that troubles me. I probably should have said something when we did the Tarot reading, but I couldn't be certain then."

"And now?" Gemma said, encouraging her friend to be out with it.

"I do know a few things about magic." Leti hesitated again. "Gemma, you need to be careful. Magic is neutral. There is no bad or good intention to be found in the magic itself. But you seem to be receiving magic unawares. You did not summon it, as far as you know."

"No. I thought I was going bonkers. I certainly didn't summon anything."

"Perhaps the Artist summoned it. But if she also does not realize what she's doing, there could be danger."

Gemma studied Leti's face for some change. Her expression remained thoughtful and cautious. "What kind of danger?"

"I don't know what kind of danger, but magic is never free. Energy can never be created nor destroyed. It takes great energy to manifest this kind of magic. You are essentially possessing the Artist when you have these spells."

Gemma nodded slowly. She was possessing the woman her husband loved...who was pregnant.... It was more than she could digest already, and now Leti was warning her of some unforeseeable danger. She gripped her brandy glass, *At least this one object is solid.*

"If the Artist does not know what she is doing, then she is not exchanging anything for the magic. She's not making due payment. Sooner or later the magic will extract its dues."

Gemma laughed, an unruly outburst. She slapped a hand over her mouth. "I'm sorry, Leti, but you made it sound like the mafia just then."

"Hmmm," Leti nodded. "It is rather. Suppose a chap called Tommy walks in the shop and offers me protection. I didn't ask for it, but I get it anyway. Sooner or later I'll have to pay Tommy for the protection. If I don't pay, he'll take his payment one way or another."

"Leti, should I be scared?"

"Concerned, dear. I would be concerned. I believe this Artist is the one who needs to make things right. Just be careful, Gemma. Somehow you've been pulled into someone else's dealings and I'm not sure how that will play out, for any of you."

"Is there something I can do in the meantime?"

"Be grateful."

"Be grateful," Gemma repeated. "Be grateful."

Chapter Thirty

SIMONA STOOD SURROUNDED BY Clarice, Rosa, Alma, Marguerite, and Flora Blanca, all staring at the mural. The women she painted were complete but one, the central figure. Simona had roughed in the background, the quilt on the clothesline with the ancient apple tree, a breeze ruffling its surface just enough to show movement. She had completed the tree and over half of the quilt in meticulous detail, more than was strictly necessary given its distance from the viewer.

"Who are you going to put in the middle?" Marguerite asked.

"It sure must be someone special," Alma said.

"Maybe she hasn't decided yet," Rosa said.

"Oh no, she knows," Clarice said. "She's just holding out on us."

Simona looked at Clarice, her head tilted to one side. "Holding out? No. I'm saving her. The best for last...that sounds childish, doesn't it?" She shrugged away her confession that there was someone better than them, someone she longed for.

"You better hustle, or you won't get much time with this best-for-last person." Clarice's wink was accompanied by a knowing smile.

Simona sighed and Flora Blanca slipped her hand into Simona's. Simona looked at her and smiled, this woman-child who was so innocent and made her feel better with a touch. Flora Blanca put her head to Simona's shoulder and her hand on Simona's belly, where it remained.

"I'm nervous about it. I feel like I have to paint her last. Am I wrong?" she asked Clarice.

Clarice shook her head. "Follow your heart, baby."

"It will work. She will come out." Simona's voice raised a note, belying her certainty.

Clarice didn't confirm, but looked again at the mural. "I sure do like that quilt."

Flora Blanca pressed a warm hand against Simona's abdomen. The baby turned over as though to get away from the hot spot under that slender palm. Simona looked at the hand, gave Flora Blanca a squeeze, then moved to climb the scaffolding.

As she worked, she felt the eyes of the spirits on her. Watching.

It was three in the morning before Simona crawled into bed with Peter and curled against his side. He slipped his arms around her and kissed her neck. She slept through his leaving in the morning, though he kissed her and her belly. Peter left a note next to the toaster. "I'll see you for lunch," it said.

"But can't you paint during the day?" he asked.

They were eating out of bento boxes, their chopsticks clicking against each other. Two egrets stood in the lake, their long necks curved into Ss. One of them picked up a foot, its knee bending backwards as the leg folded against itself.

"No, not really." Simona plucked a slice of pickled radish out of her box. "I get energized around midnight and do my best work then. I need to maximize that."

"I don't think it's safe, you being alone all night. What if something happened? Your cell doesn't even work in there."

"I'm not..." she was going to say alone, "...worried. I'll be very careful. There's a phone in Hal's office."

Peter continued to protest while Simona looked at the egrets, admiring their stillness, their tranquility. She wanted her life to be like that, if only on occasion. "You have to trust me. It won't be for much longer," she said.

"Fine." Peter held a piece of sushi before her. "But you have to eat more. You look too thin for the third trimester."

Simona opened her mouth and let Peter feed her. The seaweed broke up as she chewed and the creamy avocado blended with the soy and sesame flavors. This moment, she realized—with Peter, a park bench, egrets on a spring lake—was tranquil. Simona leaned her head against Peter's shoulder and placed her hand over the baby nestled inside her. "I love you," she said.

Chapter Thirty-One

DAILY RAINS AND INTERMITTENT sunshine—just enough to warm the city, get the flowers out, and clear away winter doldrums—meant spring was indeed well under way. Gemma had always loved the spring, rejoiced in the freshness of cleansing rains, all the drabness of winter's gray suddenly replaced by spring blooms. It was a tradition of hers to tour gardens each year with the Yellow Book, something she'd missed the last two years because even the freshness of a new season couldn't wash away the dismal funk of her depression. That, thank goodness, was over now. Gemma sat on her lawn chair in the back garden, the catalogue on her lap, planning her route. A Sunday in Kent seemed ideal, and she thought she'd ask Leti along.

The women strolled along the gravel-packed path past a closed knot of dwarf box. The hedge had been shaped in geometric patterns of interlocking diamonds and filled with bright primroses and snapdragons. Behind them rose a stately early-eighteenth-century manor.

"I used to love these knot gardens," Gemma said. "I couldn't get over the intricacies, the planning, the design. But now, it seems...."

"Confined."

"Yes."

"Think about this garden. What does it really say?" Leti spoke without turning to look at Gemma, her gaze cast over the garden while she walked with her hands loosely clasped behind her back.

"Control."

Leti nodded. "And wealth and power. This isn't a labor of love. It's an exercise to demonstrate man's ability to rationally order his world."

Gemma thought of her own garden, once neatly boxed into bordered beds, trimmed and clipped and orchestrated into something controlled, now growing unkempt and wild, her design lost when the borders were overrun, the edging tumbled, and her plants returned to their own Darwinian struggles. She admitted it could use some tidying, but she would never go back to the way things were.

"Come on," Gemma said, stopping on the trail. "Let's go find a nice, unstructured cottage garden."

"Lovely idea, but first, I'd like some tea."

The hostess poured from a china pot with petunias decorating the sides, then set it next to the tiered cake server on their table. The dining room looked as though it hadn't changed since The War with small pastoral oil paintings on the walls, lace curtains, patterned carpet, and cozy floral cloths on every small round table that dotted the room. Leti selected a lemon tart from the server. Gemma chose a small cake with a marzipan daffodil laid across the icing.

"I feel like we've stepped back in time," Gemma whispered across the table.

"Yes, we should have worn skirts and drawn lines up the backs of our calves."

"And bicycles parked outside, leaning against the side of the building."

"This was a lovely idea." Leti smoothed back her silvery hair, then twisted it into a knot at the nape of her neck, which she secured with a stick from her shoulder bag.

Gemma took a sip of tea, then set it down to squeeze a lemon wedge over her dainty cup.

"I'd like you to buy the shop," Leti said.

"What?" Gemma's hand went astray and she squirted lemon juice onto her blouse.

"Gemma, my sister just found out she has cancer. I'm going to move in with her and I'll need to sell the shop."

The sudden news of Leti's departure made Gemma go cold. "But you could come back to it, once she's better. I'll run it for you until then. With your oversight, of course."

"No, dear. I'd like for you to have it. Run it until you're through with it. Do what you will." She picked up her cup with the pansies and smiled over its scalloped edge. "I'll be carefully constructing one of those unstructured cottage gardens."

"But..." Gemma was unable to smile at Leti's comment, her mind concerned with how the proposal—if she accepted—would completely change her life.

"I've been able to retire for years now, but I didn't have two things: a reason to leave London, and someone to take over the shop. Now I have both."

"Leti, I can't just buy a flower shop. Can I?"

"Why not?" She took a delicate bite of her lemon tart. "This is quite excellent."

"I have to think about it."

"Of course."

"There's the money."

"We'll work it out."

Gemma moved her hands atop the table, glanced out the window at the sunny village square, and lifted her fork, held it poised over the cake. "I don't know how to run a business."

"You do this one."

"Yes but," she slid the tines into her cake, "there are things."

"I'll teach you." Leti smiled at Gemma with soothing confidence.

Gemma set down her fork and began to wonder if it was actually possible and what Peter would think. Abruptly, she realized Peter was no longer a consideration in her life. After all these years, she only had to ask herself what she wanted. "All right, then." Gemma held up her tea cup and smiled at Leti. "I'll do it."

As Leti raised her cup in return, her smile expanded as though to say, *I knew you would.*

The women sipped their tea and ate their sweets, sealing the bargain. Gemma's head swam with options, the possibilities of a new life, the choices she'd have to make. By the time they'd each drained their second cup of quiet tea from the demure china and left nothing but polite crumbs on the small plates, their resolve was firm, and both women had moved beyond the worries of possibilities to the comfortable drifting thoughts of how good it would most certainly be.

May

Chapter Thirty-Two

SIMONA NUZZLED AGAINST PETER'S shoulder. They were having a Sunday morning lie-in, as he called it, and she had agreed not to mention the Center or the mural until after lunch. Peter was still dozing, only conscious enough to wrap his arm around her shoulder when she slid her body into place. That required more effort these days with the swell of her belly in the way. She still wasn't used to how a small movement required so much more effort than she expected. She got winded on a flight of stairs. The baby made her sore, insisting tiny feet be jammed up against her ribcage so the only way to sit was as though she had a rod up her spine, making as much room for the baby as possible. Lying here was as comfortable as she'd been in days, except for when she was at the Center. For some reason, when she was working, nothing bothered her. Her body felt like her own again and she was able to go long hours with hardly a break. Simona kissed Peter's shoulder. Then she kissed his chest. He mumbled a good morning and kissed the top of her head. He rolled onto his side and opened his eyes. Simona was greeted with his smile, the kind green eyes, the mussy hair. She put her arm over his shoulder and drew him closer, as close as he could fit. She felt him stirring down low.

They made love tenderly. His hands twined in her hair. Her fingers stroked his face, then played over his chest. They kissed and pressed their bodies together, arms wrapped around each other, hands finding shoulder blades and the little knobs of vertebrae separating them. His foot slid along her calf. She folded her knee between his legs. When they had finished, they remained together, facing each other, holding each other, kissing.

Simona stroked Peter's brow as he dozed again, then left him to sleep and went to shower. When she came back, her hair dripping on her shoulders, the towel she wore parted over the swell of her belly, Peter had risen. He stood at her dresser, absent-mindedly fingering the ivory beads of her mother's rosary. The crucifix dangled above the dresser, and Simona saw that in the hands of another it was only a trinket. Her smile faded. She took the rosary from Peter and put it in the jewelry box, closing the lid with a snap.

"Hey," Peter said, "what's that all about?"

"Nothing."

"It was laying out. Have you been praying?" He reached for Simona's neck and she jerked her head away.

"No. I don't pray. Not anymore." The water from her hair had begun to run down her back in a cold trickle. She lifted the corners of her towel from her chest to squeeze out the ends of her hair. "It was my mother's."

"Ah...I'm not allowed to touch it?"

"No. Of course. Peter, it's not a big deal. I just wasn't ready to see someone else handling it. You know? I would have liked you to know what it means to me first."

"It's all right, love." Peter hugged Simona to him, sliding his hand to the back of her neck. "I didn't mean to upset you."

"I'm sorry." She put her nose to his chest and inhaled the scent of their bed. "I'm going to paint her."

Peter sat on the edge of the bed and guided Simona to join him there. He held her hands, waiting.

"I know we haven't had lunch yet." She smiled apologetically. "I've decided to paint my mother into the mural."

"That's great. Isn't it?"

"Sure." She wrapped her hair in her towel and Peter reached around her shoulders to dry her back with the trailing ends. "I'm just nervous about it. I mean, she's been dead since I was born. A ghost. A hole. A...I don't know what. But now, with the baby coming, I feel like I need to paint her. Maybe it will bring some kind of..." she paused, having no way of saying what she hoped it would bring her, "...some closure. Or some peace."

Peter held Simona to him. She loved him for being understanding and patient, for the smell of his skin, for holding her. Yet, she had kept her secret even now. They spent the entire day together and in the afternoon the rocking chair with the carved and painted swans was delivered—a surprise for the mother-to-be. Simona sat in it next to her bookcase, delighted by Peter's extravagance, and wanted more than ever to tell him about Clarice and the others. She wanted to tell him that when she painted her mother, she would finally get to meet her. She rehearsed what she would say, that meeting her mother would fill a hole she's lived with her entire life. That it would make her a better mother to their daughter. That it was the magic of creation and she didn't know why, but she had been given this gift and she couldn't waste the opportunity. Each time she thought it through, she imagined Peter's face falling in disappointment. And she was afraid that if he didn't believe, it would spoil the magic. At the end of the day, she fell asleep in his arms without mentioning her work a second time.

Flora Blanca pushed herself up from the floor and lumbered across it, her crooked teeth jumbled into an excited smile. Upon reaching Simona, she threw her arms about her waist and laid her head against Simona's belly. "Baby," she said. "My baby." Simona nodded and placed a hand on Flora Blanca's head, then exchanged greetings with the women.

With Flora Blanca cooing against her abdomen, Simona's hand tenderly stroking her hair, she stared at the mural, filling the central gap with the essential portrait, imagining its completion with the fear and hope of great expectations.

While Marguerite and Rosa argued over the best way to roll out flour tortillas—with a pin or by patting and spreading with the hands—Simona arranged her paints. When she began her work, Clarice was playing pat-a-cake with Flora Blanca. The tuneless hum came and went from her notice along with the women's conversation while she worked on the quilt. When Simona climbed down for a break, she rested on the blanket with the others, drank water and ate a banana. Nothing was said for a long time. They gazed at the mural, lost in their own labyrinths of thought.

"Everyone should know the story of how they came into this world," Clarice said, ending the long silence. "It's the first beginning, the one that sets a precedent for all the beginnings to follow."

"I'll make sure to write it all down," Simona responded.

"You be sure to do that for your baby. It is important. But I was talking about you."

Simona looked up, her face opened in surprise.

"Oh yeah, baby. I can tell you your story."

Simona crossed her legs and leaned forward, resting elbows on knees, her body shaping itself around her belly. The other women settled themselves as well, and Flora Blanca lay down with her head in Rosa's lap, ready for the story to begin.

"Your mama didn't speak any English when she and Gilberto arrived in America, but she tried to learn. Every time she saw anyone in the hallway or outside, she'd say, 'Word, please.' So we, her neighbors, would tell her something. If we had a bag of groceries, we'd pull something off the top to show her. Apple, or rice, or cookies." Clarice chuckled. "She learned pretty quick to only ask the adults after Johnny Fellows told her a hot dog was a penis. She decided to go to the store and get herself some of them for dinner."

Simona smiled at the harmless fun, the thought of her mother's confusion and embarrassment when she learned what she'd actually requested of the grocer. She imagined her mother would have told this story herself, laughing at the folly.

"Now, your father got the work visa to come over here from a distant cousin who hired him to work in his butcher shop. You knew that?"

"No. Gilberto never talked about the past."

"Shame." Clarice shook her head before continuing. "Your mama was real sweet. She made friends fast in the Italian community, and all the while she was working to fit in her new American home. When it was time for you to be born, your folks had only been here about seven months. A midwife was called in to do the delivery. This woman had a mother and grandmother and great-grandmother who were all famous midwives in their village in the Alps. Since coming to America, this woman, Anna, had been called on to deliver babies by several immigrants who neither understood nor trusted the hospitals here. Afraid of being handed some outrageous bill and thrown in prison when they couldn't pay it, they called on other immigrants with a hand or two in the healing arts, like Anna."

Simona was at last learning something of her own history, that dark spot her father had so neglected finally illuminating. The humming sound had grown louder and become a sort of undercurrent to the tale, rising and falling with Clarice's voice, stopping when she paused and resuming when she did.

"Anna was a good woman who had delivered several healthy babies in the area. But what was not known, what she did not say, was that she'd never had a true apprenticeship with her mother. She had, in fact, scorned her heritage and neglected her talent through some perverse aversion to following in her mother's footsteps. When she came here, she was called based on her forebears' renown, and once she held that first, slippery newborn with the cord still pulsing, and the grateful parents named the baby Anna, there was no refusing destiny. So she did not dwell on the past, assumed the things she'd picked up watching her mother would serve her well enough, and she all but put out an ad."

Marguerite clucked her tongue and shook her head. "Why must children always believe the parent's life is not good enough for them?"

"Sometimes it isn't," Alma said. "Just depends."

"Anna was called to deliver Carina's baby. And that was her first real test as a midwife. The baby came breech. Carina was in terrible pain and could not deliver. The pushing phase lasted over five hours with Anna only coaching Carina to push and push more. Finally, Anna figured out how to put a hand on the baby's rump and pushed it back inside its mama. She turned the baby with one hand inside and the other outside. It took a lot of doing, but she eventually got that baby turned. I always believed it was her mother or grandmother working through Anna's hands, doing what she didn't know to do.

"Poor Carina had been exhausted before, and now was too weak to even complain. She suffered, barely able to stay conscious while Anna beat her from the inside and out. Her assistant was a friend, another recent immigrant who trusted in Anna's lineage so completely that she responded to the woman's every order and never thought to question her."

Simona wrapped her arms about her belly, her baby, and although she knew the story's outcome, was afraid.

"When Anna withdrew her hand so that the birth could continue, it was followed by a rush of blood. Blood that had been filling the uterus, corked in by the baby, and then midwife, soaked the bed. Carina managed to push a few more times before passing out, but was so weakened from the exertion and blood loss that she was ineffectual. Anna's assistant straddled Carina and pushed on the uterus with the heels of her hands until the baby delivered. Carina regained consciousness long enough to kiss her daughter on the head, smearing her lips with blood from her baby's crown. With those lips stained red, Carina named her daughter before she died. Simona Maria Casale."

Simona wiped tears from her cheeks, as did Rosa and Marguerite. Alma smoothed her skirt over her legs and shook her head.

"You were delivered to your father with your name and the news of your mother's death. Gilberto beat the midwife, slapping her with one hand, while cradling his infant daughter in the other, his tears splashing onto her bare head.

"Gilberto Casale," she continued, "quit the butcher shop after that because the sight of blood reminded him of his wife's death bed and made him want to cut out his own heart with the knife in his hand." Clarice looked at Simona and waited for her to look up. "Your father gave you that extra name you dislike so much to honor your mother."

"He never told me anything," Simona said. She continued to cry for her mother and her infant self. She looked through bleary eyes at the blank space at the center of the wall and promised herself that she would meet her mother.

Chapter Thirty-Three

LETI DECIDED TO CLOSE the shop for a couple of days while she moved out of the flat above, insisting that the business not officially change hands until after she had left. Gemma tied a scarf over her hair and rolled up her sleeves. Her hands were dingy with newsprint as she wrapped one glass and then another. Leti's furnishings were hardly spartan. She'd been in the flat a long time without a proper clean-out, and the number of things packed in such a small space amazed Gemma.

"What about this?" she asked, holding up a small glass swan.

"Oh, goodness." Leti scratched her head and looked at the ceiling. "I can't recall where that fellow came from. A niece, I believe." She threw up her hands and let them drop to her sides. "Gemma, you'd better just pack everything. I can sort things out when I unpack. And then if that little bugger is from my niece, I'll be sure she sees that I've kept it."

Gemma smiled and took up another piece of newspaper. "What a good aunt you are!"

Leti laughed. "Yes, indeed. And if it's not from her, I can put it in a rummage sale then."

Gemma was packing up a lifetime of trinkets, so little of it valuable, only sentimental, and only some of it. She looked around the flat, soon to be hers. The kitchen was small and the appliances were not up-to-date, still, it would function. The dining room opened onto the living room, which had a lovely bayed window that overlooked the street. A small parlor sat off the living room, separated by folding doors with gold-colored windows, one of the more charming original features of the flat. It also had a window overlooking the street. Leti used it as a music room. The movers coming for the furniture would take out the piano. She had already packed up her viola and music stands. She offered to leave the large potted plants for Gemma. She accepted. The room was to become her art studio and she liked the idea of keeping the greenery in tact. The bed and bath were upstairs. At some point a wall had been removed to make one suite of two smaller bedrooms. It felt spacious with windows at both the front and back, and a fireplace in the middle of the room with a green-tiled mantle. The more of Leti's things she packed away, the more excited Gemma became about settling in.

Leti took her out for a curry at the end of the day. Gemma wanted to buy their supper since retirees needed their savings, but Leti insisted. It was a celebration of change and she would have time to become cheap once she had moved. Back home, Gemma wandered through the house. She ran her finger over the sideboard. She opened the buffet to look at the formal china with the gold edge, the crystal goblets. She considered the dining table and chairs. The sofa and end tables. The marble lamps with raw silk shades. She would not miss any of it.

The next day, she and Leti finished packing. They stacked boxes in the living room near the furniture that had been emptied, stripped of cushions, or padded with moving cloths. Gemma wiped sweat from the back of her neck and pulled her t-shirt away from her back. She had done the heavy lifting, more than she should have, but she wanted to feel things were truly done and organized for the movers. Leti came next to her and put an arm around her shoulder so that together they could survey the nearly empty place.

"I'm getting all soppy now." Leti wiped a tear from her eyes. "I've had a lot of good years here, Gemma. I'm so glad it's going to be yours now."

Gemma hugged Leti, feeling a little soppy herself. "Me, too."

"Come on. I could use a cold pint much more than a cry."

Leti took Gemma across the street to a pub and ordered them fish and chips and stout. They found a table in the window where they could keep an eye on the street for the moving van pulling up to the flat. Gemma drank, the rich bitterness of dark beer catching her by surprise. "It's been a long time since I've had a pint."

"Well, you've earned it today, old girl!" Leti raised her glass and toasted Gemma.

"I'm going to miss you, Leti."

"Likewise. But we'll keep in touch." Leti nodded her assurance.

The barman called Leti's name and she went to retrieve their food. Gemma watched her, a woman in her sixties wearing dungarees and an old sweatshirt like some college kid, as unassuming as they come, chatting with a barman half her age like they were old friends. Leti and her shop were a part of this neighborhood, Gemma realized, and she would be missed by more than herself.

"Gemma." Leti waved her up to the bar. When Gemma stood beside her, she told the barman, "This is Gemma. She's taking over the shop and the flat, too. You be good to her for me."

"Pleased to meet you." He held his hand across the bar. "I'm Jake." Jake had a ruddy complexion, heavy freckling. His reddish-blonde hair matched his skin tone, making him appear an all-over pink.

Gemma found the square jawline and day or two of ginger beard surprisingly attractive and also found herself lingering as she took him in. "Hello, Jake."

"I hope you'll come in here for your dinner sometimes. It's the best way to get to know your neighbors."

"I'll be sure to pop in."

The women carried their baskets of food back to the table. "He's a nice one," Leti said. "He'll look after you if you need anything." She poured some vinegar over her chips. "Now, Gemma, I want you to do a little something for me. Well, for yourself really." She pulled dried sage from her bag, the leaves of grayish green tied with a thin red string into a tight bundle. "It's called smudging. Once the flat is empty, light this and walk through the place, letting the smoke bless the rooms and clear them of past energy."

"But Leti...really? Is that necessary? I mean, if there's anyone's energy I like, it's yours."

"You're very kind, dear. But I've made mistakes like everyone else. And you're starting over. You should do everything you can to ensure a clean slate."

"All right." Gemma accepted the sage, feeling silly, especially when she noticed that Jake was watching her take the bundle from Leti. Too late for pretenses, she slipped it in her pocket.

Chapter Thirty-Four

SIMONA SAT IN FRONT of her window, a sketchpad laid across her lap, staring at the neon sign across the street. The pink tubing had been bent into the word *girls*. She would have chosen a different view if one had been available. Living in the warehouse district surrounded by artists and entrepreneurs had been her dream. It made her feel successful and cool. She had a historic photograph of the street below framed and hung beside her window to remind herself it wasn't always like this—this Urban Hip. Her building had been a garment factory, one of several in old Minneapolis. *Her* building had been the one where girls were exploited, not that one across the street with the pink neon. Some factory workers, mostly newer immigrants from just across the river in North Minneapolis, were as young as eleven. They would have walked or bused in horse-drawn trolleys across the Hennepin Avenue bridge, seeing the old Grain Belt Beer sign coming and going, past the beautiful Gateway Park, and then a few more blocks into the warehouse district. Large brick buildings filled every block, ready to swallow up the working poor. That hot pink sign could have hung over her building's front door. And across the street, a blue one for the men, old and old-before-their-time, who lived there. Now a strip club sandwiched between a bar and a restaurant that had once been a meat packing plant, it was then a flophouse for winos, the single men who lost everything during the Great

Depression and became drifters and drunks. Simona couldn't imagine placing such men in closer proximity to their greatest temptations: a bar next door and factory girls across the street. It wasn't until the 1950s that the city decided to clear out its Skid Row and clean up its image, beginning decades of transformation. The Gateway Park was long gone. The Grain Belt Beer sign still stood, an historic icon, overlooking the Mississippi. The warehouse district became a place for entertainment. Clubs, bars, restaurants, and theaters moved in as industries moved out. And eventually, developers saw big profit in converting old warehouses to new lofts. Distressed wood floors, brick walls, and exposed beams became all the rage. Simona had been lucky to get into an artists' co-op when she did.

Peter touched her shoulder, startling her out of her reverie. She hastily flipped the cover shut on her sketchpad and wiped the tears from her cheeks. "What's wrong, sweetheart?" Peter knelt in front of her, the light from across the street framing him with a pink halo.

"Nothing, really." She shook her head, trying to clear the melancholy thoughts that had made her cry. "See that photo?" She pointed to the historic piece and explained her neighborhood's past. "I don't know why I was crying, but I got to thinking about the factory girls and those poor men. They were so hopeless. And then I realized we'll have to move. We can't raise a daughter across the street from a strip club." Simona's voice cracked and she started sobbing. "I love my loft," she exclaimed, "but that's a strip joint, and those little girls weaving shirts right here, and the winos!" Her hands gestured jerkily like puppets dancing on strings, helpless to control themselves or anything else.

Peter chuckled and took Simona in his arms. He drew her against his chest and shushed her, stroking her head. "Darling. Darling. It's all right. I promise it is."

"Really?" She looked at Peter with wet eyes. "You promise?"

"Yes. Look here." He stood and closed the curtains over the window, blocking out the neon sign. "Right?" Simona nodded and sniffled. "We'll have our baby and this will be her first home and everything will be perfect. We can move any time before she's two. There's plenty of time."

"And that will be all right? She won't be scarred by living in sight of exotic dancers?"

"She won't even notice."

"Oh." Simona put her hands on her belly and rubbed circles over the mound of baby. "It seems so simple now." She laughed. "I got pretty carried away, didn't I?"

He kissed her brow. "It's allowed once or twice when you're carrying around an extra person. Expected even." Peter put his mouth next to Simona's belly. "Hey, you in there, it's Dad talking. Try not to make your mum too crazy, all right?" He kissed Simona again. "Now," he said, "what have you been drawing?"

"Nothing."

Peter frowned at her.

"Well, I drew something, but it's nothing. It's not ready to be seen." She smiled at Peter, grateful for his kindness when she was being so ridiculous. "Shall we eat?" Simona rose, leaving her sketchpad on the chair and led Peter to the kitchen.

Simona had filled the sketchpad with drawings of Carina Casale. She was almost done with the mural's background, which would leave only her mother's portrait. When she painted Clarice and Rosa, she'd painted the women she remembered. It had not occurred to her she could get it wrong. Now, that was all she thought about. The pages were full of half-drawings, variations of a woman who was impossible to know. The only one she could be certain of was the drawing from the photograph, in which her mother's face was too shadowed to be seen clearly. The more drawings she made, the more she feared she had it wrong. She began tearing out sheets of paper and crumpling them up in frustration. When she slept, her mother came to her, stepping out of the painting the way Clarice did. Simona rushed to embrace her, but stopped short. Her mother's face dissolved into a black vapor, followed by her reaching arms and the rest of her body. Simona woke from those dreams damp with sweat, aching to be held by her mother and to hold her own daughter, as though one were the other and the two were the same.

Simona was again drawing and discarding portraits of her mother. This time at the Center with the spirits sitting around her, talking to each other in their way, letting Simona concentrate on her art. Except for Flora Blanca, who stood beside Simona's chair, one hand on the back of the chair, the other on Simona's shoulder. She watched Simona draw, fascinated by the marks of graphite taking shape, becoming a face.

Simona drew that one face over and over, now with a pixie chin, or full cheeks, or high brows, or hair down, or back. There were a million possibilities and she couldn't seem to settle on the right combination. It seemed to her a daughter should know her mother. If only she drew the right face, she would know somehow that it was her mother on the page, a feeling would descend, contentment or love perhaps. And if she got it wrong....

Flora Blanca leaned in over Simona's shoulder so the hairs that strayed from her braids tickled Simona's neck, her breath warm and moist against Simona's skin. Simona wriggled loose and adjusted the neckline on her top to cover more of her shoulder. Flora Blanca repositioned her chin over Simona's shoulder, this time her braid fell forward and lay across Simona's chest. Simona looked at it, irritated by it because she was irritated by everything when her work wasn't going well. She put her hand on it to move it aside and paused. Her daughter was going to have dark hair. Someday long. Someday in braids. Instead of moving the hair, she reached up to pat Flora Blanca's head. "Sima," she said, and reached around to put a hand on Simona's belly. The hum that filled the air when the spirits were present increased. Simona tilted her head to rest it against Flora Blanca's, who cooed pleasantly at the touch. The baby kicked against Flora Blanca's hand.

"Did you feel that?"

"Baby," Flora Blanca said.

"That child have a name yet?" Alma asked.

"No. I'd like to meet her before I stick a name on her."

Alma huffed. "Stuff and nonsense. A name is a name. Just something to call a body by is all."

"Well, Mama, I'm glad you put some thought into naming your children."

"Clarice is a pretty name and perfectly serviceable."

"Like you," Rosa said, giggling. "The Perfectly Serviceable Clarice."

Flora Blanca's hand wandered from Simona's belly and rested over her breast.

"I think it is nice to see the infant first," Marguerite said, with a nod to Simona.

Flora Blanca's hand was hot through her shirt, causing an unfamiliar ache in her breast. She moved the hand and stood to stretch. It was time she got up that scaffold and started painting.

Simona came out of the bedroom in her bathrobe, moving groggily into the kitchen. "Good morning," she said and yawned.

"What time did you get in last night?"

Simona didn't like the question. It felt like an accusation. "I don't know." She poured herself a cup of coffee and looked at Peter, sitting across the loft in front of her aquarium. He had a newspaper open on his lap, his glasses in place. *The picture of the man at home,* she thought.

"I bought us pastries," he said. There was a white paper sack on the counter. Simona took out a plate and opened the bag. She put out the chocolate croissants and blueberry muffins, then carried the plate to the coffee table and set it before Peter. She stopped to feed the discus before joining him on the couch. "Thanks," she said, selecting a croissant, then turned to face him and put her feet up on his lap, crunching the newspaper under her heels.

Peter dragged the paper out from under her and folded it. "How much longer?" he said.

"Really? Can't we just have breakfast?"

"Really. You don't look healthy. These long hours are taking a toll on you."

"I feel fine, and I'm almost done." She pulled apart the layers of her croissant and licked her fingers. "You said you could handle it, me working a lot before the baby comes. This doesn't feel like you're handling it."

"Working, yes. Being gone all night, no. Losing weight, no. You should be plump and rosy now."

"Plump and rosy? Jesus, Peter, I'm not Donna Reed."

"Who?"

"It's not the 1950s. I have a career. I'm almost done with the mural, so just...*wait*."

"Just wait? For what?" Peter closed his mouth, stopping the flow of whatever words were coming next. He took up Simona's foot and massaged it, working his thumbs into the pads on the ball of her foot. "I'm worried," he said with forced calm. "You're unreachable. That building's a dead zone. What if something happened?"

"Nothing will happen. I'm safe there."

"How are you safe?" His thumb pressed deep into the soft spot between the firm pads of her feet.

"Ow." Simona scowled at Peter and pulled her feet back. She crossed her legs and stuffed a hunk of croissant in her mouth. She had to trust him. Didn't she?

"What if you got hurt and couldn't get to the office to phone out?"

"I won't."

"You could. And what if you do? Simona, you're too important to me to lose, and so is our baby. Just work during the day, when other people are around. If you're almost finished that should be enough time.

"I can't."

"Why not?" His voice strained with tension.

"I just can't," she insisted.

"Why not?" he shouted.

"Because the spirits only come out at night!" she yelled back at him. It wasn't how she'd meant to tell him, but now it was out. Peter's expression was dumbfounded. His mouth hung open, words seemed caught in his throat. Simona got off the couch with some effort and stood by the fish, watching them swim about so Peter couldn't see her face. She imagined Peter removing his glasses and running his hands through his hair the way he did.

"The what?" he finally said.

"The spirits."

"The spirits?"

"Some of my subjects come out of the painting when we're alone. At night."

"And then what?"

Simona could feel Peter looking at her back. She continued to talk to her fish. It was easier that way, to say things that sounded crazy even to her. "We talk. They watch me work. They're like...they're like muses."

"But, Simona, that's not possible." His voice sounded brittle, the air between them full of the friction between belief and disbelief.

She turned to face Peter. His glasses were on the coffee table. His face was constricted with worry. "I'm not alone."

"Simona?"

"I'm safe. That's what I'm trying to tell you. They would help me."

Peter shook his head. "No. No. No. This can't be happening."

"I know it seems impossible, Peter. I didn't believe it either. But I can touch them. They're solid. And warm! Flora Blanca has the hottest little hands..." Peter's face was an impasse, his jaw set in stern defiance of every word Simona spoke. She stumbled, trying to imagine the words that would convince him. Nothing came to her, and she slumped into the new rocking chair near the bookcase. "I'm not crazy."

"Are you sure?" He spoke slowly, without the hint of a joke.

"Yes."

Peter put his head in his hands and held it there for ages while Simona waited, giving him time, she hoped, to accept the idea. When he looked at her again, his eyes had lost some of their warm fondness. "Let's go see the doctor today. Maybe this is a hormonal thing, pregnancy-induced delusions or something."

"They're real."

"No, they can't be. It's the hormones."

"Clarice told me it's the baby. Her creation inside me is a kind of magic. Like fission or fusion or something. There's so much energy."

"There. You see?" Peter slid off the couch and knelt in front of Simona. He clasped her hands in his. "The baby. Hormones. It can all be explained. By the doctor." His grip on her hands tightened.

"Why? I don't want it explained. I know they'll stop coming once the baby is born. That's soon enough, Peter."

"Simona, darling. If the doctor can explain it, I...*we* will know the cause of this, this whatever it is, and then you'll know it's not safe to be alone there all night."

Simona shook her hands free of his grasp and stood up from the rocker. The tags swung against the arm with the soft clatter of paperboard. "Peter," she snapped. "Listen to me. I do not want to see the doctor. Nothing is wrong. I am safe and fine and this will all be over very soon. I'll finish painting." Her voice strained, "The baby will be born. You'll get your divorce. And we'll live happily ever after!"

Peter went around the coffee table to face Simona. He gripped her elbows inside the wide sleeves of her bathrobe. "That's my baby in there, too. I say she needs to see the doctor today."

Simona flung her arms in the air, freeing herself once again of Peter's grasp. She stormed past him into the bedroom and slammed the door. She flung open her closet, shoved Peter's things to the side, the hangers scraping across the rod, and threw a cotton top, leggings, and a belted cardigan onto the bed. "She's still in *my* body, you know," she shouted through the wall to Peter. "And I say everything's fine. You have some nerve trying to pull that parental rights bullshit on me when you've got a wife and a house and a whole life overseas. How do I..." Simona pulled the shirt over her head. "How do I even know you're really staying with me? Maybe this is all just a test run. Low commitment and all while you hang onto your wife back in London."

"Simona!" Peter threw the door open. "Don't be absurd. Low commitment...really? Is that all you think of me?"

Simona tugged on her leggings, then sat on the bed and crammed her feet into her cowboy boots, reaching around her belly to hold the tops, and stomping each foot down hard to drive in her heel. "Then believe me." She paused her furious movements to glare defiantly at him. Peter opened his mouth, but when a moment passed without him speaking, she stood and pushed past, grabbed her purse from the coat rack beside the door and slung it over her shoulder.

"Where are you going?" Peter called as she slid the steel door open.

"To the Center. I'm going to finish the damn mural before I come home again." Simona stepped into the elevator lobby and punched the button. "Don't wait up!"

Peter slammed the loft's door behind her, rattling the track and frame.

Chapter Thirty-Five

GEMMA FELT RIDICULOUS WHEN she lit the end of the smudge stick. But, she decided, having all those visions, inhabiting the Artist, hardly left her in a position to doubt. The flat felt different devoid of Leti and her possessions. It seemed bigger. It also seemed vacant. The blue-gray smoke curled and twisted away from the sage as Gemma carried it from one room to another. *Cleansing,* she thought. *Out with the old. In with the new.* As Gemma moved, following Leti's instructions to get the smoke into the corners where energy collected, just like dust and cobwebs, she found her self-conscious apprehension replaced by excitement. She decided she would paint the walls, update the range, at least, and change some of the light fixtures. She adored the fireplace in the living room, its mantle tiled in a deep gold that matched the glass in the folding doors. Gemma would furnish the flat and move in right away—the expense would be modest and could be factored into the divorce settlement.

The slow-burning herb filling her home with aromatic smoke, a blessing. And why not? What religion didn't use incense of some kind in its ceremonies? She no longer felt foolish or self-conscious, only pleased that she was doing something for herself. When Gemma had finished moving the smoke through the flat, she set the smudge stick on the tile hearth and lay down on the floor. She had never had her own place before. During school there had been flatmates, and then Peter. She put her palms flat on the wood and swept them across the boards. Her floor. Her bedroom. Her smudge stick...the smoke was becoming overpowering. It smelled like sweet marijuana. Gemma rolled over and reached for the bundle. She ground it out against the hearth tiles.

Whether it was magic or just the power of suggestion, Leti was right about cleansing energy. The place already felt like her own.

Chapter Thirty-Six

SIMONA WORKED ON THE scaffold, painting the last of the quilt. There wasn't much of it left and she intended to finish it that day. She also intended to stay at the Center until she was finished with her mother's portrait, even if it meant sleeping on the floor. She was furious with Peter for forcing her to reveal her secret, for neither trusting nor believing her. She had to push all of her anger aside now in order to paint. The quilt was meant to be warm and inviting, not tense and edgy. After nearly three hours of work, she had almost forgotten their fight. Almost forgotten that he insisted she see her doctor. He probably didn't realize the depth of her upset, the way he'd done it, what he was implying! She pushed the thought aside for the hundredth time and picked up cerulean blue on her sable brush. Then, Hannah walked in.

Simona set down her brush and palette beside the small cans of paint, cups, and rags she kept handy on the scaffold. She leaned on the railing and looked at Hannah without even a smile for her best friend. "Well?" she said, shouting down.

"I'm taking you to lunch," she returned, calling up.

Hannah had cut her hair since Simona last saw her, a chin-length bob with long bangs that swept to one side. With the length gone, her hair had some wave to it. It was cute, but Simona wasn't ready to say so. Not yet. "You're on a mission. Sent by the enemy."

"He's your fiancé, not your enemy, and so what if I am? Come on, Simona. I'm buying."

"Oh, all right." Simona checked that her paints were all sealed and wrapped her brush in plastic wrap so it wouldn't dry out. When she reached Hannah, Hannah linked her arm through Simona's and turned her toward the door.

"Cute hair."

"Nice mural."

They hit the café right before the lunch crush. The line for the counter ran back past Simona and Hannah's table, so that Simona was uncomfortably aware of someone hovering over her shoulder. Two different people bumped her with their bags. She picked at the grilled crust of her panini. A large woman with a little boy sat at the table nearest them. She had her head bent toward her phone, all but ignoring the boy while he chattered noisily, sometimes launching into nursery rhymes in singsong without a recognizable melody. "Hickory dickory dock, the mouse ran up the cock..." Simona was drinking just then. She laughed and wound up choking down her ginger beer and coughing into her napkin. Hannah laughed, too, while the boy finished his song and the people in line inched along behind Simona's chair. The woman dropped her phone in her purse with an exaggerated sigh, gathered up some of their mess, including the boy's barely touched grilled cheese sandwich, and delivered it to the busing station by the door. She came back for her purse and her son, sidling her large frame through the line for the counter. The boy was content to sing to himself, having moved on to Jack and Jill tumbling down a hill. Once she had him by the hand, the woman looked at Simona, who had only just finished coughing and was still collecting herself, and said pointedly, "Good luck, honey."

As soon as she'd turned away, Hannah tossed her purse on the vacant table. She and Simona transferred their things, moving away from the line of customers. "Thank you," Simona said. "One more bag to the back of my head and I was going to lose it."

"I could tell." Hannah rearranged her lunch, setting her food and drink precisely where she'd had them on the first table.

"Feeling OCD today?"

"Hey, this lunch is about your issues, not mine."

"I almost forgot." Simona grabbed a hair band from her bag and pulled her hair into a ponytail. "So, why didn't he come himself?"

"Because you would have kicked him out."

"Yeah, there is that. I know Peter means well, but I need him to back off. I'm almost done."

"What did you say that got him so freaked out?" Hannah looked at Simona with the knowledgeable gaze of a best friend. She would know if Simona tried to pass off a half-truth.

"What did he say when he called you?"

Hannah shrugged, speared some spinach onto her fork with a cherry tomato. "He's worried, wants to know if I think you're all right."

"I am."

"I can see that. What's going on?"

Simona went back to picking at the edges of her sandwich. "He thinks I could get hurt and doesn't want me alone at the Center."

Hannah laughed. "That's it? That's pretty reasonable, isn't it?"

Simona knew better than to argue with Practical Hannah. There was no way to convince anyone she wasn't alone there, and no way to convince Hannah that Peter was being in any way unreasonable. "Maybe. I work best at night. I like being there alone. And I'm so *close*. What difference could a few more nights make?"

Hannah made her scowly face as she considered. "It all depends on what happens, doesn't it?"

"Hannah!" Simona felt the anger rising again. Was she over-emotional? She couldn't trust her reactions these days. She certainly wouldn't have cried over a textile factory that shut down decades before, or the Skid Row bums all long since dead if she weren't pregnant, so maybe she was the unreasonable one. Still, the emotions were real and she had to be alone to be with the spirits. That much she knew. "You're both treating me like a child. I've been doing this for months and I've been pregnant for months. Anything can happen at any time, and I'm not going to give up this opportunity because you two are worried something *might* happen. I could slip in the shower, too."

"Simona!" Hannah was superstitious enough to be alarmed by the mention of a specific misfortune. "Don't say that." She sighed and composed her face again. "Fine. It's your life to risk as you see fit. So be it." Hannah leaned back and crossed her arms over her chest.

"I know you don't mean that. I can see it." Simona waved a hand at Hannah, gesturing at her posture and expression. "Stop worrying. I'm fine. I only need a few days. Maybe less."

Hannah uncrossed her arms. "What should I tell Peter?"

"Tell him, I'm not crazy and I'll be fine."

"Not crazy. Fine," Hannah repeated.

They ate their lunches and talked about work, life, love, and the baby. Hannah teased Simona about settling down, and Simona reminded her that was precisely why she needed a little freedom now. Though not precisely true, it seemed to satisfy Hannah. Simona excused herself, and when she came back, Hannah's phone was on the table. It chimed as a text came in. "Did you tell him?"

"Yep. Not crazy. Fine. You have three days."

"Thanks." As Simona bent to hug Hannah the baby gave a solid kick. "Oh! Feel this." She put Hannah's hands on her belly, positioning them to feel the jabs and punches.

"Wow. Do you have a name for her yet?"

"We've got a few, but we want to meet her before we stick her with a label." Simona sat again.

"Like a UPC code?"

"Yes. We're thinking of tattooing it on her head.

As the friends joked and chatted, Hannah's face lost its slightly drawn look of concern and warmly opened, regaining its natural state. Her eyes, in particular, filled with an inviting radiance. Though Simona would never have articulated it, she cherished this quality of her friend's. To always broadcast your feelings in your expression was to be sincere and guileless. They finished their lunch talking about Hannah's life and the new man in it, or almost in it. When they tired of the loud café and both felt the tug of their responsibilities, they left for the Center.

Like good Minnesotans, they remarked on the weather as they walked down Washington Avenue. "April showers bring May flowers" was no longer dependably true. They had snow in April the year before and winter's hibernation had seemed eternal. This year's spring brought relief and a sense of justice, as though the earth owed the people a beautiful season after the trials of the past year. On this day, the sky was lovely and the air light, cool in the shade of the buildings that lined the street, but warm wherever the sun came to rest. They talked about crossing the street just to walk fully in the sun, but didn't bother. Though they couldn't see it, the Mississippi River ran nearby, flowing fast, carrying the debris of spring's runoff. Simona decided she and Peter should go back to the Stone Arch Bridge, where he had proposed, and watch the river. St. Anthony Falls would be impressive now.

When they reached the Center for Women, Hannah and Simona hugged. "Call Peter," Hannah said. "Whatever you said this morning, it scared him."

"All right. I will."

"And go home tonight when Hal does, would you?"

Simona considered for a moment, weighing the importance of each option. "Sure," she nodded.

"Really?"

"Really." Simona could paint her mother's portrait tomorrow and meet her then. One more day wouldn't matter. She watched Hannah head off, reaching for her phone, working before she got to work. The sun warmed Simona's face and she stayed on the limestone steps beside one of the columns. She rubbed her baby bump. "We're almost there, baby. We're almost there."

When she turned to go in, she paused to once again admire the bronze sheafs of wheat that formed handles on the large wooden doors at the center of the portico. They were a fitting emblem of Minneapolis' past, once the flour milling capital of the world. *And now*, she thought, *they grace the entrance to the Center for Women, still fitting. Wheat becomes flour, which becomes bread, or sometimes tortillas.* She smiled and thought she would mention the wheat-shaped handles to Clarice and Rosa when she saw them next. Simona went to the far side of the portico and swiped her keycard.

She waved to Hal as she entered. He was at his desk with the blinds up on his office windows. When she stood some thirty feet from her work, Simona stopped to take it in. The scaffold blocked the far edge of the mural. She would climb it for the last time today and finish that corner. Tonight she would go home and be with her fiancé. Tomorrow, she would paint her mother's portrait, and tomorrow evening she would meet her mother for the first time in her life. The thought of it caused her stomach to flutter on top of her lunch and she burped. Gas aside, they were excited nerves, not fearful. She wondered if she would dare share her excitement with Peter as she took hold of the scaffold's ladder and began to climb. She wanted him to be excited for her, but that was probably asking too much. She would tell him after their baby was born. Simona unwrapped her brush and got to work.

At five o'clock, she climbed down the scaffold and crossed the lobby to knock on Hal's door.

"Simona, how are you?" He was standing at his desk, putting paperwork in his briefcase. Hal had hung a print of Monet's garden behind his desk, showing the small arching footbridge over the creek which reflected the lush greenery that hung over its banks.

"Have you been to Giverny?"

"Yes. And when I get frustrated, I find gazing at that scene is the best remedy." He glanced behind himself at the print and when he looked back, he was smiling with less end-of-the-day fatigue on his face than had been there a moment before.

"I'll have to get one of those for my wall."

Hal moved from one cluttered corner of his desk around to another. "I have to tell you," he said with a businessman's earnest expression, "our tenants have been clamoring to get in here and see the grand entrance, *especially* this mural. I have dutifully prevented that. We're saving your mural for a big reveal."

"Really?"

"Oh, yes. There's talk of hanging a big curtain in front of it and dropping it during our grand opening reception."

"Wow. That would be some serious fanfare."

"Well, maybe I shouldn't have said that. The budget will determine whether or not we can hang the curtain and all."

"Sure." Simona loved the idea of her work begin saved for the grand opening party, with or without a curtain. She was flattered and couldn't wait to tell Peter about the reception and big reveal.

"Looks like you're almost finished, which is good. The lobby furniture is due to arrive in about four days and the café will have to move into its space." Hal took up his jacket and came around the front of his desk. He paused by the door to his office and looked at Simona.

"I came in to use the phone," she said.

"Of course. Help yourself. Good night."

Hal left her as she picked up the phone. While she dialed, she watched him cross the lobby, pausing to look up at her work before leaving the building. "Peter?"

"Hello, darling."

There was a pause. Simona didn't know how to get around the morning's fight, so after several long moments in which Peter was silent, she decided to pretend it hadn't happened. "I'm almost done. I'm going to finish up one little thing and then I'll come home for the night."

"Good." She could feel the tension vanish. "What time do you think?"

"By the time I clean up, I'd say an hour."

"Are you hungry? I could cook supper for us. Pasta?"

"Pasta sounds good." She coiled the phone's cord around her finger while enjoying the receiver's smooth solidity in her hand, like that solid connection she again felt with Peter.

"Excellent. See you soon."

Simona began to hang up, but heard her name. "Yes?"

"Look, love, I'm sorry about this morning."

"Me, too."

"Right. Well. I love you."

"I love you, too."

So this is a relationship, she thought, *arguments and apologies included.* She felt better. Even if Peter didn't believe her, he loved her. In a day or two, it wouldn't matter if he believed her. She would have met her mother, Carina Casale, and then she would move on with her life—with *their* life.

Simona set the phone back in its cradle and paused to stretch her arms to the ceiling, to twist and bend her spine with a satisfying crack. All the work she did, standing, bending reaching—and with this melon of a baby in her belly—made her ache. The baby seemed to be asleep right now. Simona pictured her curled up, her skinny legs crossed, feet curving to hug herself into an egg shape, one thumb tucked into her mouth, suckling already. The downy hair—lanugo, if she remembered correctly—covering her brow, eyelashes already thick and dark. Simona didn't picture hair for some reason, maybe because the other things she could be certain of, but hair she could not, and she didn't want to be disappointed. If she pictured a full head of black hair and the baby was born bald...well, it wouldn't matter. Still, hold off expectations and let it be a surprise either way. She walked her fingertips across the swell of her abdomen and watched them traverse the high point of the mound where her navel sat, once concave, the perfect size to hold a blueberry, and adorned by a silver hoop, it had been stretched flat and looked like the end of a hot dog where the casing had been twisted shut. The belly ring had to go weeks ago, her first concession to motherhood. Next she'd be chopping off her hair because she didn't have time to wash it and she'd spend all day in sweat pants covered in spit up. Simona laughed at herself and the sound was louder in that small office than she'd expected. She looked around the room as though she might have startled the walls themselves.

The blinds were up on the row of windows that faced the old grain exchange floor. Simona went around Hal's desk and leaned over the bookcase that lined the wall, its top shelf level with the window. She felt the power of being on-high and surveying those below as the finance managers, men with arm bands, stiff removable collars, and waxed mustaches, must have felt watching the bustle of commerce on the floor below. Of course, Simona's floor was empty. From her vantage point, she could see part of her mural. It was good to see it from afar. When she was working, her mind filled with doubts and criticisms. Being the one making them, she was keenly aware of every flaw in the work. This shade was too dark, that line strayed from its course, and if she was feeling doubt, the quilt was trite. But now, seeing it from this new vantage point, Simona decided it was beautiful. "All right, you," she said, pulling back from the glass, "don't get a big head."

She shut the office door quietly and went down and across the lobby, her cowboy boots scuffing against the maple floorboards. When she began to climb the scaffold, the heel struck the piping with a clang. As though called forth by the sound, Clarice, Rosa, Alma, and Marguerite came out to stand before the mural. They formed a wide semicircle and watched Simona climb to her platform. She felt their gaze on her back and heard the hum that always accompanied them, like the low frequency buzz of a transformer. Simona paused at the top of the ladder to consider the massive voltage of a transformer and wondered if that was an apt analogy for her spirits, if they were in fact coursing with high voltage. The image of a metal sign with yellow lightning bolts surrounding the word *danger* in the unmistakable pattern of a jolt flashed in her mind as she climbed over the lip of her platform. Maybe she would ask Clarice about the hum before she left tonight. Simona turned to wave hello to the spirits. They smiled up at her.

It took fifteen minutes to finish painting the sky above the quilt in that corner. So little, it seemed silly she hadn't finished it before going down to call Peter, but her body had urgently demanded a break, the way it did these days. No matter. It was done now. Simona found herself eager to see him, glad to be done with this rig of steel pipes. She could go home and tell him from now on her feet will stay on the floor. She knelt and fit the lid on the can of cerulean blue. The lip had wet paint on it, and she came away with a line of blue across her palm. She was headed to the sink, anyway. Simona picked up her brushes and stood as Flora Blanca burst through the wall.

"Sima!" she cried, her arms spread, braids flying over her shoulders. Flora Blanca hurtled into Simona, wrapping arms about her waist, throwing her off balance.

Simona's mouth opened, gasping in surprise. She rocked back on her heels and threw her arms out for balance. She groped with her right hand for support and let go of the paint brushes. Their wood handles knocked against the safety railing before falling to clatter against the floor. The sound echoed in the empty hall.

Clarice and the others remained in their semicircle, their faces lifted to watch, masks of calm. The hum went up in pitch as the frequency of the vibration increased, as though with excited anticipation. Clarice held her arms out, and the spirits linked hands.

Simona was aware of Flora Blanca's head pressed against her belly, her arms wrapped around Simona's waist in an embrace of fierce love. Flora Blanca's momentum carried them both backwards. As Simona flailed, she noticed the pale line of scalp where Flora Blanca's hair had been parted so perfectly straight. She felt the hard round railing like a kidney-punch as she struck it, her back arching. She grabbed at the steel frame. The blue paint on her palm transferred, smearing as her hand swiveled around the pipe and came free.

Flora Blanca clung to her as she fell. The heat of the embrace enveloped Simona, who thought irrationally, *She's eating me.*

Simona's back struck the floor first, and the wind was knocked out of her with a great *Ooof!* Her head struck next, then snapped forward, chin to chest, and back again with a heavy thunk. The impact cracked her skull, making a piecemeal depression just like cracking an egg; her head left a comparable depression in the floor. A gurgling sound came from her throat. She was aware of her spirits standing around her, looking at her. Simona said *my baby my baby my baby,* but no words came out, only a raspy sort of moan and another gurgle.

Chapter Thirty-Seven

GEMMA HADN'T BEEN ASLEEP long when she woke with a start, sitting bolt upright in bed. Drops of sweat clung to her body everywhere they hadn't been flattened against the sheets. Her heart raced and she looked around the room like a rabbit searching the shadows for a fox. "My God," she said, as the pieces fell into place. She grabbed the bedside phone.

Chapter Thirty-Eight

PETER ADDED TWO CLOVES of minced garlic to the pan with the onions and a splash more olive oil. He would turn on the burner under the pot of water in ten minutes, maybe fifteen. He stirred the garlic into the onion and then lit a candle on the breakfast bar behind the stove. His phone rang. Gemma's ring tone, a snatch of a John Wesley Harding song they both liked. It had been weeks since they'd spoken, which had given him hope she'd moved on as well. *Not now*, he thought. Peter pressed the button to silence the ring and send her to voicemail.

He began chopping bell pepper. His phone resumed her song. He picked it up and held it, staring as though the caller ID, a picture of her from different times, could tell him what she wanted. The ringtone started over, and he pressed the answer button.

"Peter!" she shouted before he could say hello. There was panic in her voice and his gut clenched with the old dread that had begun to characterize his marriage. "Peter," she said again. "Listen. Where is the Artist? Is she there with you?"

"What? What artist? Gemma, I—"

"Peter!" she cried in exasperation. "There's no time. S. Casale. The Artist. I know everything so don't bother playing stupid. She's hurt. I think she is...she...oh God, I don't know—"

"Gemma, slow down." The oil sizzled and Peter turned down the flame. "What are you talking about?"

"She fell off the scaffold at the mural."

Peter's body went cold. He lowered the phone from his head. He almost dropped it, but Gemma was shrieking his name from somewhere far away. He shook his head and blinked himself back to reality and stared at the phone.

"Peter! Peter! Are you there?"

"Yes," he said. "What do you mean Simona fell?"

"Simona? I never knew..."

"Gemma, how do you know this?"

"There's no time, Peter. You have to get to her before the spirits take her." Peter had the sensation that his body had just been pushed under ice. Gemma was yelling at him. "Go, Peter! Go!"

Peter called Hannah as he ran down the stairs. The call was intermittent as he moved through the stairwell with its concrete walls, and he lost her once he went underground to the parking garage. She had repeated back to him that Simona fell and that she would call 911. That was good enough. He flew out of the garage in his rented Audi without checking for traffic or pedestrians. All along Washington Avenue he ran the lights, blasting his horn as he went, hunched over the steering wheel. He swerved around cars and was aware when a moment of panic broke through his adrenaline-fueled determination that a woman had leapt out of the crosswalk as he tore past. His jaw clenched so tightly that one of his molars cracked, though he wouldn't realize it until the day after next when he tried to eat a piece of baguette and a corner of his tooth fell out. Five blocks from the Center, a police cruiser caught up to him, lights and sirens blaring. *Good,* Peter thought. *Clear the way.*

He slammed to a stop in front of the Center and cut the engine while still in drive. The Audi lurched and died with a shudder. Peter ran up the limestone steps to the door.

The windows were papered over, the doors locked. "Simona!" He banged against the heavy wood as the cruiser pulled up right behind him. It's red and blue lights flashed their colors over the Greek columns and neoclassic facade of the building. An officer ran up the steps with gun drawn while his partner covered him from the car. "Get down! On the ground. Now."

Peter spun around to face the officer. "She's hurt!" He saw the gun pointing at him and raised his hands, realizing that he was the wrongdoer, the menace to be overcome, and that there were actually two guns pointed at him. He bent a knee to the ground and, as he lowered himself, saw a corner of the nearest window was uncovered where the paper had torn or been torn for a view to the outside. He could see Simona, or enough of her to know Gemma had got it right. He began to scramble toward the window, but the officer shouted. "Look," Peter pleaded. "She's there. She's pregnant." He pointed at the window where the unpapered glass caught the red and blue police lights, flashing with each strobe. "Look. Please, God, please. Look!"

The officer's radio cracked with voices and he spoke into the transmitter at his shoulder before stepping closer to Peter. In order to see, he had to get down low and he shoved Peter hard to the stones by the back of the neck before bending to look through the glass. Peter's cheek caught between his teeth and now he tasted blood. The stone was gritty and cool under his skin. More sirens. This one was different—an ambulance. The police officer spoke into his transmitter again. "We got a body in here. Grab the kit." He gave the back of Peter's head an extra shove. "You're still in trouble, mister." He got up, holstered his gun and ran to the doors.

"Over there," Peter pointed them to the security door at the far end of the portico. The second officer ran up the steps with a medical bag in each hand. She grunted as she set them down. "What do we got?"

The ambulance pulled up to the building and cut its siren. Hannah arrived right after them and rushed to where Peter and the police stood at the door. The EMTs climbed the stairs behind her with a gurney and medical bags. The first officer was radioing dispatch to get access to the keys in the Knox Box, but Hannah went around them, an access card in her outstretched hand. She swiped it and the officer swung the door open as soon as the lock clicked. The officer with the bags went through, followed by the EMTs with the gurney. The other officer went in, releasing the door behind him. Peter grabbed it and looked at Hannah. Her eyes were red from crying and her face showed as much misery as he felt.

Peter broke into a run. He didn't know what he was going to do, only that he had to be with Simona.

Wuf! Something like a brick wall blocked Peter. He folded in half, his chest caving. Arms and shoulders swung and locked him into a two-person stronghold. "Easy, buddy. You'll just get in their way," the officer said, her voice a shout in Peter's ear, yet barely registering over his panic.

He flailed against them before realizing they were right, he was helpless. He pushed his weight backwards now, away from Simona and their grip. "All right. All right. I'm okay now." They eased up as he stopped his struggle.

Hannah came beside him and made a choking sound, her hand over her mouth. Peter grasped at Hannah's other hand and when he squeezed, she squeezed back.

The policewoman stood beside Hannah, rubbing the shoulder she'd used to block Peter. The policeman was on his radio to dispatch again. The EMTs knelt beside Simona working fast. She already had a collar around her neck and they had established she was unconscious. One leg bent back and up, the hip rotated strangely inward. Her arms were askew, though less unnaturally it seemed to Peter. Her long curls fanned out around her head, crown-like, while ruby-blood seeped out near her left ear to pool on the floor. Her face looked peaceful, but for the trickle of red from the corner of her mouth.

The EMTs cut open Simona's shirt. Her ring on its long chain had caught up in her bra strap near her shoulder. Peter found himself staring at the little star of her navel. "My baby," he said. Hannah gripped his arm. He hadn't realized he'd spoken out loud until he felt her fingers clutch at his biceps. She made a sobbing noise at his side.

The EMTs worked each to one side. Their sturdy white shirts bore the blue Star of Life on their sleeves. While the first checked her blood pressure, the other picked up Simona's hand, held her thumb and dug his nail into her cuticle, watching her face. "No response to pain," he said with the dull note of routine. His partner announced, "Heart rate one-twenty. BP one-ten over seventy." They continued speaking in code while Peter and Hannah watched, horrified and praying. *Please, Simona. Please, Simona. Please, please, Simona.*

One of the EMTs shifted Simona's leg. "Oh, shit."

Peter froze.

"She's bleeding out vaginally. Let's scoop and run."

The EMTs loaded her onto the gurney and ran for the door. Peter found himself staring dumbly at the floor where Simona's blood had seeped out. The blood from her head pooled in a shiny puddle the shape of a kidney bean, its viscous edges perfectly rounded. The other stain had smeared when the EMTs moved her. Her black leggings must have absorbed most of it, which is why they didn't see it until the leg was moved. Peter continued to stare, trying to understand what was happening, while the EMTs exited the building with Simona.

"Peter!" Hannah shouted from across the lobby.

He snapped awake and ran after them, watched them load Simona into the rig. "You family?" the EMT asked. Peter nodded. "Climb in." He started an IV as his partner shut the doors behind Peter. A moment later, the siren came on and the ambulance pulled out into traffic.

It was a short ride to Hennepin County Medical Center. Peter sat perched on a small vinyl seat, rubbing his palms on his jeans. When the medic asked a question, he answered, otherwise he was useless, sitting there sweating and crying, swaying with the movement of the vehicle. The EMT radioed ahead to the hospital. "We have a fall from twenty feet or so. Female, thirty-two, thirty-eight weeks pregnant. Pupils dilated, barely reactive. Probable skull fracture with subdural hematoma. She's bleeding out vaginally."

"Fetal heart rate?" The person on the other end of the radio asked.

"One-seventy."

Peter tried to record the details. They were important to him, something he'd want to get straight later, when he told Simona what a scare she gave him, how he'd almost lost her. A sob caught in his throat and the EMT glanced up, met his eye briefly. Peter wasn't ready to give up hope. He looked away, then reached out to touch Simona's fingers. When the EMT didn't correct him, he took hold of her hand and saw a smear of blue paint on the palm.

Simona was rushed into the ER, where the shock-trauma team waited to meet them with a neonatal cart. Peter was blocked from following them into the trauma room, but before they closed the door on him, he saw the concerted efforts of a team of professionals, like every move had been choreographed and rehearsed before their arrival, and it gave him some relief. One person cut away Simona's bra. Another squirted her abdomen with antiseptic. A fist was placed on her sternum, the knuckles rolled up between her breasts. Simona's arms rolled away from her body. The sight of it made Peter queasy, though he didn't know why. As the doors were shut on the trauma room, Peter glimpsed a scalpel in the doctor's hand.

And the mural was complete.

Chapter Thirty-Nine

THE SMELL OF CHARRED onions hit Peter as he entered the loft. He went through to the kitchen, turned off the burner and looked at the pan, ruined after six hours over a flame. He walked around the breakfast bar and opened the window by Simona's easel. Across the street, pink neon flashed at him. *Girls. Girls. Girls.* He balled his hand into a fist and punched as hard as he could against the window screen. The mesh stretched taut over his knuckles and tore from its aluminum frame. He drew back and punched again and again, now with two fists. The frame bent and became disjointed, popping loose from the window and tumbling three stories to bounce on the sidewalk below. A sound deep within Peter welled up, first as a rumble in his gut, then a growl from his throat, and by the time it burst from his mouth it had become a cry of pain and rage. Peter grabbed the window frame on both sides and thrust himself through the opening to roar into the night. People on the street stood and stared up at him, uncomprehending and stupid. Peter's anguish took the shape of a word as his scream finally ran thin. He gulped in air and shouted to the world, "Fuck! Fuck! Fuck you! Fuck you! Fuck you!" His rage turned to helplessness, and he withdrew from the window to slump on the floor, his back against the brick wall, his head between his knees. Outside, someone on the street began clapping.

When Peter lifted his head, he looked at the studio flat through bleary eyes. Across the room stood the fish tank. It glowed with the diffuse quality of a light in water. The blue discus moved in slow motion as though dozing. Only Red George showed any signs of life, popping up to the surface to gulp at some floating speck, then thrusting himself back to the bottom to scrape along the blue pebbles. Up and down. A fish with a neurosis. Beside the tank, caught in its cool glow, sat the rocker. One of the swans was visible, its wings spread in flight. Making a backdrop to the rocker were the spines of Simona's books. It was idyllic in its way, the rocker sat so expectantly, waiting to hold the mother who would hold the baby. And it was so tragic, Peter couldn't stand it.

He grabbed his keys and left. There was a pub across the street, the one Simona told him had been a part of Skid Row some eighty or ninety years before.

Being close to closing time on a weeknight, the pub was dark and quiet. Round tables crowded the front of the establishment, while a row of booths with high-backed wooden benches lined the wall across from the bar. Peter slid onto a stool and tossed his wallet down in front of him. The bartender approached and stood before him, waiting. When he looked up from the heavily varnished wood, Peter found himself staring at a phoenix rising from flames that curled up from the deep scoop of a loose-fitting tank top. The bird's wings spread along her collar bone, its head bent, beak open in a squawk, presumably triumphant, at the base of her throat. The flames spread over the tops of her shoulders. "Is that a metaphor?" he said.

"Isn't everything?"

Peter's eyes rose along her throat to the face. She wore a lip ring at the center of her lower lip. Other than mascara, her face looked naked, fresh and unblemished. She was pretty, if one looked past the ring. And the hair, which had been shorn. Another tattoo showed through the fuzz of hair over her ear. "Doesn't that get in the way when you kiss?"

"No. Actually, it's great for fellatio." She let the tip of her tongue protrude on the A sound in fellatio, and Peter saw the glint of another piercing.

"My fiancée died tonight."

"Oh..." Surprise. "Oh..." Recognition. "That was you. Screaming. Fuck. Fuck. Fuck." She turned away from Peter and poured a scotch, which she set in front of of him.

"Thanks."

She paused, bounced a little as though about to say something, but thought better of it. She left Peter to his drink.

He finished the scotch quickly and pushed the glass to the edge of the bar. The bartender returned with the bottle and tipped it. Peter put his hand over his glass and she stopped. He took the bottle, checked the label and set it down. "Have you got anything older?" She turned to the rows of bottles arranged behind the bar, the mirror reflecting their neat tops back into the room. She selected from the far row a Laphroaig eighteen-year-old. Peter nudged his glass toward her when she returned. She left the bottle on the bar and went to clear a table. He watched her in the mirror. She picked up glasses and garbage with practiced efficiency, moving everything to the bar. After she wiped the table, she turned up its chairs, her shoulders and arms flexing with practiced ease. A couple of blokes near the door stood to leave and she wished them good night, but not without glancing at the note they left on the table. Peter was too far from her to make out the tattoo that spread across her shoulder blades, especially in a mirror. She left the table she was wiping to lock the front door behind the customers and click off the open sign before grabbing their cash and collecting their glasses.

She came around the bar again, the washcloth dangling from her hand. Peter lifted the bottle. "Do you mind if I have another while you close up? I'd go home, but there's nothing to drink there."

She faced Peter, her hands on her hips, and raised an eyebrow.

"She was pregnant. My fiancée."

She recoiled, the expression of good-natured tough fell away, and the bartender looked momentarily wounded. "Fuck. I'm really sorry."

"Me too."

She set a glass on the bar and poured a scotch for them both. She picked up hers and swung its heel against the lip of Peter's glass. The thick-rimmed clink was not unpleasant. "Better days ahead," she said and took a drink. She didn't wait for conversation, but turned to her work and began loading a dishwasher tucked in beside the sink. When she bent forward, Peter saw that the tail feathers of the phoenix extended into her cleavage.

"No," Peter said.

"Huh?" she looked up from the dishes.

"Not everything is a metaphor. Even the things that should be aren't always." Peter was remembering the fight they'd had early that same morning—technically yesterday. The spirits. He thought Simona was going mad, the way Gemma had—first a nonexistent baby, and now this painting. It seemed at the time like it was happening to him. These women and their hysterical fantasies had become his curse. Over the course of the day, he'd decided to give Simona a chance, to finish the mural, to have the baby, to let her hormones normalize. He convinced himself the hormones were the problem. The bartender turned on extra lights around the bar and put on a Radiohead album, filling the somber place with a new energy. She grabbed a broom and swept. That call. That bloody call. The only way Gemma could have known was if they were real...and if they were real, why didn't they protect her the way she said they would? He snorted as a wave of sorrow overcame him, tears and snot suddenly flowing. Peter grabbed a bar napkin from a nearby stack. Thank God he had told Simona he loved her. He took off his glasses and blew his nose. The bartender tilted her tall garbage can forward and Peter tossed in the napkin.

"Do you mind a question?"

He shrugged one shoulder.

"What happened to the baby?"

Peter lifted his face to meet her eyes. She was the first person he'd looked in the eyes since he saw Simona laying on the floor, her leg bent like some cheerleader jump gone wrong. The bartender had blue eyes, large and heavy-lidded. They made Peter think of the discus and that he needed to feed them when he got back. "She's alive."

The bartender exhaled a rush of air. She began to smile in relief, but stopped herself, her eyes darkening with new concern. "And? Is she okay?"

"I don't know. She's full-term, but the fall...."

She stepped away from Peter, watching him as though she might change her mind about him. She pulled a bar stool over and straddled it. She took up her scotch and sipped, watching him closely. "The fall?"

He smiled sadly. "Do I look guilty?"

She had one hand on the edge of her counter, close to a panic button, no doubt. She raised her glass in her other hand. "My brother is a cop."

Peter chuckled. "I think he shoved me to the ground today. Or one of his friends did." He drained his glass and poured another.

"I have cameras all over this place."

Peter described the rush to the Center, borrowing the explanation Hannah had given the police before joining him in the hospital waiting room. He'd been on the phone with Simona when she fell. The police took his license and impounded his rental car. The bartender finished her drink while he recounted events, now with both hands on her glass. She poured them another.

"The baby's in the NICU. A nurse offered to take me to her." Peter fell silent. "I couldn't." He drank. He looked at the bartender and was surprised to find her wiping tears from her cheeks. "I'm a bad person, aren't I? I should have seen my daughter. Shouldn't I?"

She nodded. "But you'll go tomorrow. Today. After you've slept and sobered up."

"I don't feel drunk."

"You will once you stand up. Hell, you'll probably fall over." She tried a smile, but her eyes betrayed her. "Will she...?"

"Live? Too early to tell. The nurse said she has lots of dark hair, like her mother." Peter suddenly couldn't stay there, hemmed in at that bar by so much sadness, all of it his own. He stood up and gripped the bar rail, his head reeling. He swayed and knocked into the stool next to him. "Sorry.

Sorry." He stood still, waiting for equilibrium to return. "You're right," he said, "I'm bloody fucking pissed." He carefully lowered himself onto the barstool. "That was my goal when I set out, so..." he picked up his glass once more, "here's to me."

"Mission accomplished."

Peter clinked his glass to hers and raised it to his lips, but stopped short of drinking. He set the glass down and broke into sobs.

"Are you sure?" Hannah stood with her hand raised, the key card ready to swipe.

Peter nodded. The baby slept in her carrier, a blanket tucked up around her chin. It was morning and though not cold, not warm. Peter didn't understand parenting yet and was, in fact, still terrified of it, but he instinctively felt better with her tucked in, as though the layers of swaddling soothed both father and daughter.

They entered the Center for Women and found it changed. The furniture had been delivered. Chairs and tables were positioned on rugs that marked off sections of the room. The counter, once a bank tellers' counter, was lined with stools. A new expresso machine sat on a back counter, still under a plastic shipping sleeve. Beside the old safe sat a new stainless fridge. Laid atop one of the tables, a large menu board someone was in the middle of lettering.

Peter set the infant carrier on a table and lifted out the baby. She stretched and smacked her lips together. Peter offered her the pacifier and tucked her against his chest. He slung the diaper bag over his other shoulder, and they walked to the mural. A sofa and chairs had been placed for viewing. Peter sat on the sofa, and Hannah joined him. They gazed at Simona's masterpiece without speaking for a long time.

"Could we be alone for a little while?"

Hannah nodded. "I'll go get us some coffee." She stood, then paused to put a hand on Peter's shoulder. She put her other hand on the baby's head.

Peter was grateful for her and was about to say so, when she turned and left them. He listened for the door at the far end of the lobby to open and close.

They were alone. Peter kissed his baby and stared at the mural.

The women who stood before him, with their detailed and expressive faces, told stories. Peter started at their feet. It seemed the natural thing to do. He marveled at the way such a common and homely body part could be shod with such extravagant variety. The lady with veins, blue and raised, crisscrossing her calves and the nylons rolled down like donuts circling her ankles made him smile. Simona even had the shoes right: thick-soled orthopedic lace-ups in beige. He could see in the large and knotted hands of this one, that she was a farmer's wife, used to hard labor. That one, with the glasses pushed up onto her head and the feathered blonde hair falling over a satin jacket, she was partying away the night, hoping to be discovered in a disco. Peter let his eyes roam over the faces of the women, studying the details he had never taken the time to see before. One woman, who was just a face at the back of the crowd, had gray hair and kind eyes. She looked tired, like she'd supported other people on the breadth of her back the whole of her life. She reminded him of his grandmother. Peter wondered which of these portraits were the spirits who had come to life for her and who had betrayed her in the end.

But he wasn't there to feel bitter. He had time for that later. He wanted to see the mural, to spend time with it, and to show Simona their baby.

He let his eyes trail the faces through the crowd. Finally, they found Eve, placed at the head of the rest. Peter's eyes seemed to catch on her bare breasts, as though Simona had wanted him to notice. He glanced down at the baby, contentedly sucking on her pacifier while she slept. He lifted his gaze again and looked upon Eve's beautiful face. He liked her face best of all, strong and determined without the signs of hardship and desperation the other women bore. *This* was an Eve proud of all that had been accomplished since the Fall.

From there, Peter's eyes easily caught the edge of the quilt blowing above the women. Once his sight hooked into that visual maze and began to wander, he got lost in the intricacies of the work, this fabric art rendered in paint on a wall. From the middle of the lobby, it looked like a painted picture. From ten feet away, it looked like a real quilt he could take down and wrap himself in. Up-close, he saw that each piece of fabric in the quilt had been painted on the wall with a different pattern, the way a real quilt was pieced with differently patterned fabrics: polka dots, vines, tiny flowers, swirls of color, some had gold threads woven through.... The giant quilt portrayed a great gnarled apple tree in the middle of some medieval garden, but there was no snake, no Adam, and Eve stood with the women beneath the quilt. One golden apple colored in metallic paint hung on a low branch. Here and there words were painted on the roots and branches in that same metallic gold: Love, Wisdom, Charity, Faith, Hope, Knowledge, and Progeny.

Finally, Peter allowed himself to really look at the central figure, the portrait that should not be there. Simona stood at the head of womanhood, barefoot, in a white dress, her pregnant belly gloriously swollen. Her hands held her belly—her child—and her gaze was downcast, her dark curls falling about her face and shoulders. Filled with grief and longing, Peter began to cry.

The baby squirmed against him, so he loosened her blankets, giving her more freedom to move. Peter kissed her head. "Our daughter is perfect," he said. "She's beautiful, just like you."

When Hannah returned, Peter was feeding the baby on the sofa under the mural. Hannah brought a small side table around and set out the coffee and muffins. "I'll trade you."

Peter handed her the baby, who fussed momentarily. He was relieved to stretch his arms and have a sip of coffee, though he couldn't quite relax with his daughter, only five days old, in someone else's arms, even Hannah's. It proved, he decided, that he had a parenting instinct after all.

"Any luck?" Hannah asked.

"I think so." Peter looked at Hannah so he could gauge her reaction. "Maeve Emilia."

Hannah looked at the baby in her arms, the sweet face and dark curls of hair, the tiny dimpled hands, and when the baby looked up again, the stunning green eyes. "Maeve Emilia," she whispered. "Welcome, little Maeve."

"Maeve means joy. Emilia was—"

"Simona's middle name," Hannah finished.

"She told you?"

"Years ago." Though Hannah addressed Peter, she was speaking softly down to Maeve, watching her mouth move around the bottle's nipple. "Simona Maria Emilia Casale. She thought it was weird having two middle names." Hannah smiled at Maeve, whose eyes had begun to close with sleep. She put the bottle down and cradled Maeve against her shoulder and rubbed her back.

"It was also her mother's middle name. I think Simona wanted to honor her mother."

"Then you honor them both."

"Hannah, you've been such a good friend to me. To us."

They sat together, the three of them, under Simona's mural and the final portrait that had impossibly, magically, completed S. Casale's greatest work of art. At Hannah's suggestion, the plaque that would go on the side wall nearby would explain that the central figure could equally be the artist's mother carrying the artist, or the artist carrying her daughter, making it a mysterious double, or even triple, portrait. It was fitting for a piece titled *Womankind*, that celebrates the ultimate creative act: life itself.

June

Chapter Forty

A BIT OF LUCK, thought Peter, finding the house dark and quiet. He and Maeve could sneak in while Gemma was out. Not that coming home to them would be any less of a shock than his walking in on her, but at least he'd be able to get Maeve settled. He set their bag down in the entryway and carried Maeve, resting at last, in her infant carrier up to the nursery.

He pushed the door open with his foot and stepped inside. Peter stood still in shock, holding the baby carrier in his aching arms, and stared. The room was completely empty and the walls had been painted a shade of purple. He set the baby on the floor and knelt next to her. After an exhausting flight, she was finally asleep. Her tiny fist curled next to her cheek, poking out of the blanket. Her black hair showed from under the stocking cap, and Peter knew she was perfect. How could Gemma look at her and not want her? Apart from her being someone else's child. Apart from her being the product of his infidelity. He could see the pitfalls, all the reasons for his wife to reject his child, the lifetime of problems they could bring upon themselves—that he could bring upon all of them. He was certain when Gemma saw Maeve, she would see an innocent, deserving of her love. He touched Maeve's cheek and she smacked her lips, turning her head toward his finger, even while she slept. It would be time for a bottle soon.

First, he had to figure out where Gemma had put the baby things.

Entering the bedroom, he was overcome by a sense of wrongness. Something was missing, like a piece of the room was gone. He sensed it before he knew what it was. Turning slowly, he scanned the room. Then he came to it, a void on the wall after the dresser and before the door. Gemma had taken down the painting. It was for the best. They could hardly become a family with Simona's portrait hanging over them. Even after that rational acceptance of the picture's disappearance, he felt ill at ease, as though there was something else.

Peter pulled open Gemma's dresser drawers one after the other. Empty. He opened the closet. It contained traces of her in the form of posh frocks and flashy, seldom worn outfits. All the things that were comfortable, worn repeatedly, enjoyed and appreciated, they were gone. There was no need to check the bathroom. Gemma had left him.

In the other room, Maeve started to cry and Peter rushed to her, worried that she would be upset by the unfamiliar surroundings, that she could sense something vital had gone missing. Peter held her to his chest so that her cheek rested on his shoulder, the way she liked, and his broad hand supported her neck and head with the surety and confidence of experience. His other hand was offered and she began sucking on his little finger. Father and daughter, finding themselves alone in the world, took comfort in each other.

"Hello, Gemma."

Gemma spun around, startled by his familiar voice. She stared, her lips parted in disbelief at what stood before her, then a sort of uncontrollable burst of laughter exploded from her throat, and was clipped, as though caught and restrained before the body of it could escape. Peter realized he probably should have called first. He looked about himself, took in the irises and camellias that surrounded him and the baby strapped to his chest.

"Hello, I don't think we've met," Gemma said, her eyes locked on his.

"Gemma, this is Maeve Emilia."

The infant's feet kicked, dangling beneath the baby-pack, her head mostly hidden by the supportive back.

"Maeve Emilia Ledbetter. Aren't you a pretty little thing? Just like your mama."

"You cut your hair. It's nice."

"You've changed, too." They were quiet, taking each other in for the first time. "You'd better come round back for a cup of tea. It seems we've both got a lot to tell." Gemma parted the beaded curtain behind the counter and held it for Peter, who gently rubbed his daughter's feet as they walked through.

They sat at the old table with mismatched mugs. Gemma's bore the toothy grin of the Cheshire Cat; Peter's read, "It's not my fault you thought I was normal." They talked for hours, Gemma leaving Peter whenever the tattle bells rang, signaling a customer's entrance. She told him about the visions, how she thought she was going mad, and how Leti helped her realize both that she wasn't mad and what she wanted out of life. She explained how the spirits worked, the good they did for Simona, and how they got hungry and demanded payment for all that good. Peter explained how sorry he was that he didn't believe Simona when she tried to explain about them. Maeve rested naturally in Gemma's arms, sucking contentedly on a bottle. Her hands fluttered while she drank and her eyes drifted about, catching shapes and colors where they could. Gemma set the bottle aside and shook a rattle.

"You're a natural," Peter said. "You'll make a great mother."

"I would have, you mean."

"Gemma...." Peter blew out a breath and removed his glasses before running his hands through his hair. "I know we've both changed. It sounds like you're happy. Or happier. I'm glad for you. I truly am." He fingered his glasses nervously but didn't put them back on. "I know this sounds crazy. I mean, we left each other. I realize that. We've both moved on in so many ways, but Maeve can be our child. Maybe everything was meant to happen this way. For us. Now we can be the family we always wanted to be."

Gemma lifted Maeve, held her over her shoulder so their cheeks touched. She felt the delicate softness of infant skin, smelled her sweetness. Gemma sighed, relishing the feel of that specific weight—about eight pounds—the uncontrolled shifting and flopping of body parts, and the sense of a tiny heart beating so close to her own. She stroked the fine, silken hair that swept over Maeve's head in black curls. Then she looked at Peter, made eye contact just so he could see that she meant it, that she was not speaking out of hurt or resentment. "No," she said. "It's a nice offer, Peter. But no."

Five Years Later

Chapter Forty-One

MIRANDA RICHARDSON CHECKED THE address again. It hardly seemed the right sort of neighborhood, and there was a shop at the address: The Enchanted Garden. *Well,* she thought, repositioning her sunglasses, *I've seen art come out of stranger places than this.*

She gingerly put a hand on the door, as though something contagious might linger on the handle, and pushed it open. The shop was dimly-lit by red candles, some on tall iron stands that were shaped into all sorts of contorted designs, while others sat in rock beds, neatly contained by edging that kept the smooth, round river rocks off of a path that branched out from the entrance and wound through the store.

Miranda took off her sunglasses and let her eyes adjust to the candlelight. *Trés Zen,* she thought, the corners of her mouth curled down into a look of lofty disapproval. The ceiling had been painted to resemble Van Gogh's *Starry Night.* She took a step forward, still gazing at the ceiling, observing the work with her critical eye. Her heel caught in something and she wobbled. If there was one thing Miranda could not stand, it was being off-balance. It usually went along with somebody else having the upper hand. Looking down, she realized the pathways were paved with stepping stones, and the stones had words chiseled into them. Miranda rolled her eyes, then took a step on the balls of her feet.

The stones nearest the door read, "Enter...all ye...who seek..." before the path branched off in different directions. Miranda chose the stone with "wealth" chiseled into its face, and stopped there. Before her, coming up out of the bed of rock: *The Self Less Mother*. It looked different in the shop, or gallery, or Zen garden...whatever it was. The slides Miranda had received that started her quest had been taken outside in full sunlight. This atmosphere certainly lent to the sculpture's mystique.

The structure stood taller than she'd expected, a good seven feet. It was simple, yet poignant. Reaching out, she touched the steel—such a hard metal to express such a tender sentiment. The piece was full of curves, feminine looking, but it left her with a tension at the base of her neck. She knew, had sales records to prove, that the best art was physically emotive. Her favorite component, the orb at the center, had been polished to the fine sheen of a surgeon's instrument and pierced on all sides with dagger-like pieces scorched black. *The wounded heart,* she thought, then stopped her mind from wandering. There wasn't time to stand around and soak in the ambiance. She was on business, and once she had procured the piece for her gallery, she could spend all the time she wanted musing over its many facets. She set off to locate the artist, a G. Warner.

A beaded curtain hung behind a shop counter displaying tabletop pieces. Once the strands were parted, Miranda could see across the little back room and through an open door into the garden. The grass was strewn with large pieces of metal and in the center, on a concrete pad, stood the latest work-in-progress. Replacing her sunglasses, Miranda stepped outside.

A woman worked with her back turned to the door in denim overalls, clunky work boots, and a tank top, unaware of Miranda's presence, blind-sided by the welding mask she wore. Miranda noticed her shoulders, how strong and well defined they looked. She stayed still, mesmerized by the click of the blowtorch and ensuing sparks, using the time to consider bargaining tactics. What's more, Miranda *did* have her moments of patience, such as when faced with startling a person with a lit blowtorch.

The woman finally shut off the torch and stood back from the piece, contemplating it. "Ms. Warner?"

She turned, looking through the small window in her mask for a second, then lifted it, a broad smile on her face.

Miranda looked hard in that awkward moment before recognition set in, then shouted, "Gemma? Gemma Ledbetter!"

"It's Warner again. I see you got my portfolio."

"You silly cow, why didn't you tell me?" Miranda came forward, her arms outstretched to hug her old school chum, but she stopped short and reconsidered Gemma's dirty bib front. Instead, she cupped Gemma's shoulders and gave a little squeeze with her clean, manicured hands.

"I didn't want you think I was looking for a favor." Gemma removed the welding mask from her head and pulled off heavy leather gloves. "Come inside."

As Gemma got the old copper kettle going, Miranda stood in her finely tailored suit and court shoes, looking oddly uncomfortable for such a practiced head-hunter. "You can sit down," Gemma said, putting mugs on the table. "I'll even wipe off a chair for you."

"Right. I'm still in shock. You look so...so...like an *artist*! What happened to you Gemma? Your hair's cropped and not even blonde, and you used to have such delicate hands."

Gemma held her hands up in front of herself. The nails were short and unvarnished. She had a scar where she'd burnt herself some years ago, while learning her craft in an apprenticeship. Even now her hands were always getting nicked up and scorched while she worked. Looking at those hands, Gemma felt an extreme satisfaction with their abundant imperfections. She ran one through her tousled hair. "Well, in this line of work, you know, long hair's something of a fire hazard."

"But, it's red."

"Yes."

"How come?"

"It's a fire thing. Kinship, protection from burns, you know."

"Really?"

"No, Miranda, that's total bollocks. I'm teasing you!" Gemma shook her head and chuckled. "I've changed is all. It is what you recommended last time we met."

"Goodness, I'd forgotten that. Well, this is a brilliant surprise!"

Gemma turned as the kettle whistled and opened a cupboard marked "Extra Greenery, General Silk Foliage" and removed a tin of tea. "Miranda, I know your time is valuable and you didn't come here for an old girls' school reunion."

"Down to business then." Miranda drew in a breath, readying for the negotiation. "I want *The Self Less Mother.*"

"It's not for sale." Gemma couldn't help smiling a little at the look on Miranda's face, at the thought that she was playing ball with Miranda Richardson and had the upper hand. "But I'll let you show it as part of a collection that is for sale."

"Why can't I have it?" she asked, almost pouting.

Gemma set a mug of tea in front of Miranda and took a seat across from her. "I have few possessions I intend to never part with. One is that sculpture, and the other is a painting of the same title."

"Painting? Gemma Led—Warner, what are you hiding?"

"The painting and I have an intimate history, but I never really understood it until my mum passed away."

"I'm so sorry."

She shrugged at the polite condolence. "It was over a year ago. Mum and I had grown quite close after my divorce, then she took ill." Gemma paused to reflect to herself. "When she was gone, I finally understood that the painting was about longing. I borrowed the title and made my own work on the same theme." Gemma glanced at a Tarot card, the Princess of Disks, that she had framed and hung in the back room where she would see it a dozen times each day.

"We could display the two together, the inspiration for your masterpiece and your masterpiece side by side."

Shaking her head, Gemma smiled again. She didn't mind using

Miranda to further her own career, but if she ever shared the Artist's painting with the world, it would not be through that woman. "It's not really fit for a gallery showing. It's by an unknown American artist." A minor lie, S. Casale had a following in the States and her work was fetching an outstanding price posthumously, guaranteeing bright little Maeve a tidy security for her future.

"I see." Miranda sat back, her sudden disinterest in the painting apparent.

Gemma knew Miranda, better still, she knew Miranda wanted what she had. Gemma held back, waited, and let Miranda speak first. When they had finished their tea, Miranda was paying a prize commission for Gemma to create a sculpture to be permanently displayed at her gallery. They'd also arranged for an installation and a black-tie opener to which Miranda's A-list would be specially invited, all her favorite patrons simply dying to snatch up the latest thing bearing Miranda Richardson's stamp of approval.

Gemma Warner was about to explode onto the London art scene.

Chapter Forty-Two

"Aunty Gemma!" Maeve cried, rushing to Gemma's open arms.

Gemma wrapped her in a hug and lifted, spinning them round while Maeve burst into giggles. Gemma brought them back to earth, setting the girl softly on the grass before staggering, one hand reaching for Peter to brace herself.

"Steady there," Peter grinned.

"Right." Gemma kissed his cheek in greeting.

"Daddy?" Maeve looked up, a coil ready to spring away. He'd barely managed a nod, and she was racing off to the playground ahead of them.

"Come on, We've got treats." Gemma nodded to the park bench where a thermos of tea and tin of homemade biscuits waited.

"Saving seats? I thought that was against park rules."

"Strictly forbidden. Benches are prime real estate in these parts. I've already made fast enemies of the Mummy Club, but we've come to an agreement."

"Oh?" Peter pried the lid off the tin and peeked inside, "Gemma, you shouldn't have, unless you're planning to keep Maeve. She'll go mad for these."

"I didn't." She smiled conspiratorially.

"All right, spill. What is all this about?"

"Aunty Gemma!"

Gemma watched Maeve sit at the edge of the slide, scoot over the lip, then rush down an enclosed spiral to be spat out into a well-worn divot in the sand.

"Hooray!" she called back with a wave.

Initially, Gemma did not want anything to do with Peter or Maeve, feeling a clean break was for the best. But then one day, months after the divorce was made official, she met them in the market stalls. Peter pushed a stroller and Maeve, tiny adventurer, toddled along beside him. The fine baby down Gemma had stroked the day Peter returned had sprouted into dark curls. Peter was barely managing to steer the stroller, loaded with diaper bag and shopping, with one hand through a crowd of people. The sight of him bent down to accommodate Maeve, giving her as much freedom as he dared, moved Gemma. She caught them and took hold of the stroller. "Hello, stranger. Would you like a hand?" Peter looked up from Maeve, smiled, and straightened with an audible crack. "Goodness, yes. I was about to direct Maeve to the chiropractor's office." Gemma did not mind stroller management, but when Peter offered a swap, she gladly accepted. She and Maeve were instant friends, laughing, sharing sweets, swapping sticky kisses, and drawing, always drawing. In fact, as an official Aunty, Gemma never went anywhere without a small notepad and tin of colored pencils, pastels, crayons, or even sidewalk chalk. She and Peter managed to become friends, too, dear ones.

"Now, about this agreement," Peter said. "Why do I feel like these biscuits come with strings."

"See that one?" Gemma discreetly pointed across the playground at one of the mummies. "She's the boss, see? They all noticed you don't wear a ring, were starting to move in. I was getting a little frightened, actually. So, I made sure the boss knew that we're just friends, that, while I am an honorary aunty, I'm not *that kind* of aunty."

"Gemma, what have you done?" Peter removed his glasses and rubbed the bridge of his nose. When he put his glasses back, he raised his hand to wave and smile at Maeve...then saw the Boss Mummy behind Maeve, near the swings where her twin boys played, waving back.

"Let's just say, so long as you're available and I'm not a threat, I can save seats at the playground."

"Really, Gemma—"

"Amari made the biscuits. For you."

"I got that." Peter lifted his hand to wave again at the woman with the twins, who had jumped off the swings to throw dirt at each other.

Gemma laughed and rocked sideways into Peter, giving him a playful shove. "It's worth it, you know, for the bench."

"And the biscuits."

Maeve ran to the swings. Anticipating what was coming, Gemma stood up. "Save my seat." She winked at Peter, "And try a biscuit," then went off to help Maeve fly.

Gemma still dreamt of the Artist. Now it was the other way round, though, with the Artist inhabiting her. She replayed moments like this in her dreams, Maeve swinging in slow motion, her striped tights and little skirt in colors that reminded of autumn leaves, shades of rust and amber, scarlet and sienna. Those black curls flying and green eyes shining. And the laugh, best of all, Maeve's laugh. Gemma saw her hands with the unvarnished nails reaching out to connect with Maeve and give her a push, *Higher! Higher!* Sometimes the hands had a burn scar, and sometimes they had paint under the white half-moons of nail.

Dear Reader,

THANK YOU SO MUCH for reading *A Stone's Throw!* Notes from readers really do mean the world to me. If this story moved you, I would love to hear from you. I am available to meet with book clubs or give an author talk. I write, because I have a story to tell. I put my stories out into the world, because I want to connect with people. *Like you.*

Please grab a copy of the reader's guide. And if you'd like to stay in touch, I have a newsletter where I reflect on writing, life, and the writing life. That is the best place to hear about the books I'm writing, new releases, and author events. (Links below.)

Please leave a review. Reviews really help authors by growing awareness of their novels, and help readers by introducing them to books they will truly enjoy. Leaving a review can be as easy as giving stars and answering one of these questions:

- What did you like about this book and why?

- Did it make you feel any particular way?

- Who else might enjoy this book?

Thank you! Alida

Reader's Guide

You can grab a free reader's guide, perfect for reflection, insight, and discussion. Whether you just want more food for thought on your own, belong to a book club, book store, or library, you'll find questions about the novel's themes, characters' choices, and a peak behind-the-page. Get it at alidawinternheimer.com/ast-readers-guide or scan the code below.

Get the Reader's Guide

Acknowledgments

I AM EXTREMELY GRATEFUL to everyone who has supported and believed in my writing. Your encouragement and kindness has touched my life and my art, especially during those times when my faith in myself wavered. You know who you are. And Pete, who is supporting me in my purpose now. Love to you all!

About the Author

ALIDA WINTERNHEIMER IS AN award-winning writer, developmental editor, story craft coach, and podcaster, who is three times nominated for the Pushcart Prize and listed as a notable in Best American Essays 2022. Winner of the 2023 Page Turner Writing Award and Genre Award for historical fiction, she has taught writing classes many places, including prisons, and hosts the Story Works Round Table podcast, where she has conversations about craft. Alida also writes *The Story Works Guide to Writing* craft books. Join her author newsletter below for updates on new novels, a look behind the page, and more.

When she is not writing, reading, or teaching writing, you can find Alida sea kayaking, cycling, or being walked by her golden retriever around Minneapolis, Minnesota.

Find Alida at www.alidawinternheimer.com. Join her newsletter, A Room Full of Books & Pencils, for reflections on writing, life, and the writing life at booksandpencils.substack.com. Scan the QR codes below for quick links.

www.alidawinternheimer.com

booksandpencils.substack.com

Made in the USA
Monee, IL
16 February 2025

11976081R00173